Victory in Sight ...
and Trouble Below

"Sir, there's trouble below," the young midshipman said to Commodore Bainbridge. The Commodore turned from his spyglass through which he'd been observing the *Constitution*'s gunners making mincemeat of the British ship, *Java*.

"When is there *not* trouble below?" Bainbridge asked, letting out a satisfied sigh as a cheer rose from the *Constitution*. *Java*'s mizzen —her last mast—had collapsed overboard, and the battle was over.

The midshipman mumbled that the trouble was of a sensitive nature.

"Sensitive?" barked the Commodore. "Man, explain yourself."

"The powder boy who was wounded—he isn't a boy. It's a woman—and she's in labor . . ."

The FREEDOM FIGHTERS *Series*

TOMAHAWKS AND LONG RIFLES
MUSKETS OF '76
THE KING'S CANNON
GUNS AT TWILIGHT

Guns
at
Twilight

Jonathan Scofield

A DELL/BRYANS BOOK

Published by
Dell Publishing Co., Inc.
1 Dag Hammarskjold Plaza
New York, New York 10017

Dell ® TM 681510, Dell Publishing Co., Inc.

ISBN: 0-440-02919-8

Printed in the United States of America

First printing—June 1981
Second printing—September 1981

Guns
at
Twilight

The War of 1812 was fought under the most peculiar circumstances of any military venture in our history. In the first place, the British cabinet on June 1, 1812 had conceded all but one American claim. The war, however, had been declared and was carried on regardless. In the second place, there was some question as to whom we should be fighting. France had offended as grievously as England. Napoleon was regarded as the great menace to world peace. In the third place, the war was ostensibly fought to protect New England maritime rights but only the South and West were enthusiastic. New England was against it from the start. The subject of impressment, which had brought on the war, was not even mentioned in the peace treaty. And finally, the war's greatest battle, which was fought at New Orleans and made Andrew Jackson a popular hero, was fought after the treaty had been signed.

—Anonymous War Book Catalog,
late 19th century

England's disposition is unfriendly; her enmity is implacable; she sickens at our prosperity.
                    —American War-Hawk, 1811

The present situation of the commercial parts of this country is worse than any war could be, even a British one.
                    —Josiah Quincy, Boston, 1811

The sea is ours, and we must maintain the doctrine that no nation, no fleet, no cock-boat shall sail upon it without our permission.
                    —London *Courier*, 1811

PROLOGUE

Sept. 5, 1803

IT WAS A NIGHT without moon or stars. Only the phosphorescence of plankton on the water and the sporadic creaking of a spar aloft kept Kevin Kinnaird's green eyes open. With the swells rocking the ship, at times he'd fancy himself back in bed in Glasgow after a pint or two at the Black Horse. He'd crawled all the way out on the bowsprit, bare feet on the forestay yokes and calloused palms clamped to the topmast stays. All in all, it was a far sight better than serving a grade higher on His Majesty's ship *Victory*. And the pay was almost triple to boot: seventeen Yankee dollars a month. He turned his red head and marvelled at the spectacle of seaborne lightning bugs below.

On the roster of U.S.S. *Constitution* he was Jack Dranik, ordinary seaman. Only the ten dozen landsmen and boys were of lower rank among the complement of four hundred eighty. A year earlier the press gang had got him in

front of the Black Horse. It had all been quite
convivial. They had humored him and joined in
when he began to sing Scots ballads. But when
he woke up the next morning he found that he
was on a ship out of land's sight, with no choice
but to fall in or be thrown in the brig. Made no
difference whether a man became deathly sea-
sick or not. The officers and petty officers were
a breed apart; peacocks afloat on the sweat of
impressed crews.

Kevin had jumped ship off Cuba. Thanks to
a weakness for Canadian whisky, he got so lost
in an obscure series of inns and public houses
that even the King's marines couldn't find him.
He shipped aboard a coaster to Boston and became a bartender at the Fox Head, where he
assimilated American ways while waiting for a
ship to sign aboard for the return to Scotland.

In June, the American frigate *Constitution*
was working up under a new captain, Edward
Preble, an outstanding commander during the
Revolution. He had become a merchant seaman
for a time but had been recalled to duty during
the French conflict of 1799. Kevin, staring into
the inky mist as the ship's bell tolled twice,
recalled that spring day when he had signed
on the *Constitution*. As a deserter from one of
His Majesty's ships, he decided it was best to
continue to conceal his identity, even on an
American ship. He had written his first name as
Jack and then, in a panic, wrote his last name
backwards—and dropped, in his haste, a letter
or two. The good Scots name of Kinnaird be-

came Dranik . . . Ordinary Seaman Jack Dranik. When the subject of his name came up afterwards he explained that his father was a Lithuanian seaman and that he was reared by his mother's Scots relatives in Halifax, thereby accounting for his accent.

Even the safety of his new identity, however, could not prevent him from feeling some trepidation as the *Constitution* approached the British bastion of Gibraltar. Perhaps it was poetic justice that Dranik-Kinnaird, originally a schoolmaster, albeit only an apprentice, was now entering the gate to the worlds of Pliny and Plutarch. Whatever the case, as he stared out into the darkness from his post on the bowsprit he swore to himself that if he ever reached home after his year's service under Preble he wouldn't touch another drop of whisky until he was permanently employed as a proper schoolmaster. Not another drop—

What was *that*? Jack held his breath, listening carefully. There it was again. Water against "tumble home," the part of the hull that veers sharply to the rudder post.

Jack crawled back down the bowsprit boom and slipped over the forward pinrail to the deck. "Don't," he whispered to a seaman who was unbuttoning his britches and about to hop to the crew's head, a platform below the sprit with three holes port and starboard. "There's a boat out there!" He sprinted lightly aft to warn the deck officer.

Within a minute, Commodore Preble, in carpet slippers and robe, was on deck waiting for the carronades to be run out. There was a creaking of wood as twelve gunports opened on the spar deck and fifteen more on the long-gun deck below. The 32- and 24-pounders were shotted with over seven hundred pounds of metal for a broadside. When the guns were ready Preble raised his brass speaking trumpet.

"What ship is that?" he bellowed into the night.

No answer. He put the trumpet to his lips again, just as an eerie reply resounded. For a moment it seemed an echo.

"What ship is that?"

The commodore identified his ship and himself and repeated his query in accordance with maritime procedure.

Again, the same evasive answer.

Preble, now irritated, told the invisible craft that unless a proper answer was forthcoming, *Constitution* would fire a shot.

"Beware, we shall answer with a broadside," came the reply. "This is His Brittanic Majesty's ship-of-the-line *Donnegal*, of eighty-four guns, Sir Richard Strachan, Commodore. Send one of your boats."

"We will not—repeat, will not send over a boat," Preble shouted. "We have forty-four guns and we're about to use them. Blow on your matches, boys!"

An almost interminable silence ensued. All along the port spar deck glowing ropes wavered over the flash pans, waiting for the order to fire into the blackness. The matches moved closer as a succession of sounds came through the darkness: muffled voices, creaking and then a rhythmic splashing.

"Belay the matches, boys. Bosun, make ready for boarding." Preble's steward eased him into his uniform jacket and took the speaking horn as the port gangplank was lowered.

"Sideboys one and two . . ." The bosun smartened his crew and piped the *Donnegal's* emissary aboard. Preble waited aft, near the wheel, flanked by two battle lanterns as the British officer was escorted past the glaring gun crews.

Jack had been relieved as for'd lookout and caught the jist of the conversation before going below.

"I beg your pardon, sir, for this ruse. Our ports were dogged and we needed time. You might have been French or Spanish. Being a light frigate of only thirty-six guns, our captain was justified. We had no intelligence of an American warship in these waters . . ." The embarrassed young officer spoke with the mechanical inflection of a puppet.

"Did I sound French or Spanish to you?" Preble demanded, much to the amusement of those within earshot.

"It's not for me to say, sir. And now if I may beg your leave . . ." The young officer looked around, his eyes resting momentarily on the nearest carronade and its smartly turned out crew.

Jack Dranik stayed in the mizzenmast's

shadow, as if fearing the unfamiliar British officer might recognize him.

"Jack, m'boy." It was Aarney, his Finnish shipmate. "The bastard lied to us. *Donnegal* eighty-four, my arse. It's the puny *Maidstone*. Ran across 'er off Cuba last year. Her captain's a queer duck—too fancy to come up on deck."

Captain Leigh Merry cursed as the ground glass stopper of his port wine decanter refused to budge. Damned this asinine, inopportune encounter with, of all things, an American man-of-war. The *Constitution* to boot! Damnation. Only a week to Portsmouth and transfer to command of a seventy-four. How to face his cousin Anthony, just appointed minister to the United States, how to face his officers at the next mess. . . . What to tell the enquiry—and there would be one. He had too many enemies aboard, and they all wanted his position.

He drew a lace kerchief from his velvet pocket and caressed the glass stopper. "Thank God for this." Merry poured liberally, drank deeply, hiccoughed once, and turned up his oil lamp. He pulled a morocco-bound volume from under his bunk pillow and immersed himself in it. *Memoirs of A Woman of Pleasure* . . . a Spenserian flourish . . . *H.E. Cleland.*

In the wardroom, one deck below and slightly forward of Merry's cabin, Lieutenant Duane yawned and swung his booted feet up into his bunk. "We're bloody lucky not to have been blown to kingdom come," he commented to the other three lieutenants of the British eighteen-pounder frigate *Maidstone*.

" 'E's probably tiltin' the bottle about all this," chuckled Crenshaw, "what with 'is promotion comin' up. Say, Burdette, what did this Commodore Preble look like?"

Lieutenant Richard Burdette considered his reply. "He looked a lot more in charge than—" He pointed aft and up with his thumb. "His eyes were cold as frost, his cheeks hollow and hungry. A different sort of captain than we're accustomed to."

"What about the ship?" Crenshaw asked, inhaling a pinch of snuff.

"Very ready, and a healthy lot they seemed."

"All eager volunteers with the wages John Adams gives 'em." Duane yawned audibly. "No bloody need for press gangs and their scurvy skeletons. Look at our crew. Half of 'em would jump ship if we as much as turned our backs."

"What about their guns?" Crenshaw asked.

"Curious thing. Steele's lists American frigates with twelve-pounders on the spar deck but I'm sure I saw carronades. Thirty-two-pounders!"

"What did I tell you?" Duane roared.

"And going down the plank, I saw what looked like adjustable sights forward of the flash pan." Burdette blew out the candle and swung into his upper bunk. "It makes sense— they've got a small navy so their best bet is to stand off, fire and run if the odds are bad."

"Well, I'll tell you somethin', Burdette," Lieutenant Duane said in grave tones. "I come into this navy before ye was born an' it took me a lot of action to get my stripes. I've seen the King's navy change. It's not like it was then, when we were still sharp. We wiped the damn rebels off the waves. But we're getting fat—like the Romans. I'm up for a pension in a few years and I tell you that if we ever have to go across and fight those rebels again this officer will put in for a seventy-four at least. Where do ye think all the la-de-da admirals'll be? Not on a toothpick like this! And here's something else to give us all pleasant dreams. My uncle in Boston worked on *Constitution* in '97. Her hull is twenty-two inches thick. *Ironwood*, he called it. And us with a niggardly thirteen . . . Good night, gentlemen."

Sept. 10, 1803

WHITE SMOKE curled out of the bubbling black iron kettle and rose toward the square opening in the longhouse roof. This was Ga-oh's fire. It was flanked by two smaller fires that helped to warm the Seneca families and reflected in the brown eyes of the children who hid in the background. It was the time of year when the star hunter and his dogs overtook the star bear, the time for hunting the white-tailed deer. But this red-leaf time was not the same as the last; it was a time for Raising-the-Tree.

Sa-da-wa-sun-teh, called Midnight by the white man, was the oldest warrior of the village by O-hee-yo. He turned his weathered head feebly, good eye toward the fire. Thrilling inside, he counted on his bony fingers: one, two, three Feasts of the Dead had passed since the last time of Raising-the-Tree, since Midnight had run with Handsome Lake and Red Jacket behind the redcoat cannon to Sko-har-eh and the big river. He closed his eyes and remembered the victorious return; scalps for which the redcoat gave silver, and something more than mere white dog's heads for Hanging-of-the-Kettle broth. He chuckled while watching his daughter, Wind Spirit, push the dog head down into the bubbles with a stick. The Six-Nation Council had become a council of squaws. He looked at the young boys peeking wide-eyed from behind the elm posts and reed partitions. It was at such a feast long ago that he, childson of Swift Lizard, looked into the broth kettle and saw the Frenchman's hand with the gold ring. It was the time the redcoat major vomited.

Ga-oh held up the sacred wampum belt and spoke to it, her voice strong and steady. "Oh, Ah-ka-to-ni, it is now that we raise the tree. To raise it high for our slain brother, Little Stone. Ah-ka-to-ni decrees another in place of Little Stone. It was the white man from Gen-nes-hee-yo that shot him for fishing near house. Ah-ka-to-ni, my brother . . . his brother." Ga-oh was in a trance, lips quivering, eyes closed. "Oh, Red Knife, our brother, do you heed and honor A-gris-koue . . ."

The twelve families of the longhouse paused and listened. Only the distant low whistle of the saw-whet owl was heard through the door that faced the rising sun.

Slowly, one of the braves stood up above the cross-legged silhouettes. He breathed in deeply before he spoke, first smoothing out his scarlet meeting robe which had been given to his grandfather many feasts ago by the Great King across the big waters. "Yes, my sister Ga-oh, Red Knife does heed and honor A-gris-koue and accepts the privilege of Ah-ka-to-ni."

Ga-oh fell to her knees and gave thanks. The twelve families echoed her words as she put the sacred wampum back into its beaver purse and drew out a red and purple feathered sash. Ga-oh stepped up to her warrior brother and slipped the ceremonial sash over his bowing head, then tied it loosely at his right hip, over the black buckskin he wore under the scarlet robe. She motioned the twelve families to raise their arms in praise to the heavens, then stirred the steaming broth. Her younger sister held a wood platter as she ladled the white dog's dripping head out of the kettle. The head, a delicacy and symbol of faith in the Great Spirit, was laid by the knees of Red Knife along with a bowl of broth.

Breakfast over, sun's rays now streaming through the high elms and dappling the bark-covered longhouse, Red Knife led his hunting party into a clearing a short distance from the village. Eleven braves, one from each of the other families of the longhouse, formed a circle and raised their English muskets.

The white man's thunder reverberated through the valley of the Gus-ha-wa-ga by the River Al-egh-eny, two day's travel from the River Gen-nes-hee-yo. The hunt was on.

Sept. 12, 1803

T HE SWIFT GENESEE sparkled gold on smooth,
mossy stones as the late summer sun broke
through the clearing known as *Canadea*, or
the place "where the heavens lean against the
earth."

"Good fish for *masque-alonge* here!" Standing
Branch guided the elm dugout canoe between
submerged rocks and lodged its bow firmly on
a sandy landing. The young Seneca jumped cat-
like from the stern into waist-deep water and
held the canoe while the four white men went
forward and jumped onto dry land. All lent a
hand and dragged the craft onto the bank.
Camping provisions and equipment were put
ashore and the boys, Carson DeWitt, sixteen,

23

his brother Caleb and Jamie Hunter, both fourteen, set to building a lean-to while Jamie's father, Robert, tended to the fire and mounted guard, content to have the Indian guide catch the evening meal.

Robert Hunter, the eldest son of Douglas Hunter, and owner of a large tobacco plantation in Charleston, South Carolina, was staying with the DeWitt family at Hastings-on-Hudson while looking into new harvesting equipment in New York. He'd taken the boys on a hunting trip, first traveling to Elmira where they were met by Standing Branch, who escorted them the last fifty miles to Belvedere, the Genesee River home of Philip Church, whose father was an acquaintance of the DeWitt family in London. There they provisioned and borrowed a canoe for the twenty-mile trip to Portageville. They'd stopped and hunted unsuccessfully for deer, then decided to camp at the clearing.

The young brave had not interfered with Hunter's technique of deerhunting, not wishing to hurt the vanity of his employer. But as for fish, Hunter readily agreed that although he knew the ways of croaker, shad and perch, he had never gone for the vicious "long-mouth," called *masque-alonge*. Standing Branch had been born in this valley and shortly returned with a huge specimen that he'd speared upstream.

"Yes, the 'long mouth' is bony, but one eats the meat on its back, which is good. For this reason it is important to catch a large fish." The

Indian expertly cut and apportioned the fish which he had cooked on a flat rock over the fire.

Later, around the glowing embers, while the elder Hunter slept, Standing Branch mesmerized the boys with tales of the Seneca nation. He passed on stories told him by his great-uncle, the prophet Handsome Lake, and by Red Jacket and Farmer's Brother. He told them of rituals, war parties and bear hunting, of scalpings, fort burnings and battles with the Frenchman. He was careful not to frighten the boys with stories of the settlers and white farmers; he emphasized that, thanks to President Adams, the Treaty of Big Tree seven years earlier had ended the Senecas' skirmishes with the white man.

As the summer crickets raised their night songs and wild turkeys crawed in the bush, he told of the secret rituals of his family's clan of the snapping turtle. He fanned the fire and showed the boys the hidden tattoo at the base of his spine and they eagerly asked to be made brothers of the clan, to accept the code of the snapping turtle, "Ka-ny-ahte-h."

Standing Branch, hardly a year older than Carson DeWitt, sharpened a *masque-alonge* vertebrae bone into an awl by grinding it on flint. Then, as the boys lowered their britches and lay by the firelight, he inscribed on each the outline of a tiny turtle. After each tattoo, a series of close, light punctures, he wiped away the blood and rubbed in a mixture of charcoal and red sandstone.

"Now you will go to the river and cleanse the

tattoo with the waters of Gen-nes-hee-yo and when you return to the fire I will ask the Great Spirit to accept you as my brothers."

"Ha, Mr. Trout, you are a worthy adversary, but I must warn you that my father and his father before him have taught me your ways." The bronzed Seneca poised his steel-tipped spear high over the rushing pool waters—then stopped his thrust abruptly, letting the fish dart off.

Standing Branch ducked behind a bush and held his breath. He'd heard a strange sound. There it was again. Not Nyak-wai, the bear . . . nor Noti-nyokawi-yo, the spotted deer. He peeked out among the clumps of blueberries, his brown eyes waiting. The foot-sounds were accentuated by crackling twigs and water sloshes. Yes, they were on the river bank, going downstream—toward the campsite. There would be no breakfast this morning. Clutching his fishing spear, he crawled up on a rock ledge overlooking a river bend and he saw them.

A war party! Standing Branch knew by the three white stripes on each warrior's cheek that they were Iroquois, but their dress was not of the tribes of the Gen-nes-hee-yo or the Al-eg-heny. Nor did he recognize the leader. Now they had stopped to bathe and to eat from their packs, but soon they would be moving and they would find the camp. Strange, thought the Seneca; those orange and white belts hanging from the tomahawk heads . . . Where had he seen them before? Then it came to him: Gus-ha-äh, the burden strap with which captives were bound. Never had his turtle clan owned such a strap; not in his memory.

First he thought about interceding, diverting the braves and their wicked fire-sticks away from the campsite. But he sensed danger. The boys and Mr. Hunter might be in greater peril if he were caught. Certainly this was no affair between tribes, for then the chiefs would have taken their grievances to the Council of Condolences at Ton-a-wanda. No, it was a one-house affair, to replace, to kill, or do both—to avenge a lost warrior.

Standing Branch crawled quietly down to the riverbank and sprinted downstream.

"But I thought the treaty put an end to all this." Robert Hunter picked up his Ferguson breech-loading rifle and followed the Seneca who'd ushered the boys ahead into the dense forest above the lake.

"Hurry. Do not stop to look back . . . I will explain later." Moving to the front, Standing Branch led the small column through thick underbrush infested with giant mosquitoes from the lake swamp. They were attacked mercilessly by hordes of the buzzing insects; they stumbled blindly, swatting at the insects and pushing away the thorn vines that left bleeding cuts on their skin. "Here, put mud on face for mosquitoes . . ." There was a chance that the war party would not relish following them into this swampy hell, teeming with the dreaded copper-head snake. "Better bug's bite than tomahawk," he muttered to himself as they moved relent-lessly on. Panting, they filed out of the woods near a waterfall and ripped off their infested rags to bathe and cleanse their raw skin.

Suddenly, Carson turned pale. "Mr. Hunter," he gasped, "Caleb . . . he isn't here. He was right behind me and Jamie in the swamp . . ."

Robert Hunter stared at him, then stood in one swift motion. "I'm going back," he said grimly. He broke for the swamp, brandishing his rifle, but Standing Branch leapt after him and brought him down with a flying tackle.

To the horror of Jamie and Carson, the In-dian and white man began to wrestle, tumbling among the rough stones and into the stream. Hunter's rifle clattered to the bank. Rolling over, he drew his knife and was about to use it when Standing Branch broke free. He beat Hunter to the rifle, raised and cocked the hammer. The piece was leveled at the Virginian's gut and the Indian's finger moved the trigger slightly.

Hunter froze, dropped his knife. "You too?" he said, glaring at the muzzle.

"Hear me, please, Mr. Hunter," Standing Branch spoke entreatingly. "Master Caleb has a better chance of living if we do not follow. We wait for some hours and then we look. Iroquois will kill captive if they see us. If we not find boy by next sun we tell Fire Council at Ton-a-wanda. They find boy; pay much wampum for release."

"He's right, Mr. Hunter," Carson said. "The Iroquois will listen to the council, especially if Standing Branch speaks for us. If they're riled up more, Caleb will be tomahawked and scalped. I know that my father would agree."

"All right, Standing Branch. I'll do as you say. I hope the Indians up here are different from the Shawnee."

The next morning, Standing Branch led them back to the campsite, retracing the swamp route. A chill fall wind had discouraged the mosquitoes. There was no sign of Caleb. Arriving at the clearing, they found the canoe was gone. In the soft riverbank clay where it had been, the sharp-eyed Seneca noticed a scrawl. He called the others to look.

They were the initials *C* and *D*.

1812

January 4, 1812

IT WAS the day before Christmas, bleak and cold in St. Petersburg, capital of Russia. The hoary arctic sun refracted rainbows through gigantic blocks of ice sawed from the frozen Neva and neatly trimmed for summer storage. Potted firs had replaced the pontoon-boat bridge that led from Falconet's celebrated equestrian bronze of Peter the Great to Vassilievki Island's cultural complex.

A mist shrouded the south bank below the ponderous Winter Palace. It clung to the pier that extended from the grounds of Koborov's neo-classic Admiralty edifice, a symphony in gold-trimmed wan yellows.

The great organ of the fortress cathedral

Peter and Paul boomed out songs to the glory of
Nicholas, the patron saint and protector of children, scholars, merchants and sailors. The organ
music reverberated among the white marble sar-
cophaguses of Peter the Great, who'd built the
city; his second wife, a Livonian prisoner who
became Czarina Catherine II; and poor assas-
sinated Paul, the insane, and father of Czar
Alexander I.

Voices of the devout rang into the bell tower
and over the fur-coated holiday throngs that
skated and promenaded on the glacial-still river.
The music hummed through the spars and
shrouds of the ice-bound merchant fleet, moored
off the Muscovite Quarter, and filtered down to
the deck of the *Periwinkle,* topsail schooner of
fourteen guns and chartered by DeWitt & Co.
of New York Port.

Thanks to England's enmity with Spain and
France, American merchants such as DeWitt
& Co. were making unheard of profits through
trade with Russia. Early in 1806, an American
merchant ship carrying cork and madeira from
Barcelona to Havana—with an interim stop at
Derby Wharf in Salem—was declared to have
broken the blockade law designed to prohibit
trading between England's adversaries, Spain,
France, and their colonies. The interim stop was
no longer an acceptable means of circumventing
the blockade law and the ship was made an
example of, its cargo confiscated before reaching
Havana. The Essex Decision, named for the
American ship, drastically cut into American

mercantile profits and turned many a Massachusetts businessman from Tory into Patriot. Under the new interpretation of the blockade law, a "broken voyage" was to be considered a continuous voyage, regardless of the disposition of cargo. It remained for crafty merchants to arrange a coastal voyage by a different ship and a complex transference of goods, with a consequent rise in handling costs, to confuse the British authorities enough to carry on even a fraction of the pre-*Essex* colonial trade with the continent.

In response to the British maritime restrictions, President Jefferson initiated an embargo that forbade American vessels from leaving American harbors for foreign ports, a pretense of protection for such ships. Of this, a newspaper printed:

> Our ships all in motion once whitened the
>   ocean,
> They sailed and returned with a cargo;
> Now doomed to decay, they have fallen a
>   prey
> To Jefferson—worms—and embargo.

The Embargo Act encouraged smuggling and garrotted the independent ship-owners, while the large Boston merchant fleets such as that of William Green continued to ply the trade routes rather than return to home port. The majority of ship-owners rebelled against the embargo, especially the ban on East India and China trade since there was hardly a question of danger to our ships there and the ban only allowed the British merchants to prosper. Jefferson had lost the support of the northern merchants, and repealed the Embargo Act on his last day in office, March 3, 1809, in order to help his party.

Commerce boomed again, but largely for New England, whose merchants maintained financial ties with England, ties that continued well into the War of 1812! America supplied the British army against France in the Peninsular wars, incurring Napoleon's enmity and causing a blockade of the continent. Over two hundred New England vessels were trading with Russia as a result of the French blockade. Profits of a thousand percent were common. Yankee captains and businessmen were forced to burn the midnight sun oil, carousing and drinking with a new breed of merchants, the Russians.

Carson DeWitt scanned the ships from his vantage point until he saw the *Periwinkle*.

"There she is—the tops'l rig with the green ports."

"Right smart boat." William Bainbridge climbed into the cupola atop the five-story-high wooden scaffolding as an attendant helped a lavishly dressed woman onto a short sled. "I counted five hundred steps." The elder American puffed wisps of steam as he took in the colorful panorama. "What's the complement of a schooner?"

"You'll have two officers and seventy men.

Henry Spencer is building it—a variation on *Enterprise*—if you don't mind being a privateer."

"I'll sail your father's ship to Hades to get out of debt." Bainbridge took a sled from the stack and set it on the icy track as the fancy woman was pushed off, screeching down the incline. The two former naval officers waited as attendants poured warm water on the ice. It froze as it flowed down.

Carson had been sent by his father, Schuyler DeWitt, to get a share of the burgeoning Russian market resulting from the Czar's misalliance with Napoleon. It was his first trip to the continent and he marvelled at the splendors around broad Nevsky Prospekt below him. It was lined with stalls and shops and with long, fluttering penants, and reeling with rides, games and dancing bears, almost forty thousand people having turned out for the Christmas festival.

Suddenly they were on the sled, screaming down with ever-increasing velocity, cheering and waving like schoolchildren. They sped by fleeting faces, yapping dogs and scurrying skaters, queues of staggering men at spirits barrels, whistling tea kettles . . .

Joining the promenade mainstream between the ice incline and the carriage sled traffic of the well-to-do, Carson and Bainbridge walked toward the Admiralty. Reaching a footbridge, they crossed over to merchant's row and wandered through the flea markets and shops. Carson absentmindedly bumped into a pretty girl who was browsing through a stall of books and knocked her book to the packed snow. He picked it up and dusted it gallantly, then bowed as he placed it in her gloved hand. Their eyes met and she burst into a merry, playful laugh. Before Carson could get a word out, a dour old woman had pulled her by her elbow into the tumultuous crowd.

"Next time you pick one who's brought her sister, and a connoisseur will show you how it's done." Bainbridge, a commodore on extended leave from the United States Navy, slipped a leather-covered telescope out of its case, raised it and focused on the top of the ice incline where petticoats were being blown over silky knees on the descents. "I just got an idea for a lucrative sideshow," he murmured. He set the instrument back on the display table—much to the disappointment of the stall keeper. "But there are too many petticoats in the winter . . ."

Above the two men, on a wooden balcony, a small band played "Wenceslas" with an excess of tinkling Tartar cymbal. Carson DeWitt felt a tinge of homesickness and envisioned his mother cooking delectable cakes and breads in the beehive brick oven by the roaring fieldstone fireplace . . . And his sister, Catherine, sledding down the slope all the way to the Hudson River, as he had done . . .

Bainbridge shoved his friend ahead. "I know the feeling, boy, but after twenty years and twice as many foreign ports you get over it. The old pictures disappear; you carry your life in a seabag and you're happy to get on *and* off your boat. Oh, sure, you go home to see the folks, but it's not the same as it was—you come home one day and you don't fit in anymore. Even your old dog growls at you, because you're now different. Might as well have sprouted fins and grown breathing gills." Bainbridge paused and snatched a newspaper from a rag-swaddled peasant boy, flipping him a coin and refusing the change. "French edition of the *Novoye Yremya.* Comes out a week later than the Russian. The Czar has to censor it first." He folded and stuffed the paper into his side coat pocket.

"I wish I could read French better," Carson said.

"Learned mine spending fourteen months in the bey's dungeon at Tripoli. Say, how about a drink?"

"Not for me. Too cold. It must be ten below." Carson stomped the caked snow from his furred boots.

"There's a place we can get a free vodka—indoors," the commodore suddenly exclaimed, grabbing Carson's arm and hurrying him along.

A boisterous crowd had collected around a forty-foot-long papier-mâché whale that was festooned with gold and silver trappings. Revelers of all descriptions tore at it to reach the delicacies that were stacked within: caviar, dried sturgeon, smoked carp, garnished with pickled crawfish and onions. Others were dipping tankards and ladles into rows of casks containing beer, wine and spirits. The well-swept ice skating square was bordered with rides on which suspended wooden horses and sleds whirled the braver townsfolk in screaming circles. A knot of young men was taking turns shimmying up a greased pole, falling off repeatedly in their quest for the 20-ruble gold piece on top.

Suddenly a loud report, like a cannon shot. Another. The rockets burst, flaring and then raining sputtering sparks over the snow-capped state buildings. It was the signal. The forty thousand celebrants took their cue and drank a toast to Christmas, Alexander I, Petrograd and Mother Russia. A second rocket display signaled that it was time to eat, but the papier-mâché whale had already been torn asunder and consumed.

Splendidly attired military officers, proper businessmen, flirtatious ladies and workers in their holiday best crowded the street. Even the nobility turned out for the festivities, accompanied by dwarf mistresses or lovers, as was the current fashion in the court.

Leaning their cossack fur hats to the north wind, Carson and Bainbridge walked to the end of Nevsky Prospekt to the Admiralty Park, where they were dutifully impressed by the enormous bronze of Peter I atop its sixteen-hundred-ton granite pedestal. Crossing the river between the potted firs, Bainbridge mused that the pedestal weighed more than America's largest warship, U.S.S. *Constitution*. Heavier by five hundred pounds. The two men clomped with the crowd

to Vassilievki Island, the seat of Russia's arts
and sciences. Elaborate carriages with steam-
snorting, long-maned horses waited outside the
Bolshoi while the coachmen huddled in round
"fire pavilions."

A stuffed mastodon stood in the square before
Peter's pride, the *Kunstkamera*—or Cabinet of
Curios—a long two-storied marble building.
Bainbridge had been right. They were each
handed a large glass of vodka as they entered.
Another inducement for the museum-goers was
the hospitable white-tiled heating kiosk in the
foyer.

The main attraction, as indicated in three lan-
guages, was: *Skin of a Frenchman, tanned and
stuffed*, testimony to the mood of the time. Napoleon, it was rumored, had amassed an army of
half a million troops at the Niemen River near
Russia's western border.

Carson was especially taken by a stuffed
zebra. "I've only seen one in picture-books." He
was tempted to run his hand over the animal's
smooth fur but was deterred by the stern glance
of a uniformed guard. He wandered on to admire the precious stones—the lapis lazuli, amber,
the beryls, emeralds the size of hen's eggs—and
then rejoined the commodore, who had cajoled
a second vodka and was leaning on the warm
tile stove, engrossed in his newspaper. On the
back page, a woodcut of a sailing vessel caught
Carson's eye.

"It looks like one of ours."

"Damn if it isn't." Bainbridge scrutinized the tiny print and translated its accompanying article.

"'American frigate *President*, forty-four guns . . .' That was *my* ship," Bainbridge exclaimed and gulped down his vodka. "' . . . engaged the British sloop *Little Belt*, twenty guns, on 16 May off Cape Henry, Maryland. The British ship suffered many dead and wounded, while the Americans were unscathed. Commodore Rogers said of the battle, which took place at night, that his frigate was in pursuit of H.M.S. *Guerriere*, a 38-gun frigate, and that he was justified in firing because *Little Belt* did not identify herself upon hailing and could have been *Guerriere*, which had earlier been reported in the same position. Captain Bingham declined Rogers's offer to repair the damage the next day, many of *President's* shot having passed completely through and out of the unfortunate sloop, which then made for Halifax, Nova Scotia.'"

Carson whistled. "Damn, and here it is January. We may already be at war!"

"I'll be hell-fired!" The commodore slammed his vodka mug onto a table with such force that everyone in the foyer was startled. "What am I doing here? On the beach, jammed in the ice!"

"Does that mean you don't want the job?"

"I've got a bigger job, boy. You're talkin' to Commodore William Bainbridge; he's just re-enlisted. I'll send my regrets to your father and I'll make good the advance money as soon as I get back."

"There's a transport sledge that leaves for Helsinki and Turku on the first of every month."

"I can't wait. I'll go beserk not knowing." Bainbridge twisted his newspaper angrily.

"Let's *buy* a sledge. We can sell it when we get to Turku, or when we find a port that's not iced in. Or we can go in style by hiring a proper rig with a driver and second man."

"*We?* Did you say *we?*" The commodore's face brightened.

"Aye, aye, sir!"

"*Meza! Meza!*" the driver shouted, snapping his long hide whip over the team's ears. The magnificent Arabian stallions charged over the frozen road, brass and silver studs flashing, scarlet tassels streaming and loose snow flying at every curve.

"What's he saying?" Carson DeWitt struggled out from under a profusion of rich, warm fur blankets inside the *kibitka's* cozy canopy.

"I think *meza* means border . . ." Bainbridge rubbed his sleepy eyes and tried to look out of the elliptical isinglass back window. Nothing but a white blur. He rubbed it in vain with his fur mittens, then slumped back into the nest of fur blankets.

"Not the border with Napoleon's troops!"

"If so, we're done for. We should be almost halfway to Helsingfors. Five more hours is about all I can take. First thing, a good strong drink, hot food and then a steaming bath . . . Carson, boy, wake up! Don't you know it's a thin line between sleeping and freezing to death? That's it, give yourself a good rubbing now and then. Get the circulation going. I was saying earlier that these Russians are crazy, but they've sure got the right idea about bathing. Did you go to a communal bath in Saint Pete's? No? You don't know what you missed. My, my, we've got to find one tonight. Why, my last time I could hardly concentrate on my own body for the beauty of those fair young girls. Almost went daft in hiding my pego's passion. First time I've blushed in years. Even now, just the thought of it arouses me. Too bad you're not a girl, Carson!"

Carson laughed. "It's far too cold to even think of taking a bath," he said, pulling the fur closer about him. "Do you think Turku will be iced in?"

"Even if it isn't, we'll hardly find an ocean-going ship. Mostly coasters. If Turku is iced, Stockholm will be too and we might as well bypass the city and go cross-country to Göteborg. It's the only port in Europe that has a regular trade with the States."

"Napoleon's blockade is successful, then?"

"That's what the Russian Admiralty told me, boy."

"I wish these days were longer. Dark depresses me."

"Carson, we'll have to fix you up with a Viking woman before we sail. It'll be another month before—"

"*Volk! Volk!*" the brakeman screamed from his slat seat behind the vaulted, half-round cab.

"*Skuh-reh-yeh!*" shouted the driver. The sledge lurched crazily, careening over a snowbank and almost tipping over. The startled passengers were thrown about as the driver stung his lead horse with savage whiplashes.

Bainbridge crawled forward and unfastened the leather door, admitting a flurry of icy wind and snow. He swung his stocky body out behind the driver, ducking for fear of being swiped by tree limbs. The swish and roar of the sledge's passage through the bleak uninhabited whiteness was broken by a shotgun blast. And then a second report. Bainbridge leaned further, hanging far out from the icy oak frame of the sledge.

Wolves! A pack of vicious grey wolves, scourge of the tundra and largest carnivores of continental Russia. They ran as one dark blur, gaining . . . gaining. The brakeman, having reloaded his Mortimer double-barreled blunderbuss, fired again at the pack. One of the two lead wolves spurted red on the snow and fell back, staggering and baring his teeth at the passing pack, squaring off for his crippled finale with two hungry young wolves as the rest, some dozen, continued after the other leader—and after the sledge. Suddenly, the sledge caught and slowed in a drift and the wolf leader, almost two hundred pounds of claw, tooth, muscle and glistening fur, leapt high and onto the brakeman. The final shot went into the air, snapping off a tree limb as the wolf's four-inch canines ripped into the brakeman's heavy coach coat at the elbow. The man screamed and pleaded for help as the wolf clawed for a foothold on the reeling sledge, clinging and snarling ferociously, wet black jaws locked into leather, fur lining, inner coat coarse linen and warm flesh.

"Carson!" Bainbridge reached back into the cab. "My pistol! For God's sake, hurry!"

"It's cocked." DeWitt slapped the warm Regia walnut stock into the grasping hand and tried to climb out, but he was unceremoniously pushed back in.

Bainbridge, gun in hand, crawled over the cab top, then swung dangerously out as the sledge turned sharply, spraying an avalanche of snow over wolf and man alike. Reaching the rear, he leveled his cannon-barreled *J. Waters* flintlock and inched the muzzle toward the salivating jaw. Savage red eyes blazed at the steel muzzle as it pressed against the beast's ear. Enraged, the wolf lunged at Bainbridge's bare wrist simultaneously with the flash and penetration of a .59 ball into its neck. The swipe tore a bloody gash on the commodore's forearm.

Clinging to the stretched leather atop the *kibitka*, the great wolf bared his teeth for the death bite. He sprang—and so also did a tensioned triangular bayonet, its ten inches flashing out from under the pistol's barrel, piercing the red-ribbed roof of the wolf's mouth and jabbing back through his head. The ensuing bloody howl mingled with the wind as the wolf slid back and off, past the dazed brakeman. The snow reddened where the animal fell and the hungry pack pounced on their writhing leader, tearing him to shreds while a flock of ravens, trailing the wolves for carrion, swooped down, a black cloud, snatching up remnants.

The party stopped at Hamìna village, site of the Finnish Officer's Military Academy, and found a retired surgeon to tend to their wounds. The brakeman's condition was worse than Bainbridge's; his arm was broken and required setting, as well as cleaning and bandaging for the wound. The commodore, son of an eminent New York physician, Absalom Bainbridge, recalled a time when his father had treated a hydrophobia case, and prevailed upon the old surgeon to obtain and apply lunar caustic as a precaution, wolves being potential carriers of the deadly affliction.

Fortified with a pot of lamb stew, courtesy of the doctor's kerchiefed wife, and with horses rested and fed, the group continued toward Helsingfors, taking turns in place of the injured brakeman. For a stretch, both Russian peasants were allowed to enjoy the fur-swaddled luxury known only to their masters, the rich and the military. The two grateful men responded by further easing the trip with a round-robin bottle of heretofore hidden Spanish brandywine to warm the blood.

Carson and Bainbridge were on the high seas by the middle of January, bound for Boston on the *Catherine*, a topsail sloop that was part of the fleet belonging to William Green, the former

lieutenant governor of Massachusetts. It was
during that voyage that Carson first heard the
commodore speak of the troubles in his past—and
that the older man resolved to put those troubles
firmly behind him in the American cause.

On their first evening on board they sat at the
captain's table for dinner. They were joined by
Lieutenant James Eldridge, a courier for John
Quincy Adams's St. Petersburg delegation.

"I might as well call you *Lieutenant* DeWitt,"
Eldridge remarked after the introductions were
made. "The navy is very short of experienced
officers. Welcome aboard." The dark-haired
young officer raised his wine glass, drawing an
interested glance from a pretty girl amidst a
group of dour merchants at the other end of the
table.

For a moment, Bainbridge thought the girl's
eyes were on him, then realized differently. Did
his twelve years seniority show *that* much? Perhaps he should trim his side whiskers. Yes, that
was it . . . The merchant now glaring at him had
long whiskers. Must be her father.

"My experience is inconsequential compared
to the commodore's."

"*Captain's*," Bainbridge interjected. "The rank
of commodore is only a little joke. I'm the oldest
in-grade captain in the navy."

"Imagine," Eldridge said, side-stepping a deli-
cate subject, "me, a noncombatant messenger,
having supper with one of 'Preble's Boys.' He
was from Maine, you know, just as I am," the
young officer said proudly.

Bainbridge went on as if Eldridge hadn't spoken. "Losing a frigate takes a lot of living down, especially when an experienced officer runs one onto a reef . . ." He drained his sherry.

"But the reef at Tripoli was uncharted. It wasn't your fault—" Eldridge almost said "sir."

"Lieutenant, I could have stood off, sent in a boat to sound, bought shore intelligence—but I *didn't*. No matter how you cut it, I was in charge. I fell for the savage's trap. So I'm starting from scratch. At least *one* man made rank because of my debacle."

The younger men were quiet, knowing that Commander Stephen Decatur, five years Bainbridge's junior, made captain in 1804 after leading a brilliant attack and blowing up Bainbridge's captured frigate *Philadelphia* under the bey's guns. Decatur was next in line for the coveted highest naval rank, previously held only by the father of the navy, John Barry, and his protegé Edward Preble.

"Now, now, gentlemen," Bainbridge said cheerfully, "the Barbary Wars are over and we won—even if we bought the bey off!"

"*And* the bey's boss, the sultan of Istanbul," Carson added, "with a cargo of dancing girls, tigers and gold."

"I'll admit it was my most interesting command—until the sultan took my boat as well," Bainbridge reminisced.

"War is expensive." Eldridge winked at the merchant's daughter, who turned away in embarrassment. "But you should see how much the politicians spend even in peacetime! Why, John Q. keeps a house in St. Petersburg with twenty-one servants *and* their families."

"When in Rome, I guess . . ." Bainbridge enjoyed the change of subject; he had said too much. "I hear he and the czar often take long walks together. And they talk in French."

"You'd talk with John Q., too, if you needed American goods," Eldridge laughed. "And merchants don't care what language is spoken so long as it translates into dollars. We're a new nation and we've got to expand. I've seen great lands west of the Mississippi, all untouched, unplanted, just waiting for settlers and prospectors. We'll need lots of gold and the only way to get it is by free trade. You've seen what blockades can do. Unless our navy is as strong as any at sea, we'll be strangled. The great lands will be taken by the strongest."

"But we've got some fine ships. We can outgun and outrun anything afloat, ton for ton." The "commodore" lit a long white clay pipe with a candleflame. "And we're building more."

"You've been away. You haven't heard?"

The veteran officer blanched. "Not war. Not yet . . ."

"No, not yet, but Madison has been talking to the secretary of the navy."

Bainbridge's voice rose. "That imbecile? What does a governor of South Carolina know about naval matters!"

"He's getting what he wanted! The same

thing his crony Jefferson wanted . . ." The lieutenant set the bait.

"Dammit!" Bainbridge slammed his brawny fist on the heavy oak table, scattering silverware and turning heads. "Not the gunboats again!"

"I can just see," Eldridge taunted, "*Constitution, Constellation, President*—all snugly anchored in harbors. No sails, no masts, guns on one side only, ready to repel the enemy and protect our isolationism, while scores of little one-gun cockboats flit to and fro, anxious to fire their one eight-pound shot at a fleet of His Majesty's 74s. And all the while our merchant fleet is being decimated on the high seas, our sailors impressed and flogged . . ."

Captain William Bainbridge thought of his wife and their five children in New York, of his father's dedication to his work, of Tripoli's dank dungeons . . . of the imperious British officers he'd met, of the cost of bread . . . and tea! He ground his teeth and his blood roiled within. Then he growled, "Not if Preble's Boys have anything to say about it!"

21 March

Caught a sturgeon yesterday while fishing through the ice below Tower Ridge. It was almost seven feet long, and is now in the smokehouse.

My family is disappointed at not meeting the commodore, *but he had urgent business in*

Washington. There was time, however, to stop off at our offices and recommend several captains for our new schooner. He was gracious enough to post a letter on my behalf to Captain Isaac Hull of the frigate Constitution, *just arrived from Cherbourg and lying off Annapolis pending a refit and careen. Great growths of clam, barnacles and seaweed had been generated while on Mediterranean station, the bottom being so fouled as to impede the vessel's speed by several knots. Commodore Stewart, whom we met in New York, told us also that Captain Hull had sent a package of selected marine specimens from the sheathing to the secretary of the navy as evidence for appropriating refit money.*

Bainbridge and I were fitted for new uniforms at the naval store in Broadway and I will pick them up on my way to Washington in a fortnight. My compatriot was mortified at the increase in his girth since his last fitting after the Tripoli imprisonment. However, his breeches were on the "snug" side even then, as I remember. Fate works in curious ways. I met Bainbridge when I was an eighteen-year-old midshipman at the Navy Yard in Bruecklyn, and he the commandant. That we were both in that frigid city of Russia at the same time will no doubt have great impact on my future. But for him, I'd still be languishing in Russia, waiting for the thaw before becoming inextricably involved in my family's business. It was time. I am twenty-five and my parents had made certain con-

*nections with a family of influence who hap-
pened to have a darling daughter. I am now
absolved of this relationship, no small dividend
of my rekindled friendship with Bill Bainbridge.*

*If Bill and Commodore Stewart cannot pre-
vail against the secretary's gunboat plan, I shall
have to wait long for a proper assignment, for
an anchored warship needs only half the complement of a sailing warship. In that case I might
best apply for a more remote sanctuary; the
prospect of being cornered in matrimony goes
more and more against my grain.*

5 April

*Arrived at Washington Naval Yard. Dined in
spanking new blue with the trio of Preble's
Boys. And good news! President Madison has
changed his mind—or the Boys have done it for
him. The era of gunboats and isolationism is
over. Enter America as an aggressively defensive
sea power! Captain Hull had come over from
Annapolis where Constitution lays careened,
stripped of stores, ballast, guns and rigging. He
got the appropriation for refitting, his evidence
having been smelled as well as seen. Providen-
tially, the frigate's original sailing-master,
"Jumping" Billy Haraden, is yardmaster and taking special pride in fitting a new copper bottom
as well as new planks and more efficient spars.
He's intent on making her the fastest afloat.*

*I'm fortunate in that a major part of Captain
Hull's crew has been mustered out and he is
currently recruiting. He's assured me of no less*

than fourth lieutenant, since his fourth has left for an indeterminate leave and his fifth is rather undependable.

Commodore Stewart and my friend have at least one thing in common; neither has a command at present and both are anxious to obtain one. In the meantime, they frequently laugh heartily together about past service, deeds and superior officers.

11 April

But for an odd package delivered to my quarters, I might have forgotten my birthday, what with my new station and all its requirements. It was from Bill; he remembered. But then he had made rather a point of it on the crossing in Catherine. *I opened it eagerly and found a wooden case. I knew instantly by the heft and the dimensions, by the maker's burnt imprint on the wood. It was the bayonet pistol that I had so admired after our encounter with the wolves in Russia!*

There was a note pinned to the green velvet lining of the lid. "Left for Boston as expected. I won't need this for a while. Not expecting any 'Barbary boarders' to attack the Boston naval installation!"

Feeling a pang of remorse for him, I examined the pistol. Perhaps his new command was for the best, a time to temper anger and sharpen his considerable skills. A chance to fit in again—to find luck instead of the adversity that has been his lot.

I flicked and retracted the spring bayonet, tested the trigger and lock. Then I saw it: a brand-new lockplate, inscribed with curlicued script:

Lieutenant Carson DeWitt, U.S.N.

June 20, 1812

Pinpoints of red and white light flicked in geometric patterns against the darkness that was sleeping Annapolis—reflecting on the calm river, interpreted, memorized and passed on from night lookout to the duty officer.

Below, nineteen-year-old Midshipman Elias Lovett II laid his quill pen in its drawer and carefully sprinkled drying powder over his precise handwriting. His calligraphic talent had been inherited from a succession of instrument makers, first from London, and then from Salem. Next to his quills, a leatherbound volume beckoned, tempting him from his duty as log officer aboard U.S.S. *Constitution*.

First looking around to see if he was alone, he

lifted the heavy book, opened the cover and read the dedication on the endpaper.

> For Elias Junior,
> Who would be
> An Arithmetick sailor like me.
> May this gift speed your safe return.

Elias eased the treasure back into its place, its gold-tooled spine glinting in the light of the oil lamp. NEW AMERICAN PRACTICAL NAVIGATOR. The boy sighed and turned up his lamp, diligently reading his entry for mistakes. It had been an unusual day—but then it *was* Midsummer's Eve. Even Jack Dranik, with nine year's service aboard this ship, even cool Jack had said he wasn't surprised that it had happened on this day, of all days.

". . . In the captain's absence, our commanding officer, Lieutenant Read, had the crew turned up, and read to them the declaration of war between the United States and the United Kingdoms of Great Britain and Ireland that had passed the Senate, authorizing Pres. J. Madison to employ the armies and navy of the United States against the above powers. The crew manifested their zeal in support of the honor of the United States by requesting leave to cheer on the occasion (granted them). Crew returned to their duties—"

"Lovett." The voice behind him was staccato and definitely "quarterdeck."

The midshipman pushed back his chair and snapped to attention.

"At ease, Lovett. I'll take the log if you're through."

"I am, sir."

"We've just received a semaphore that the captain has left the dock. Considering the hour and circumstances, he'll prefer to see the log in his cabin."

"Aye, sir." Lovett blew the powder off and handed the log book to the duty officer.

"Thanks, Lovett." Lieutenant Carson DeWitt started aft, then turned, his blond hair catching the lamplight. "By the way, the captain is pleased with your performance. He might be interested in a demonstration—if done in the presence of our navigation officer—of your Arithmetick Navigation method. It might be considered as an adjunct to normal procedure."

"I understand, sir. Thank *you.*"

"Well, how does it feel to be at war?" Carson scanned the log entries, then slid the book under his arm.

"Sir . . . I . . ."

"Don't be afraid to say it, Lovett. I felt a shiver go up *my* spine, too, this afternoon."

To my taste, the women of Baltimore have more charm than the rest of the fair sex in America—their white skin, slender figures, beautiful little hands . . . and dainty feet . . .
—*Baron de Closen, 1780, on a visit.*

Captain Hull watched Carson DeWitt's reaction as he read the anecdote. Lieutenant Morris had already been tested and Hoffman, Wadsworth and Morgan were not old enough. Read and Shubrick were on duty.

"But that was before I was born." Carson handed the book to the steward.

"Those women all have daughters by now," Hull snickered as the steward topped up his sherry.

"And sons *and* husbands," Morris chimed in.

"So much the better. Sign 'em all up, DeWitt, so long as they can walk and see over the gun'l. We'll need near three dozen recruits. Speak to Lieutenant Hale; he's also in need."

"How much time do I have?"

"How much will you need?" the captain shot back.

"The ship sails tomorrow, gets its guns lashed and ready, rigging done . . . Why don't I meet you at Norfolk, *with* the recruits, and *with* extra powder and carronade shot?"

"We'll be at Norfolk by the thirtieth."

"I'll be there, sir."

"Fine, we should be worked up enough by then to take on the British. And while you're at it, we're one below authorized strength in officers. See what you can do. The navy yard couldn't help me out."

"I'll look around, sir."

"Excellent. We'll certainly expect you at the holiday mess in a fortnight."

"Wouldn't miss the Fourth of July for anything. Can I bring some fireworks? Baltimore is the country's biggest—"

"Already requisitioned. You'll need money. See the purser and take what you'll need—but no more than what you have coming . . ." The officers laughed; it was just like old Hull.

"I understand, sir. I'll be on the first launch."

"Good, we'll weigh after Sunday services . . ."

FRIGATE CONSTITUTION!

To all
ABLE-BODIED and PATRIOTIC SEAMEN
Who are Willing to serve Their Country
and support its cause
THE PRESIDENT of the United States
having ordered The CAPTAIN of the
Good Frigate CONSTITUTION, of 44 Guns
now Proceeding to the Harbour of Norfolk,
where it will take on provisions and such
personnel as will put said ship in ready state.
NOTICE is hereby given that a
House of RENDEZVOUS is opened at the
Sign of The JOLLY BOAT in Fell's Point
for Seamen and Boys, and at
Mr. Chatworth's on Gay Street for Marines.

At the former, seven ABLE and eleven
ORDINARY Seamen, and five BOYS
will enjoy the opportunity to enter the service
for one year, unless sooner discharged by
the President of The United States.

To all ABLE hands the Sum of 17 Dollars
and to all ORDINARY the sum of 10 Dollars
and to BOYS the sum of 8 Dollars will be given
per month, and two months' advance will be
paid by the recruiting Officer if necessary.
NONE will be allowed to enter this honorable
service but such as are well organized,
healthy and robust, free from scourbutic
and consumptive afflictions.
A GLORIOUS Opportunity now presents to the
brave and hardy Seamen of THE SOUTH
to enter the service of their country—to
avenge the wrongs—and to protect
its rights on the Ocean.
Those brave lads are now invited to repair to
the Flagg of the CONSTITUTION,
now flying at the above places, where they
will be kindly treated, handsomely
entertained and may enter into immediate pay.

—Isaac Hull, Captain

Lt. DeWitt will preside in Fell's Point,
whereas Lt. Hale will enlist 1 Sargeant,
1 Armorer, 1 Drummer, 1 Fifer, and 8 Privates.
None can be enlisted that are not
5 feet and 6 inches high.
Privates will receive 10 Dollars, and
others up to 20.

Transportation to Norfolk will be arranged
at no charge.

Carson proofread the first handbill. "Sorry to make you work on Sunday, but there's a war on."

"Don't make any difference to me, Lieutenant, so long as I get paid extra for openin' up an' missin' my sleep." Old Ezekïel Hammond waited expectantly, grizzled hand on the press turn-screw.

"No mistakes that I can find," Carson said, finishing his reading. "Run me off three dozen."

"Might I make a suggestion—for my country?"

"Yes?"

"Yer goin' to recruit again?"

"Maybe. If we don't sign up enough this week, we'll try again in Norfolk."

"For a dollar extra, I'll run off another dozen, *without* quantities or addresses. Then, when ye get to Norfolk, ye can write in the new particulars without havin' to set type all over agin."

"Zeke, you're a genius. President Madison can't argue with that. Another dozen it is."

"You kin thank Ben Franklin fer that. I remember something from *Poor Richard's Almanac*. My first job—I was a thirteen-year-old printer's devil, same age as Ben when he started in Boston on the *New England Courant*, run by 'is half brother. What a genius he was. Too bad the *Almanac* stopped printin' before th' war. I mean the big war. This 'un ain't a war; it's a merchant's squabble, fanned up by drunks and Republicans. What was it? I set the type m'self. Never put off . . ."

". . . till tomorrow what you've already done today," Carson joked, picking up a newspaper as the old man rolled ink onto his type platen and pushed the pressure lever.

"Quite an article," Carson exclaimed, "' . . . Without funds'," he read aloud, "'without taxes, without a navy or adequate fortifications . . . our rulers have promulgated a war against the clear and decided sentiments of a vast majority of the nation . . .'"

"Yup, that's Jake Wagner and his cohort Hanson. What might ye expect from the inheritor of a newspaper and the son of the chancellor of Maryland? As Tory as they come!" Hammond loosened the pressure lock and raised the platen. "They'll be run out of town before th' week is out. I'm glad I don't do business any closer to them."

"Why?"

"I heard that after the paper appeared last Thursday, a right lot of roughnecks bought a lot of grog that night and stayed at the saloons till all hours." Zeke pulled his first proof carefully and handed it to Carson.

"Just a lot of noise. It'll probably simmer down . . . Whereabouts would you post these?"

Zeke took the proof and hung it to dry, then set up a blank sheet and repeated the procedure. "I 'spect you'd post most of 'em between here and Fell's Point. Most of the smaller, independent boatmen are off the Hook, and they're a rowdy bunch, given to little loyalty and quick

to jump their ship for a stake. Hell, a year ain't that much time anyway compared to a trip around the Horn."

"Could you recommend a respectable inn on Fell's Point?" Carson asked, reaching into his travel bag. He drew out a purse and laid the payment for the handbills on the printer's cluttered desk.

"There ain't no respectable places on the Hook." Zeke cackled. "Every doorway has a night lady leanin' agin it. Gettin' so crowded with ladies that the place is becoming famous for it. Girls got their own names. We call 'em Fell's Pointers or Fell's Hookers—Hookers or Pointers for short!"

Carson laughed along with the old man and then plucked a proof from the drying rack and handed it to Lieutenant Bruce Hale, who'd been quietly waiting in the background. "What do you think, Bruce?"

"It's right good-lookin' but some 'o the words are too big, if you don't mind my sayin' it."

"You may, Bruce. But don't tell the captain."

"Captain's had more book learnin' than me."

"Here's the first proof, Lieutenant," Hammond said.

"Brilliant, brilliant, Zeke. We'll have a crew that's the match for any British crew at sea. Now, all that remains is to find a place to stay in Fell's Point."

"Yes, of course. There is one place. It's called The Blew Brig. Run by a poor widow, Beth Lewis. Husband lost at sea on Ash Wednesday

last. Two sons to sea already. She works the place with two kids and a hired man. Sad story. Tom Lewis was a good man around these parts."

"Where is it?"

"Shakespeare Alley, off Market Street. I'd take care walkin' those parts by night, especially if I was a man of means." The printer peered over his spectacles at the money on the desk, then cleaned his matrix and plucked out the numerals, replacing them with blank wood fillers. He then re-inked and printed.

DeWitt and Hale waited for the last handbills to dry, then divided them equally and walked out into Gay Street, where Sunday churchgoers were streaming home. Carrying nails and hammer, Lieutenant Bruce Hale rolled up his handbills and walked west on Baltimore. DeWitt turned east along the old waterfront, stopping and posting his handbills near public houses and markets.

He crossed the bridge at York Street and turned south, walking along the tidal flats. Looking west, he saw the high masts of the big Baltimore packets and schooners of the burgeoning Far Eastern trade, swift boats that had rounded the stormy Horn of South America and brought back Souchong tea, sandalwood and exotic silks. Tied up at the Pratt Street wharves, they represented the most prestigious names in shipping and were challenging Boston and Salem for world markets. There would be little recruiting from those ships. Even in the current post-embargo boom, seamen would rather sign up on privateers; it was a more lucrative and far safer choice. Privateers, built on the lines of fast pilot schooners, were meant to challenge lesser armed merchantmen and outrun His Majesty's warships. The fledgling frigates of the United States Navy were an unknown quantity in battle with the British, and the odds were that our navy was too little and in bad repair.

Ahead, beyond the claptrap wooden houses on the Hook, loomed an array of small rigs. There were coasters, brigs and small schooners carrying sugar, rum, raisins and coffee from Martinique, Havana and Dominca, ships crawling with scorpions and banana snakes, ships whose bottoms were rotting from the terado borers. It was from these ships that crews would be found, men who might commit murder for two months' advance pay—for twenty pieces of silver. Lieutenant Hale would have little trouble recruiting his marines from among these disgruntled and leaderless men, from among the roughnecks who'd rather risk death engaging an enemy once a month than spend day after day on honest sea-duty. The plan was that the men Hale signed up would function as a legal "press gang" to Carson's seamen—who would no doubt spend their advance money carousing in the Hook's public houses and brothels and would need "assistance" in finding the ships they'd signed on for. Another good point—made by Hale, and he should know—was that a squad of marines from Baltimore would know all the best hiding places.

The peeling paint on the edifice caught the sun's noontime rays. Once yellow, the pigment had weathered away unequally, giving the house a splotchy, feathery appearance. Flanking the entrance were two windows, one exhibiting a small, handwritten sign behind a cracked pane:

ROOMS BY THE NIGHT OR WEEK, REFERENCES NEEDED.

The white-curtained windows overhead looked out on Shakespeare Alley, with a view of a one-storied public house across the way that gave certain outward evidence of a thriving and raucous nighttime trade. Pink garter lying in the wagon ruts by the entrance . . . broken bottles swept into a hasty pile against the wood-planked curb . . . a three-legged dog sniffing along the foul-smelling alley between the public house and the next building . . .

Carson glanced back at the weathered, yellow building. The Blew Brig, Inn and Tavern. Entering the front door, he found another, to his left, locked. He peeked through the glass; it was the tavern, closed because of the sabbath law. The door on the right was ajar; he elbowed it open and set his bag on a captain's chair in the foyer.

Soft, quick footfalls drew Carson's eyes up the steep, bare stairway. He saw small feet and remembered the French baron's words about Baltimore women. The feet stopped and abruptly aboutfaced, retreating upward. Several minutes passed and the feet pattered down again, in shiny patent dancing pumps. They stopped at the earlier level, then descended in a more measured gait.

The young girl had seen his reflection in the mirror next to the entrance when she first came down. It had not been the usual staggering, tattered sailor, but a handsome, well-shaven naval officer with clean boots and cap in hand. She had seen a gentle but strong face, and something had fluttered deep within her. In that instant Sarah Lewis had made up her mind. This was the man. Never before had she lost her breath like this. While she was hurriedly putting on her best shoes she fantasized that here at last was the prince in blue who would spirit her away from the wrong end of Baltimore. He would take her to a mansion with columns and trimmed hedges, where she'd find closets of dresses from New York and Paris, where he'd read poems to her from a gilt-edged book with purple page ribbons. Sarah Charlotte Lewis took a deep breath as she descended the last stair and set her mouth in a way she knew would make her look older than her seventeen years.

The officer twirled his cap, whistling a tune under his breath as Sarah strode haughtily across the hall to the desk. She attempted to lift the counter-gate with one hand, the way her mother always did, but had to use both. Carson watched in amusement and craned to see her face, but her head was bowed and her chestnut hair hid her features. She raised her head abruptly.

There was silence, Carson staring into her violet eyes and unable to restrain a surprised and appreciative smile at her beauty.

"May I help—" Her voice faded to a cracked whisper and she colored in embarrassment under his scrutiny. "Excuse me," she finally said, her voice faint. "I need a drink of water . . ." With that, she hurried from the room.

Carson hardly had time to wonder at her shyness before a young boy popped behind the counter, freckled and towheaded. "What can I do for you, sir?" The boy leaned over the ponderous ledger.

"I'm looking for a room. Be here for a week or so. Is your mother here?" Carson talked in a serious tone, man to man.

"She's at church, sir. Up on Calvert Street. She's helpin' with the strawberry festival, but I can write. See?" He printed carefully, almost upside-down with his left hand: SETH LEWIS. He poised the pencil over the register and examined his handiwork, chin hardly higher than the counter, and then turned the register around. "I'll get the key."

Carson wrote down his name. "I'll give your mother my references when she comes home."

The boy had climbed up on a chair and taken a key off the board. "This is the good room." He handed it to Carson, who admired the whittled boat hull attached to it. "My daddy carved it," the boy explained. "He said that if a sailor dropped it overboard it would float back to us.

That'll be fifty cents in advance. And a dollar includes breakfast."

Carson took a silver dollar out of his pocket and spun it on the counter, to the delight of the boy. "I'll take breakfast."

Seth caught the coin as it clinked down. "Do you have a sword, sir?"

"You can call me Mr. DeWitt. And yes, I do have a sword. But I don't wear it much."

"Only when you fight the pirates an' th' lobsters?"

"Lobsters?"

"Redcoat marines."

"Of course, lobsters!"

"I'm gonna enlist an' be a boy on the *Constellation*," Seth said proudly, pushing the whittled boat along the counter.

"A powder boy has to be fourteen to enlist."

"Then I have to wait." He counted on his fingers. "Four years?" Seth pushed the boat away, annoyed and crestfallen. Then his eyes brightened. "Do you like fishin'? My father takes me—" Seth's elation suddenly changed to sadness. "It's the room near the stairs. Breakfast's at seven and we don't serve supper on Sundays. They do up the street at the Jolly Boat and their saloon opens at six." The boy turned to leave, then added, "And Mr. DeWitt, the toilet's back near the woodshed."

"Thanks, Seth." Carson wanted to tell the child that he'd take him fishing, but he didn't know his own schedule and it would be best to talk to Mrs. Lewis first.

Upstairs, he bolted the door and spread out his notes on a small gate-leg table, deciding in what order to call on the recruiting agents in the morning. James Hooper, grocer on Thames Street . . . John Cloney, spirits shop . . . George Needham, tavern-keeper of the Jolly Boat . . . Ben Morrow, lawyer, Market Street. Amazing, he thought, how many occupations thrive on war. Now even the procurement of sailors at a dollar-fifty a head . . .

Carson kicked off his boots and stretched out on the quilted bedcover. Bright reds and yellows, strips of calico, corduroy and occasionally violet velvets made up the quilt pattern. It was warm, like his home on the Hudson River; friendly, unlike the starkness of warships. He ran his fingers over the fabric. Alone. No over-eager midshipmen. No sweaty bodies and duty rosters. He closed his eyes and multicolored, transparent particles traversed behind his heavy lids; visions of the sea, of rigging, of people. Of Sarah and her violet eyes . . . She was in the same house, perhaps even on the other side of the wall, he thought sleepily. He stared at the wall, at the block-printed repeat of pale yellow flowers on grey-blue. A face materialized, a hand . . . a young girl's body, fresh like spring, wearing nothing but transparent yellow wildflowers. She came through the wall and lay down next to him, her body touching his. . . .

When he awoke from the dream he thought again of the girl with the violet eyes—and suddenly knew that she had brought about an irrevocable change in him. He'd felt lust for her, yes; but for the first time in his life it was overshadowed by something else, displaced by a deep concern for another's welfare, and a tingling feeling of recognition.

It was night, a warm Chesapeake night that promised lazy summer days on the bay. The sounds of menhaden rippling the moonlit water as they fed, the distant hoo-hoo of barn owls and squawking of herring gulls could be heard in the stillness. The aroma of strawberries was carried by offshore breezes.

Carson strolled along the narrow beach off Fells Street, sated after a supper of softshell crabs at the Jolly Boat. He'd posted a few bills and agreed to terms with the agent and now he wanted time to think, to walk and watch fireflies among the roadside peonies and listen to croaking in the beach grasses. It felt good to be out of uniform, simple linen shirt billowing in the salt breeze. He was at peace with the world, thanks not least to sweet, heady Jamaican rum—more than he was accustomed to. He followed his shadow on the wet sand until it was overtaken by a smaller one.

"Lieutenant." The voice behind him hesitated. "My mother wants to know if you prefer coffee or tea for breakfast, smoked kippers or eggs . . . and . . ." Sarah stopped as he looked at her, wet feet glistening in the sand, seaweed clinging between her toes. Standing four-square and looming over her, he took in her clinging, simple dress, pressed against her woman's body by the warm wind, against her breasts, belly and legs. The moonlight shone through the fabric and he cursed himself for looking, for moving a step for a better view, for allowing the rum to affect him. He closed his eyes.

"Is something wrong?"

"No, it's just that everything is too right. Perhaps I've been working too hard. Not used to relaxing anymore."

She looked at him quizzically and she understood. He was not like the others, the swaggering mates and bosuns, the nasty captains. She'd seen them all, had sidestepped their groping paws, ignored their smutty words. "See that ship over there?" She jutted her chin proudly toward Tenant's Wharf, where a spanking new schooner lay. "My father built it, and now everyone's copying her. He worked for Mr. Tenant and was going to start his own shipbuilding business."

"I'm deeply sorry. I heard—"

"I don't think he was just drowned. There were other people on the boat, and there was no storm. He wouldn't just *slip* from the bowsprit . . ." Sarah's voice had faltered and now she covered her face with trembling hands and sobbed. When she stopped, she was clinging to Carson, her head on his chest. She tried to push away but was pressed closer, closer and tighter until she felt limp. She felt his heart beating against her cheek, his body against hers, and she felt safe. Then she made a slight movement away from him and he released her.

"My father built boats," Sarah said, choking her tears away, "in privateer fashion, and 'sharp built,' based on solid pilot boat construction. He was the first to do so—even before I was born, he said. But he never was a businessman and he got into debt. He was the first to build decks strong enough for cannon, with a privateer waist. They promised him a partnership but nothing ever happened, so he was about to borrow and start on his own when . . ." Sarah wiped her eyes with her sleeve and walked toward the schooner. "We called it the *No Name* because the buyer would give it his own name. Mr. Tenant is finishing it with another builder. Peculiar, how things happen. Dad got a loan from Mr. Tenant on our house. Now he's dead and nobody knows how much he was offered in partnership. And guess who the landlord is?"

"Mr. Tenant?"

"Funny, we're Mr. Tenant's tenants now."

"Do you have a lawyer?"

"And what do we pay him with? Come on, have you ever been aboard a real Baltimore pilot schooner?" Sarah laughed and ran to the wharf, from which she lithely jumped onto the schooner's deck. "C'mon, Mr. DeWitt, relax!" She pushed her long tresses back over her shoulder and pried up the aft companionway hatch. "My older brothers worked on this one with father. Then they joined up."

"Privateer?"

"Jeb is on the *Rossie*, workin' up with Commodore Barney, and George has gone to Washington. He's on the *Constellation*."

"Very fine commanders they'll have. I've met Captain Stewart, and Commodore Barney is considered by many to be the equal of Barry and Preble as father of our navy."

"With so many fathers, I pity the mother." Sarah climbed down, swallowed by the schooner *No Name*. Carson followed down the companionway while Sarah found a match and lit one of the gimbaled oil lamps; she held the match live and also lit a lantern which she handed to Carson. "Just look at the joiner work, and the bad-weather handholds." She demonstrated, and in doing so found herself yet again in his arms, the lantern set aside. He flipped open several buttons on her back and his hand slipped inside her dress. It sent shivers through her as it moved down. She pushed him from her with a playful smile. He reached but she danced away from his grasp.

"Just look at the hammock stanchions. And the shot stowage. I'll bet your navy doesn't do as well." Sarah bolted aft, into the captain's greatcabin. Carson was fast behind her. "Here's the chart-box . . . Dad built it as a pass-through like a cupboard so the cox'n wouldn't have to enter to be given a chart . . ."

The brass door lock clicked shut and Carson set his lantern on the deck, next to the captain's railed bunk. He drew the transom curtain snug. Sarah stared at the bunk. Was this going to be *it*? She tried to say no but she was quiet as he advanced upon her, holding her firmly by her elbows and sliding her down, her back against cool mahogany, her dress unbuttoned. There was a curl of a smile on his lips as his mouth came down on hers. She felt her dress slipping over her shoulders, felt her back touching the rug as he lowered her to the floor, and a coolness on her inside thighs as they were gently forced apart.

Sarah kept her eyes closed, a semi-smile on her lips; she was in a kind of ecstasy of submission, content in the knowledge that she was as much the hunter as he. She let him do what she'd heard tell that men do. She dug her fingernails into his neck, pulling him down, moaning and arching her pelvis into him. When he could stand it no more, he reared back, lifting her, forcing her knees over her shoulders . . .

A string of firecrackers and roman candles burst in their heads as he thrust, she biting her lips in anticipation of the pain they said would come. She wanted to scream for delight but didn't.

There was no pain for Sarah.

Her man, spent, collapsed onto his elbows, then lightly rolled over, touching her arm with his fingers. They lay for long minutes, watching the stars through the skylight hatch as the boat slowly rocked in the rising tide.

His hand found hers and pressed it reassuringly. She turned, studying his profile in the moonlight, and gave his hand an answering squeeze.

Monday, 22 June
Settled for fried eggs with ham. I promised Sarah last night that we would be married and she was happy as a mockingbird. I must make it clear, however, that it will have to wait a bit. My parents would expect a proper letter from me and I would like to have their blessing. Dare not tell Captain Hull about it yet and Sarah has vowed secrecy as well. I must purchase something on Baltimore Street tomorrow, something she can keep as a token of my intentions after we sail.

As is my habit in daily accounts, I have started with the morning—though the most calamitous event happened much later, and I will deal with it in due course.

Sarah insisted on accompanying me on my rounds this morning and this afternoon to post the handbills. Past five, she agreed to leave me alone to pursue my mission. There are some places that a woman should not frequent, and the Jolly Boat is one such place. Mr. Needham, a picturebook rake, brought a Frenchman by the name of Claude Chassagne. Needham no doubt hoped to be five dollars richer for the introduction, for officers are as rare in recruiting as hen's teeth. Chassagne, a ruddy, stocky type with an eye for the barmaid, had of late been a lieutenant in Napoleon's navy. And of all things, he was just involved in capturing a British warship off Federal Hill point, across the harbor. The Frenchman had been advanced money enough to buy and equip a schooner, and upon leaving the bay he had encountered, fired upon and taken the brig Othello under Captain Glover, inward bound from London on 13 May. Having no prize crew, Lieutenant Chassagne had been obliged to let the Englishman go.

This act of piracy was too much, even for this "den of pirates" as the British call Baltimore, and an expedition was sent to bring the brigands to justice. The courts could not agree on which law, if any, had been broken, so the Frenchmen were freed and their boat confiscated, Chassagne retreating to his financier, a Baltimore lady who was once married to Jerome Bonaparte, younger brother of the emperor. This is the same prominent lady whose sister-in-law (after the death of her husband) married the Duke of Wellington's brother. If Lieutenant Chassagne is as good an officer as he has been an entrepeneur, Constitution should be fortunate. The Frenchman, however, has expressed a desire to become an officer only after pulling a seaman's duty for a month—in order to prove himself and not anger others with his claim to the rank. This is a matter for Captain Hull to decide upon.

It was almost seven and I'd signed up several

seamen, giving them cash advances, when the calamity occurred. Word came of a riot on Gay Street! Needham promptly closed his tavern and all Fell's Point proceeded uptown. Merchants, grocers, barbers, seamen, prostitutes and priests —as well as my new French friend and I. A rowdy mob was raiding the offices of the Federal Republic, the newspaper that had decried the war. Ezekiel Hammond's prediction had come true. Printing type was strewn underfoot in the street, presses were being smashed and pieces thrown out windows and paper was scattered like a Boston snowstorm. A man fell and broke his neck while pulling out a windowframe on the second floor. After the man died, the mob, shouting for tarring the yellow-livered editors, put hooks to the building frame and tore it apart. Several houses were burnt and plundered, ships were looted at their wharves and rigging and sails were slashed on the rumor that the ships had British licenses—a not uncommon practice of penurious tradesmen. The mayor and several magistrates were among the onlookers; there were no arrests.

If this action reflects the will of the people of our country, I can begin to understand why the Congress declared war. It reminds me of the stories I heard from my father and from his friends John Langley Hunter and Matthew Bell about the American Revolution.

I am looking forward to a more successful re-

cruitment on the morrow. But can I sleep? I must.

"Carson, I just had to show you my private island. It can only be reached at the lowest spring tide like this . . ." The couple waded through sun-warmed shallows. Sarah splashed playfully, scattering snapper fingerlings and frightening conchs back into their mossy spirals.

"I've got to get back to work by half past two." Carson stopped to roll up his white ducks and tie his boots more firmly about his neck. What a sight he must be!

"When we hear the bells strike two, we'll start back. Can't stay more than an hour anyway because of the quick tide and strong currents through here. At high tide it's over my head!" Sarah sang happily as she skipped barefoot onto the small island of sand. She darted in and out of swaying beach grasses and deep dunes, losing him at times.

"This way, over here," she teased him, crouching down to hide.

Carson grinned mischievously and decided to turn the tables. He took off his jacket and set his boots and cap on a high rock. Then he sprinted the opposite way from Sarah and climbed onto a low cliff, where he could watch her and not be seen.

She doubled back and made for the crescent beach, thinking he'd rounded the turn and was hiding. She passed him as he crouched behind a boulder and he tiptoed after her, pouncing and wrestling the astonished girl to the sand. She struggled against him, her breath coming in leaps and starts before she stretched out next to him, on her back under his strong arm.

"Young lady, you are my prisoner once more. For attempting escape there is but one punishment." Carson kneeled over her and stripped off his shirt, growling in imitation of an animal.

She pulled him down for a lingering kiss. "If I'm your prisoner, it is I who should serve you." Before he could object, Sarah had taken the initiative, wrestled him down and crawled onto him. He felt a warm hand inside his trousers and he pushed it further. She found herself holding something she dared not look at, out of modesty. His hand held hers firmly and she closed her eyes tightly so as not to appear forward or chance embarrassing him. Was it wrong that she had taken the initiative or was this what it was supposed to be like? Would it be prudish to resist? Oh God, what is right—what is wrong? Sarah wrested her hand away . . .

"The tide, Carson. Didn't the bells ring?" She turned on her stomach, wavelets lapping at her ankles, wetting her yellow polka-dotted dress.

Carson did not answer.

She buried her head in her arms and waited, not stirring at the rustle of her skirts and the warmth of sun on her legs . . . at the touch of his hand. She felt herself being lifted, pulled to her knees, and opened her eyes to brush sand away from her cheeks and arms. Sarah waited, dared not move, hardly breathing. She felt his hand under her, gentle, exploring as no one ever had before. Her body recoiled briefly, then recovered . . . pushed back at the intruder. A tiny fiddler crab sidestepped before her astonished eyes and slipped into his sandy tunnel.

Carson felt that he was taking advantage, but he couldn't control his passion. The primeval sea and sand stirred his instincts and he drove again and again. The pangs of guilt mounted and he almost faltered. But then an enormous butterfly fluttered softly onto Sarah's back, barely inches from his grasping thumbs, its lemon wings with black tracery pulsing in cadence with him . . . and he forgot the real world for the ephemeral.

After splashing in the refreshing surf they lay drying in the sun. Sarah playfully poured fine white sand on his back and brushed it off. She'd never gloried in another's body before, the soft down, the rounds and valleys.

"Carson, you have a little tattoo," she said, gingerly touching it. "In the strangest place . . ."

"The snapping turtle? My brother Caleb has one, too—if he's alive . . ." He told her the story, finishing after the churchbells rang two o'clock and they fought against waist-deep currents to the mainland.

June 29

RED, WHITE AND BLUE banners and bunting streamed from myriad mastheads, private houses, business establishments and public buildings.

A fair breeze slapped the stays and shrouds of five ships, privateers snubbed against each other on the main wharf at South Street. Captains' flags and owners' pennants curled in the wind high over the townsfolk turned out on a bright Monday morning on this auspicious day—a day that for all purposes signalled the start of the second war of independence. Independence and profit—not least the latter—were on the minds of those gentlemen sporting long Havanas and white straw hats, looking at gold watches on heavy gold chains that they pulled from their finely tailored vest pockets. They counted the shot and casks on the wharf and made mental notes of their investments. They inspected the cannon, newly forged at Dorsey's Foundry, north of town, and copied down the serial numbers for insurance purposes. They envisioned tenfold returns on their investments, which amounted to an average of forty thousand dollars per vessel, less provisions.

This was the day on which the official commissions were to be presented to the first five privateers out of the city of Baltimore, to the armed knights of the sea who would shortly embark on their mercantile crusade. Fancy scrolls had been penned by the calligraphers of the Capitol, reading in part:

> . . . BE IT KNOWN that in pursuance of an Act of Congress passed on the eighteenth day of June . . . I have commissioned . . . the private armed schooner called the *Rossie* of burthen 280 tons . . . owned by . . . of the City of Baltimore . . . mounting eleven guns, and navigated by upwards of 100 men . . . hereby authorizing Joshua B. Barney, Captain, and other officers and crew . . . to subdue, seize and take any armed or unarmed British vessel, public or private . . . and the goods and effects . . .

on board . . . to bring within some port of
the United States . . .
>   By the President, James Madison,
>   and J. Monroe, Sec. of State

Three blocks north, two coaches-and-four
quietly left the rendezvous after picking up
Lieutenant Hale and his marine recruits. It
headed west toward the Post Road, passing a
roadsign that indicated:

>   Washington — 41 Mi.
>   Fredericksburg — 79
>   Richmond — 158
>   Norfolk — 238

Arriving in Norfolk late in the evening, the
recruits were berthed at the naval barracks
while DeWitt and Hale carried on their recruit-
ment, word having been sent that the *Constitution* had been detained at Annapolis and would
not appear for some days. This allowed precious
time for the officers to procure carronade shot
and powder, which was in short supply in the
South.

On the tenth of July, after celebrating the
glorious Fourth in Southern style with grits and
chicken, Carson rejoiced at the sight of his ship
anchored off Cape Henry Light. An exchange of
semaphore messages brought in the launch while
a barge was borrowed from the naval wharf to
carry the shot and powder.

85

Thirty-seven recruits crowded into two boats and were rowed to the anchorage—some eager, some with second thoughts after a week of military confinement and some quietly resigned. Among the last were two powder boys, Nicolas Baker and his friend Lem Wilson. The flamboyant Frenchman, Chassagne, demonstrated his nautical ability by quickly untangling a line that had fouled the launch's rudder upon leaving the wharf. He was aided by Malika Tombs, part Indian, who had enlisted the previous night after a coaster voyage from New York. Originally from Long Island, he'd had valuable experience as a rigger aboard a whaler out of Sag Harbor.

Jack Dranik, on the tiller, looked up toward heaven. A motley bunch, he thought, but a body's a body and he'd be content as long as they pulled their weight.

Ship's surgeon Amos Biggs looked into their ears and mouths, then scribbled his initials on the manifest next to each name. He asked them about their medical histories, noted the replies and added his observations.

Occasionally, he'd blink and take off his spectacles to wipe at his watery eyes. It was his eyesight that kept him from becoming as competent a practitioner as his father. It was warm, too warm in the cramped sick bay, deep in the forward, third deck section by the bowsprit bitts. The Bostonians who built the frigate were not concerned with ventilation. It never got to 100 Fahrenheit in Boston!

Or was it the pills? Biggs was in the habit of trying a pill now and then, certain ones easing his anxiety and tensions. Perhaps it was a combination of heat and pills that made him feel whoozy. Perhaps he would go back to spirits. Neutral corn brandy would be best. Yes, he would assemble a distilling device in the medicine locker, labeling it for the production of rubbing alcohol. His father had used his influence to get the commission for him, and young Ames was determined to live up to his father's expectations. In a year, having proven his worth, there awaited an easy practice in Georgetown, prescribing Gascoigne's celebrated powders for wealthy senators and planters.

The deck above him and the companionway outside the sick bay clunked and clacked under a column of recruits. Biggs sighed and turned to Surgeon's Mate Yeates.

"Don't let them all in at once," he warned.

"Aye, sir, I'll notify the bosun's mate to parcel them."

"No more than five at a time." Biggs sat on a ladderback chair against the forward bulkhead, drumming his fingers on a small, round table. This was to be his first "short arm" inspection. He had planned to move his chair from left to right, sitting rather than standing and having to bend over or squat indecorously before the recruits' private parts. According to naval surgeon's instructions, it was to be expected that venereal disease among recruits from an area of high prostitution—and Fell's Point was one of the worst—would be found at a rate of one in ten. He nodded to his second mate, Armstrong, who beckoned the men inside.

Cox'n Jack Dranik, spouting Scots brogue, ushered five recruits around the suspended sick bunks.

"Up yer elbows, mates. Touch th' mon next to ye, then fur'rd and come to attention. That's it. Now drop yer trousers. Hurry now, the doctor hasn't all day." Dranik stepped behind them.

The surgeon slid his chair forward, set his jaw sternly and adjusted his wire-framed bifocals as he looked at the first candidate. He examined each in turn, nodding for a healthy, clean specimen and giving a low grunt for the opposite.

Poking his wooden tongue-depressor under a questionable appendage, Biggs shook his head in distaste. "Lesion, anterior. *P.*"

Yeates noted the statement next to *Pisano, Albert.* The stocky seaman crossed himself quickly, then gestured despairingly, palms upward.

"Chassagne, Claude." The Frenchman crowed proudly when Biggs was taken aback by his singular endowment. The rank bent over, gasped and chuckled, until Dranik restored order.

"Malika Tombs, that's an Indian name?" Biggs took off his spectacles and wiped them on the shirtcuff protruding from his coatsleeve.

"Malika is from the great Mohawk nation." Malika was not proud of his white mother, nor of his father, for diluting his proud heritage. "I am descended from Dag-ah-eoga, who was father of Hayo-went-ha and who conquered the Can-ah-see in Brueckelyn." Biggs examined the Indian a second time, lest he overlook a symptom.

Abruptly, the hull shuddered, scraping along its spine, the jolt swinging the bunks crazily and staggering Malika's group in all directions. Outside the sick-bay door, the final two groups were thrown against each other. The cox'n's mate did not recover quickly enough to notice that two of his powder boys had "fallen" behind the foremast.

Constitution's copperclad bottom had run against a shoal while hauling in the anchor cable in advance of the order to weigh. All decks and stations were notified and assured that the boat was now clear and standing off.

The inspection over, Doctor-Lieutenant Biggs summarized and sent his report to First Lieutenant Morris. There were but two cases and they were treatable, probably curable. He recommended the recruits be confined and discharged if the symptoms had not disappeared upon reaching New York.

Shortly thereafter, the double-decked capstan groaned, thirty-two men on two decks leaning into the heavers, hauling the frigate toward its two-and-a-half-ton bow anchor, buried in kelp and black silt.

"Anchor freeee . . .," cried the bow watch as he saw the cable swing to vertical from his po-

sition on the starboard cat-head. Thirty-two
voïces, starting with a few, had reached a cre-
scendo as the men plodded round and round.
Aft, the spanker loosed and luffed, then caught a
breeze and stiffened . . . The capstan song rose
into the rigging as the ship swung into the wind
and the fore mains'l was shook out.

> . . . *Oh Shenando-ah, I love thy daught-errr.*
> *Heave awaaaay, I'm bound to gooo . . .*
> *Across the wide Miss-ouri . . .*

Ship Shoal Island, northeast of Cape Charles,
was being sighted in the crosshairs of Lieutenant
Shubrick's pelorus when Dranik's hard knuckles
rapped on Biggs's day-cabin door, to port of the
sick bay. The doctor juggled a glass retort and
stowed a bowl of mashed Indian maize below
his desk. "I'm extremely busy now," he called
out, setting the retort down and putting his hat
over it.

"Then I'll put the captain's message under
your door."

Biggs picked up the envelope and opened it
with trembling fingers. "It has been brought to
my attention," he read, "that of the thirty-seven
recruits listed on the manifest and accounted for
upon boarding by Lieutenants DeWitt and Hale,
only thirty-six have been physically examined
and initialed so by you. Please compare your
report with the manifest and correct the situation immediately."

A comparison of the ship's list with his own pointed out that the ship's powder boy, Lemuel Wilson, had not been inspected. Evans called the master-at-arms of marines and the errant recruit was ferreted out and brought before him.

"But I don't have any disease." Wilson squirmed uncomfortably at the doctor's question.

"Have you had intercourse lately? Or *ever?*" The surgeon walked slowly around the boy. It was easier without a crowd; he could try the personal approach, a peripatetic bedside manner.

"No. Never!" Wilson lied, remembering the encounter the previous Sunday night in Baltimore.

"Then there's nothing to be afraid of. Trousers, please." Biggs motioned with his tongue depressor and sat down as earlier.

"I won't! You can't force me! I'll—" Wilson's voice broke into soprano as he bolted toward the door, but he was caught and dragged back by Armstrong. Wilson started to scream but the mate gagged him and pinned his arms behind his back.

"It won't take a minute, son." Biggs slid his chair forward and quickly unbuckled the struggling recruit's belt. Then he undid the trouser buttons and the stiff cotton duck slid down. The surgeon snapped the skivvies over the boy's knees and leaned close to examine him. For a moment it didn't occur to him that Wilson was different, only that he was young and immature. Biggs probed with his little wooden stick. He suddenly drew his hand back and peered over his bifocals.

Wilson was either a hermaphrodite—or a female!

Biggs turned pale, suddenly feeling faint.

"What is it, sir?" Armstrong was still restraining Wilson from behind, gagging him.

"Er, nothing." Biggs pulled up Wilson's shorts. "Let it—let the recruit go . . . No lesions, Armstrong. You can leave now. I'll make my report." Biggs waited for the door to close as Lem's violet eyes burned into him. Lem pulled up her trousers defiantly while her face turned beet red.

"I'll have to report this, Wilson."

"Call me Sarah. Sarah Lewis." She sauntered over to a mirror and poked at her bowl-cut chestnut hair.

"Miss Lewis," Biggs wheezed, ". . . look, I don't want to be court-martialed. This is a serious offense, the rules state that—" He rummaged in his desk drawer for a naval manual.

"So, I'm a girl. But I can explain," Sarah pleaded. "My family's house on Fell's Point . . . we can't meet the mortgage payments, so I had to . . ."

"Two month's advance?" Biggs exclaimed, his disbelief obvious.

Sarah nodded, biting her upper lip.

"I'll talk to the captain. We'll put you off in New York."

"When will that be?" She held her breath, thinking of Carson, of her desperation if she had to leave him.

"A week, maybe more."

"This is the damndest thing I've ever heard of, DeWitt. We'll be laughed out of the fleet." Captain Hull paced rapidly back and forth, from one cannon breech to another. "Where is the girl now?"

"In the sick bay. I've put her . . . Wilson, on temporary duty as surgeon's steward."

"You sure nobody else knows?"

"Biggs promised."

"Well, at least that's something. And on my first command . . ." Hull wrung his hands behind him.

"My fault, sir."

"How could you have known unless . . ."

"Unless?"

"No matter, DeWitt. What's done is done."

"Perhaps nobody else *has* to know."

"Make yourself clear, Lieutenant."

"Put the girl off in New York, quietly. I'll be responsible."

"It could mean your commission—"

"I'll gamble that, sir."

"All right, DeWitt. I don't know anything about it. I've got a ship to put in fighting trim and four hundred inexperienced hands. Go work it out with Biggs . . ."

Sarah and "Nicolas" stood by the scuttlebutt sipping water from a copper ladle and whispering in the dark.

"I'm to be put off in New York. If I play along

they won't press charges. Carson has accepted responsibility for me."

"*That's* not bad!" Nicolas sighed. "I'm just lucky, they'll never suspect *two* on one boat. Thank goodness they missed putting my name on the list." Nicolas slipped a plug of chewing tobacco into her mouth.

"You make a better seaman anyway."

"Thanks. Exit Lucy Brewer. I'll have to polish my act, though. Shhh, here comes the big bad bosun's mate . . ."

"Evenin', mates, I'm parched. Hope you all have saved some for me."

July 17, 1812

THRUST THROUGH open ports and resting on
elevation blocks and recoil hemp cable, the
"long 24s" did not look lethal. They were
"black metal furniture" to the corpulent Captain
Isaac Hull, furniture just like his heavy, carved
and panelled chest, his cherrywood armchairs
and polished table. His cabin, with white panelled walls, wide floor planks and a reddish
mauve oriental rug, spanned the frigate's beam,
39 feet at the stern gun deck. Behind the captain's cabin, two more 24s poked through the
thick oak hull, starred tompions in their six-inch
muzzles to protect the double-shotted gunpowder from the ocean and elements.

The brass lamp in Hull's cabin swung ever so

slightly with each swell that disturbed the calm, pale green sea. The officer, having messed alone, slid his tea service over the map, inland from the coast of New Jersey. He traced the chart visually, noting that Sandy Hook, the entrance to New York City's harbor, was over fifty nautical miles away from the last land fix at Brigantine Inlet, which they had passed four hours earlier. The morning wind had promised better, but it had diminished until there was hardly enough for steerageway. At such a speed poor *Constitution* might take days to join Commodore Rodgers's fleet in New York, perhaps arriving too late to accomplish whatever mission had been planned.

He spooned sugar into his cup and stirred nervously, thinking of other wars during the sixteen and early seventeen hundreds. Of Dutch and Russian men-of-war, of engravings in naval treatises showing becalmed ships being rowed into position to deliver broadsides. But those were kin to slave ships, those poor bastards being racked by the whip. And yet . . .

"Sail Ho," a lively shout rang out from above.

The captain sprung out of his chair, belly brushing the table, sea chart sliding and tea sloshing over New Jersey. Sucking in his stomach, he waited, arms up, as his boy buckled on his sword belt and arranged the scabbard. Catching a glimpse of himself in the mirror, he was reminded of his age: thirty-nine, ten years older than any man on the ship. Cut-away uniform jackets were hardly flattering to mature officers, he decided.

Ducking through the low door, he made his way along the gun deck, nodding at the gunners standing by, and clambered up the steep companionway into the bright glare of sky.

"Where was the sail?" He shaded his eyes and set his cocked tricorne square and firm.

"Starb'd, sir." First Lieutenant Charles Morris handed his captain the glass. "Two points for'ard. Four sail now."

"Keep silence, fore and aft." Hull steadied the glass at the white pips on the horizon. "Must be Rodgers's squadron." He looked to port; no land in sight, low haze to the west. "What's our position?"

The navigator, Lieutenant John Shubrick, scuttled to the binnacle for a compass check, then unrolled a small chart and spread it on the mizzen pinrail. The sharp-nosed young officer mumbled some figures quickly, then spoke up, his voice breaking embarrassingly. "Twelve miles south by southeast of Barnegat Inlet, sir."

"DeWitt," Hull barked at the third Lieutenant, "I want soundings—on the half-hour. We don't want to be caught inshore if that's not who I think it is."

"Yes, sir." Carson eyed the sand glass under the ship's bell. The sand had about five minutes to run through. A young boy waited, ready to turn it.

"Ahoy the masthead," called Morris through his speaking trumpet. "What do they look like?" From the quarterdeck, the distant sail was "hull down," but from the mast top a lookout could see around the earth's curvature and make out the hull.

Ordinary Seaman Malika Tombs, descendent of the proud Mohican tribe, pressed his chest against the topgallant mast, one arm holding round its one-foot thickness, the other shading his eagle eyes from the sun. "Three small sail, and one large but lying low," he called down.

"A razee," Lieutenant Morris solemnly commented, "and our navy does not possess such a ship."

"Stand by, all hands," the captain bellowed. "Calwyn, bring 'er about."

"Aye, sir." The sailing master, highest ranking non-com, jumped up on a hinged, wood-grated platform and trumpeted orders as the helmsman waited, holding the huge double wheel against the wind.

The 1600-ton frigate pointed her sixty-foot bowsprit due east. When a fifth sail was sighted, a moderate breeze had picked up, veering from northeast to southeast and allowing the *Constitution* to close in on the nearest sail. The ship, also a frigate, displayed no colors and stood off the slightly larger American vessel, sailing parallel until the sun had dipped into the horizon.

As the sun's last bright rays faded from the top royals of the distant vessels, the unidentified frigate turned away. *Constitution* followed, her marine drummer beating action stations for the long 24s. They were within range!

Aboard the *Guerriere*, a French prize frigate under British command, Captain James Richard

Dacres was very concerned. The other ship was larger, no doubt American, and he didn't know the identity of the five distant sail. It could be Commodore Rodgers's rebel fleet out of New York. It could be a trap; the American navy was green, but green forces were often cunning. Darkness solved his dilemma. At ten o'clock *Constitution* shortened sail and ran up a private signal. After an hour without response, the signal was lowered and Hull made sail under a light breeze.

Shortly before dawn *Guerriere* tacked, wore round, then sent up a rocket and fired two signal guns, startling the American gun crews out of their deck hammocks. Receiving no reply to his signal, the British commander stood away. By the time Hull noted the other's flight the breeze had died.

Colors were run up as the mist of early morning melted away. Captain Hull found himself surrounded by the enemy! The vessel he had been maneuvering with all night was *Guerriere*, commanded by an officer he'd known in Paris a few years earlier. They'd made a wager; in the event of an engagement between the two, the prize was to be the vanquished's cocked hat!

Hull recognized the squadron as that of Admiral Sir Philip Broke, one of the most competent of the British commanders. Two frigates, *Belvedira* and Broke's flagship, *Shannon*, were on his lee quarter, though out of range, and five boats were astern, including the powerful razee *Africa* of sixty-four guns under Captain John

Bastard. Bringing up the rear was a twelve-gun schooner, *Nautilus,* just captured and manned by British, her American crew interned.

Constitution lay becalmed, sails limp, with the ocean current slowly drifting her toward the enemy warships. Once engaged, Hull knew he would be pounced on by the entire fleet and forced to strike his colors—and he was determined not to. He also knew that his ship's best weapon was her speed—but there was no wind.

"I couldn't help it, I couldn't bear being away from you . . ." Sarah snuggled against Carson's chest. They had arranged to meet in the sail locker, one deck below the sick bay.

"Sarah, I'll have to go topside fast. British warships all around us, but they're still out of range. We'd make a run for it but we're almost becalmed."

"Well, aren't they, too?"

He lowered his voice upon hearing footsteps in the armory beyond the compartment bulkhead. "Sooner or later we'll drift into range of one of them."

"But at least we're together, my darling. If—"

"The captain won't risk an engagement. Nothing to gain . . . outnumbered six to one. It's not uncommon for a ship to strike colors at two-to-one odds."

"Maybe I brought the ship bad luck?" Sarah pouted.

"The surgeon told me why you did it." Carson kissed her forehead and ruffled her hair with

his hands. "You know, you look just like Seth
with your short hair."

"I was so embarrassed when—"

"I'm jealous of Biggs."

"Silly," she giggled.

"Promise me you'll stay below."

"Aye, aye sir," Sarah whispered. "I love you!"

But he was gone.

"Unship the pinnace, mates; we're putting all
boats over." Jack Dranik led a detail to the 36-
foot launch lashed down on chocks over the
spar deck hatches. "On the double, now!"

The seamen swarmed over the boat and rigged
tackle to the two smaller boats nesting inside.
Aloft, sail was taken in and the main yard swung
fore and aft over the boats; lines were reaved
through gun tackle blocks and led aft to the capstans. One by one the three deck boats were
lowered over the port waist gun'l, invisible to
Broke's squadron which lay a mile off the stern
and starboard quarter. One by one, the seamen
went over the side, coils of line over their shoulders as they worked the boats forward, close to
the hull. Over went the two whaleboats, davits
creaking, and finally the captain's gig. Once
under the bows, lines were payed out port and
starboard and into the ship's boats as they pulled
ahead. Stout hemp cables snapped taut as the
slack was taken up. Hull ordered his own boat
rowed into the current, slight as it was, to open
the distance as quickly as possible.

Meanwhile, gangs of seamen scrambled up the

ratlines, forming a bucket brigade and wetting down the sails, a practice that normally gained the maximum sail performance in very light airs. Admiral Broke's lieutenants, sharp-eyed at their flint glass achromatic telescopes, assumed there must be a breeze and called for similar measures. It was a clever ruse. *Constitution*'s "white ash breeze," as rowing was called, gradually opened the distance. At the same time gangs of sailors with axes chopped away the woodwork about the captain's aftercabin windows and rigged up two long 24s as stern chasers with an extra 18 on the spar deck above.

As Gunner Moses Smith would later tell it, "Captain Hull came aft, coolly surveyed the scene, took a match-rope in his hand, and ordered the quartermaster to hoist the American colors. I stood within a few feet of Hull at the time. He clapped the fire to my gun, and such a barking as sounded over the sea! It was worth hearing. No sooner had our iron dog opened his mouth in this manner, than the enemy opened the whole of theirs! Every one of the ships fired directly toward us. Those nearest kept up their firing for some time, but of course not a shot reached us then, at the distance we were.

"Captain Hull gave up the match to the gun captain, and we kept blazing away with our stern chasers. The shot we fired helped send us ahead, out of reach of the enemy. There was little or no wind, but we resolved to save ourselves from capture, or sink in the conflict. We soon found that we made but slow work in getting ahead.

Hull called to Lieutenant Morris, 'Let's lay broadside to them.' Admiral Broke's lieutenants had finally espied the sweep boats and were doing one better—putting twenty tow boats in front of the flagship, *Shannon*. "Since we can't outrun them," Hull said, "let's fight them all! If they sink us, we'll go down like men!' "

As a last resort, rather than put guns overboard to lighten the ship, Hull ordered most of the fresh water pumped out. But even being twenty-five hundred gallons lighter—an equivalent weight of eight long guns—made little difference. *Shannon* was closing the gap.

It seemed futile. Hull paced furiously on the quarterdeck, hoping for a miracle, a gust of wind. The captain stopped and looked along his spar deck. Twenty-five guns, shotted and with ready crews. Below were thirty more long guns, waiting for the command. Fifty-five guns . . . two hundred gunners! Commander Isaac Hull thought of his uncle, Brigadier General William Hull, Revolutionary War hero, governor of Michigan Territory, and now commander of the Western Army marching on Detroit. I must not fail, Hull thought angrily. He had to uphold the military tradition of his family's name, even if it meant using every last ounce of ammunition and still going down for the effort. . . .

First Lieutenant Charles Morris was a veteran of the Barbary Wars. Tripoli, Algiers, Tunis . . . he'd been there. He's seen commanders under stress, even Preble, Decatur and Bainbridge, and he knew the signs. Morris sensed what Captain

Hull was about to do. The first officer had also served aboard merchant ships during the years of peace, few as they had been between 1805 and 1812. He remembered being becalmed outside of Cherbourg with a cargo that would be worth more if it was unloaded before the cargo on the other ships also moored and waiting for a breeze. His captain had run out the kedges, using the small anchors to haul the ship into dock before nightfall. Why not in war too? Morris explained his plan to Hull. The other officers concurred.

"DeWitt, can you handle the lead boat?" Hull asked, his voice weary.

"I will, sir."

"Then go to it, and hurry!"

"Yes, sir," Carson answered. As he passed close to Morris, he added "my pleasure" with a wry smile. He went forward, ordered the 700-pound kedge anchor shackled and called in the pinnace.

"He's got good references, Charley," Captain Hull said, looking after DeWitt. "Carry on . . ."

"Bosun, man the capstans. I want a hundred men, taking half hour turns on both decks. Shubrick, get the second boat ready to ship the 400 kedge . . . Wadsworth, take a detail and bring up a mile of cable. If you can't find a mile of two-inch, you'll have to splice it. On the double!"

Deep in the bowels of the ship, a shadowy figure crawled past the mainmast, over barrel stores to the cable locker. Six-inch anchor cable lay coiled to the ceiling, each loop almost twenty

feet long. The lithe figure, candle in hand, went
from one corner to the other, searching for the
two-inch towing cable, candlelight casting
strange shapes as the man moved, looking high
and low behind the snaked mountains.

Bronzed hands pressed the candle into soft tallow on a cask, then drew out a knife. Its elm
handle, inlaid with blue and white seashell,
sparkled as the hand tested its grip. A thumb
brushed the razor edge before it was laid on a
cable loop halfway up the coils. The knife cut
deftly, traveling around the hemp hawser no
less skillfully than in the early years when it
earned ten dollars from the redcoat major for
each American scalp it severed.

Malika Tombs's toothless grin caught the
light as he finished. The hawser had been cut
one-half inch round its circumference, leaving
a one-inch core.

The half-breed reached for the candle, but as
he did so a huge rat that had been gnawing on
the tallow shaft sunk its needle teeth into Malika's left thumb and held on stubbornly. Knowing that to struggle would only make the wound
worse and chance a second bite, the Indian
calmly sliced through the rat's neck with his
other hand and kicked the convulsing body
away. The jaw, having loosened, was plucked
off the thumb, and Malika flung it into the dark.

He tipped the candle, running tallow into the
cut groove of the hawser, smoothed down the
splayed fibers and tucked the loop of hemp back
into the coil, deeper than the others.

He heard the click of a latch as the door opened atop the stair near the ceiling cable scuttles. Malika blew out his candle as a lantern shone down into the broad storeroom. He ducked and quietly stole aft, dodging casks and boxes, then climbed down a ladder and hid behind the barrels in the bread room.

Seaman Matthew Cox and George Adams hauled the heavy two-inch hawser off the bottom coil and set it aside. Cox felt the bottom coil and nodded to his mate.

"She's damp. May as well use this'n and give 'er a chance to dry on deck when we're through." Cox dragged the rope forward.

"With the looks of things we might be through soon."

"Georgie, always the doomsayer. Now give us a hand here, mates. Beatty, take that section. Hurry it up to the splicers. The riggers are lowering the kedge already and the boats'll be alongside in ten minutes. On the double or I'll demote the lot o' you." Bosun's Mate Symms hustled his detail up the companionway.

Malika waited until the rope detail had left, then lit his candle, opened a bread cask and rubbed flour into his thumb wound to clean it. Then he scraped green mold from a cracked stave, mixed it with saliva and applied the poultice to the wound and tied several turns of hemp twine about his thumb. Before leaving the stores deck he took one more look at the cable locker. Satisfied that the top 120-fathom coil of tow was gone, he returned to his hammock on the forward berthing deck. It would soon be eight o'clock, but even 10 minutes of rest would help exorcise the devil rat's poison before going on duty again. There was no need to see the doctor; the Mohawk medicine would cure the wound. Malika crawled into his hammock, closed his eyes and thought of gold.

"Heave . . . Heave . . ." Dranik leaned on his tiller. "Let's keep the old girl between us and the limeys," he shouted, looking up at the *Constitution* from their small towing boat. "We don't want to catch one o' *Shannon's* bow-chasers if she gets in range . . . *Shannon's* gaining, men. Lean into those sweeps for all you've got. If I've anything to say about it, we'll all draw extra grog if we can open the gap . . ."

A cheer went up from the crew and the boat spurted forward. Seaman Cox was ready on the bow, 700-pound kedge poised for a clean drop at the flip of line from a cleat after the cable was let go aft. Beatty was set to clear the cable and tend to the messenger line bent to the anchor fluke.

"Heave. Heave, mates," Dranik sang out.

"Almost payed out . . ." Carson watched the line snap taut out of the water, trailing seaweed, and then drop down again. The frigate wallowed almost half a mile back, still making way behind the other cutters. "Stand by to boat sweeps." Carson raised his hand as a signal. With the order, eight sets of oars rose as one, a forest of vertical white ash over groans of relief.

"Poor babies," Jack Dranik taunted, "ye won't

get blisters like those poor devils in the tow boats."

Carson raised his arm again. "Stand by to loose the kedge. Watch the cable . . . clear your sweeps." He waited for the boat to snub on the cable. "Cox'n, let go aft."

"All gone aft, sir."

"Let go for-ard . . ."

A geyser spouted over the bow, drenching Cox and Beatty as the cable slipped over the gun'l and followed the anchor down. The messenger line smoked the thole pins as it payed out over a hundred feet straight down.

"Messenger secured."

"Boat your sweeps." Dranik stretched out on the transom thwart. It was now up to the capstan crew to pull the frigate to the anchor. Lieutenant Morris, in the boat that was carrying the 400-pound kedge, was already standing by, lashed under the bow chasers.

Capstan turning and thirty-two men sweating, straining, singing of Shenandoah, the cable twanged free of the ocean, streaming water and kelp, stretching over the bows and along the spar deck past the fore and main masts and faired midships to the massive drum on the capstan hatch. The seamen, in twos, stepped over the inching cable as it was reeled in, first slowly, then faster as the ship gained momentum in the sea.

A white bow wave grew at the stem, under the gilded stars on the decorative trail boards, and *Constitution* magically pulled away from her pursuers.

After long scrutiny through their marine glasses the British caught on. It was not a case of quirk breezes, currents or revolutionary hull design—though the pun on the American captain's name might have occurred to the more prankish aboard Sir Broke's flagship. It was pure cunning!

Malika's dark eyes peered out next to a 24, through the port bow-chaser opening on the *Constitution*. He watched the second boat pass DeWitt's launch to carry the smaller kedge another half mile ahead. He watched the cable being reeled in. But what he was envisioning were the pieces of bright gold given to him by the old man in New York, the man called Magnus DeWitt.

He dreamed of the bald man's promise of a voyage across the sea and a prize red velvet cape given by the English king, of a uniform with bright brass buttons and large epaulettes worthy of an admiral. Malika Tombs was no longer to settle for scalp bounties. He would become a great chief of the Mohawk like Red Jacket; he would command a new name for his station and as many squaws as he desired.

Malika Tombs took his turn on the capstan, wondering when the cable would snap, wincing from the rat bite on his thumb, but singing along with the others as they went round and round . . .

"Oh Shenandoah, I love thy daughter . . ."

Shannon, by now far outdistanced, broke out her kedges and started towing as well. But even with their superior forces the gap prevailed.

The towing and kedging kept on all night. The next day, in an all-out effort, the British abandoned their tow boats for a surprise thrust in a gust of wind that soon died. They lost yet more time by stopping to pick up their boats.

On the third day, *Constitution* had a lead of almost four miles by virtue of a night breeze but *Shannon* was closing again with ship's sweeps as well as tow boats, a return to the Roman galley that only a tyrannical navy might revive in the nineteenth century.

On the American frigate the gun deck was strewn with seamen, asleep the moment they were relieved from duty. But Captain Hull had not slept. He was ever watchful for the slightest sign of wind touching water, ever ready to take full advantage. His skillful maneuvering had kept his ship to windward during the entire chase, and it was because of this that his chance finally came.

A squall was in the making. Hull, experienced in his coastal waters, read the signs and planned his move. He ordered sail taken in as the squall hurled sheets of rain, darkening the sky and obliterating his ship from view of the enemy. The British fleet frantically did likewise, reefing their large sail and heaving to, breaking formation as they battened down.

"Secure all boats and ship the kedges," Calwyn's voice rose into the gale. "All hands aloft, furl the royals and take two reefs 'n th' t'gallants, one 'n the main."

The long, inky cloud, jagged with lightning that threaded toward the riled-up waves, enveloped the heeling frigate as it pitched and yawed.

"Crack on all sail . . ."

The cry went from Calwyn's brass trumpet, spitting out rainwater, aloft to the crosstrees, repeated from ratlines and shouted into the gale at the jib stations. A hundred men in the rigging, crawling with a hand for the ship and a hand for the body, let out the main and fores'l reefs, unfurled the tops'ls, gallants and even the royals. The mainyard crew ran up the studdin' wings and *Constitution* leapt forward into the towering storm waves.

"Settle the peak . . . Stand by to wear ship . . . Trim in the main . . . Press up the helm . . ." The commands flew, mingling with the groan of straining wood and wailing of wind as the stern passed through the gale's eye and the warship shuddered onto its new tack, dipping its head to the swells and shipping ocean water over the trail boards and onto the spar deck. Seamen were washed into the foremast, against the galley smoke pipe and into the gun carriages tangled in tackle.

The sailing master clung to the binnacle, watching the fleur-de-lis of the compass rose card come to balance in its brass bowl, flat blue-steel needle quivering toward the symbol for north—and escape!

Carson DeWitt leaned into the frigate's wheel, holding it over while the aft helmsman recovered his balance. There was a quick look from the helmsman, a look that transcended rank and time, brine running from his kinky black hair and glistening in the half-light of the squall as it cascaded over his dark eyes and cheeks. "Thank you," he wanted to say. "Thank you, Master," he almost said. Will Cuffee, listed as "Mingo" on the runaway slave notice posted in Norfolk, Virginia, had used the credentials of an uncle in New York State and had been recruited as a free man along with Alex Crowninshield and Nicolas Baker.

Constitution, the pride of Boston's shipyards, tipped its log line at better than thirteen knots on a broad reach toward the coast. As the squall receded eastward, lookouts scanned the horizon from the mast tops. Two sails were all that could be seen, hull down over the horizon. Captain Hull decided to make for Boston and not chance encountering Sir Broke again off New York. The breeze held all night, and by morning, sixty-four hours after the chase had begun, *Constitution* had the ocean to herself.

As the frigate wore around Cape Cod's elbow and into a calm sea, it came across a rare sight.

"What do you make of it, Shubrick?" Morris asked.

The fifth lieutenant focused his glass and replied, "English brig with four prizes?" The men on deck were craning for a look.

"That's what I think. I guess we'd better wake the captain."

"The Englishman's striking. Now he's running up the stars and stripes . . . and so are the prizes!" Shubrick gasped, then panned the horizon. "Another sail! Can't make out—"

"Now you know why we sail without colors!" Captain Hull had hurried to the quarterdeck and took the glass from his junior officer. "Fore n' aft rig; she's a coaster and probably headed where we are . . ." He studied the ships. "Shubrick, what would you do if you wanted to play this game, too?"

The young man recognized Hull's words as an order rather than a question, and he sprinted forward toward the flag locker as the ship ploughed ahead.

Hull nodded wryly at his first officer and soon the starboard waist ports were slung up and three carronades run through. Looking up, Morris waited for the British colors to arrive at the mast top, then gave the signal. A vigorous barrage belched from the gun'l stripe, frightening the coaster to change its course and crowd on sail.

"Engagement successful," Hull mused before he went below. "Expenditure, twelve cartridges black powder, and *no* shot."

❊ ❊ ❊

"We'll have to put you off in Boston, Miss Lewis." Surgeon Biggs forgot himself and was caught staring at Sarah as she looked up from folding newly washed linen.

"Regulations are regulations, Doctor." Sarah smiled to herself. She had a plan. And she was ready to use it, if and when it proved necessary.

August 25

"AND I say the *Constitution* is no match for a British ship, even one of a lesser rating." The aged Magnus DeWitt sat with thumbs tucked under his armpits, his satin vest tight across his ample midsection. "She's shorthanded, with inexperienced crews and not enough powder and shot for more than two broadsides. It's been twenty-two days she hasn't been heard from. Why, she was due in New York a fortnight ago and wasn't there when I left yesterday. One can only assume that she's already been taken and is on her way to Halifax under a prize crew. If this war persists, we'll all be bottled up in harbors—losing our hard-won markets on the Continent, in the West Indies and in China. As shipowners and merchants, whether in New York or this fair city of Boston, we are interested in one thing. Profit . . ."

Magnus stopped; his small audience had grown. The Exchange Coffee House on the ground floor of the large brick-domed building on the corner of Devonshire and State Streets was buzzing with a Saturday crowd. With their chores and business done by noon, they'd trickled in through the inviting, open entrances to listen and discourse on the topics of the day, not the least of which was the weather. Boston was always hot during the last week in August.

Magnus lowered his voice and leaned back on the counter rail, facing a small group of businessmen. "I ask you, do we want to play soldier or do we want to do business?"

"Business, of course. Can't survive much more of this. Might sell and buy into textiles. How about privateering?"

"That's the only answer!" Gangly Jeb Stuart set his coffee cup down with a clatter. "There are three, four boats workin' up now."

"That's *not* the only answer, Mr. Stuart." De-Witt immediately wondered whether he'd gone too far, revealed too much. This was, after all, a public place.

"How did you find out the *Constitution* only had shot for two broadsides?"

"Mr. Verry, I happen to know one of the ship's officers personally."

"Just a moment, DeWitt." A polished gentleman of most extravagant summer attire turned from the ornate silver urn, a small cup in hand. "I wouldn't expect one of our intrepid naval officers to give an old Tory like you the right time o' day."

Voices trailed off. The counterman wiped his plates dry in a slower cadence. It was a rare occasion when the richest shipowner in America came down to the Exchange.

"Mister Green, how good to see you again." Magnus tried to fasten his coat across his broad stomach but a button popped off, rolled across the wide plank floor and clinked against a brass doorplate at the entrance.

"Living well, I hope, Mr. DeWitt?" A round of chuckles. "Francis," William Green addressed the counterman, "coffee for all." He sipped from his gilt-brimmed china cup, eyes piercing through the wisps of steam. Touching the corners of his mouth with a lace kerchief, he added, "What is a New York merchant doing up here?"

"One never knows when one might need an extra harbor."

"Then you expect a blockade?" Green's tone turned grim and murmuring rose among the listeners.

"Broke's squadron is not off New York without reason," Magnus pointed out.

"I take it that your brother Schuyler is well? And his lovely wife, Clarissa?"

"Why, yes. They are."

"And their children. Carson must be old enough to vote."

Magnus nodded and sipped his coffee rather

than continue the cat-and-mouse questions. It was well known that he and his brother Schuyler were on opposite sides of the political fence and that they rarely communicated. It was equally well known that Green was a master at cornering his adversaries, both at the bank and in the parlor. "Excellent coffee," Magnus remarked.

"It's *Harrari* from Somaliland, just arrived on the *Betsey*. That's why I'm here now."

Edwin Verry tasted the exotic brew. "Tastes like *Mokka* to me."

"Tastes like, yes, but costs me much less. The Africans are easier to deal with than the Yemenites—"

Suddenly, there was a clanging of bells and shouting on the street. Everyone ran to the windows and doors to watch except Green and DeWitt—a fact which DeWitt took to be surprisingly significant.

"I've heard that Boston has more fires than any other city in the states," Magnus said at last, grinning cryptically.

"Are you talking secession?" Green asked, his tone noncommital.

"I could be . . ."

"I'm afraid you're talking to the wrong man. Now if my business were smaller, say ten boats instead of ten dozen . . ."

"You tricked me," Magnus snarled.

"I did nothing of the sort, Mr. DeWitt. Just because I don't like to watch fires doesn't mean I was waiting for a moment to be alone with you, to discuss business or anything else." Green took his hat off a clothes tree and picked up his silver-tipped walking stick as Magnus stood, fuming like a maddened bull.

"And DeWitt . . ." the magnate paused and tapped his stick on a cast-iron andiron before he exited. "Give my best to your nephew. That is, *if* the *Constitution* has not been taken."

High above Boston, over the shimmering copper cupola of Faneuil Hall's octagonal steeple, a verdigris grasshopper weathervane turned its blind eyes seaward.

August 26

THE SAIL WAS first spotted near Jason Shoal,
two miles off Strawberry Point heading
nor'nor'west toward Nantasket Peninsula.
With studding wings set, she resembled a many-
tiered cloud pursued by the blinding sunrise.

White-haired Tom Wendell, up in the belfry
of Cohasset's Unitarian Church, was splicing a
new bell rope for the eight o'clock sabbath peal
when the ship hove into sight beyond the beach
dunes. After a squint, then a blink of his weathered eyes, he fairly tumbled down the ladder
and scrambled to the parsonage as fast as his
bandy legs permitted.

Trailing his vestments, Reverend Justin
Hatcher stumbled through his garden, almost

dropping his ancient telescope, and climbed into the bell tower.

At first the image shimmered upside down, as in all glasses designed for the night heavens. Thin fingers trembling, the reverend focused. Upside down or rightside up, he recognized the ship as a frigate 44. Almost abeam of the point she lofted colors to her main and mizzen, then streamed a huge flag from her spanker gaff. Stars and stripes! Hatcher inhaled with pride as he studied her lines, her billet head, galley stack, all the small variations that marked her as Boston's own progeny, the *Constitution*.

Once back down, Hatcher rang a merry peal, bringing astonished townspeople out in various stages of Sunday attire. It was rare that the bells pealed at no mark on the clock. And never had the entire population of Cohasset gathered so early on the summit of Scituate Hill.

The bells also tolled along the Charles River and in Back Bay as Captain Hull brought his ship past Harding Ledge, around Point Allerton and into the Narrows between George and Lovell Islands. *Constitution* was hailed and met by buntinged cutters as she ran up her commander's pennant on the maintop, her crew smartly turned out and shouting joyously to her escorts. A salute was fired from Fort Independence and returned in kind as the frigate rode flood tide and a following breeze under shortened sail into the crowded harbor.

Magnus DeWitt peeked out of his third-story

window above the Cocked Hat Tavern overlooking Clarke's Wharf. His eyes widened in
surprise, then narrowed as he angrily set his
jaw. He took a sheet of notepaper from his
satchel and started to write, then crumpled it.
The Indian couldn't read. . . .

The frigate nudged in smoothly at Clarke's
Wharf, a few blocks south of Edmund Hartt's
Naval Shipyard at North Battery where she'd
slid down the ways, bare of sprit and topmasts
on 21 October, 1797, grapejuice dripping from
the beard of its figurehead, a wooden Hercules,
as the ship had been christened.

First down the gangway as the crew snubbed
the cables taut from mooring heads to dock
bollards was Sarah Lewis, still in guise as a
powder boy and carrying Carson DeWitt's seabag. The assembled dignitaries took no heed
of them as they disappeared into the crowds on
Ship Street. After walking stiffly till out of sight
from the ship, Carson shouldered his bag and
gave Sarah the small one he'd been carrying.
He found a coach in front of Christ Church and
tossed his bag in after helping Sarah up. Once
in, he pulled the blinds and shouted through
the speaking hatch: "Peg Moore's boarding
house." He slid it shut.

Sarah and Carson, alone at last, fell into each
other's arms. Not having spoken with each other
for more than a few brief moments since Baltimore, almost a month earlier, they were both
speechless and preferred simply to cling to each

other. After travelling several clattering blocks along Tremont Street, Carson suddenly tore himself away, but smiled reassuringly at Sarah as he cracked open the hatch.

"Driver, can you suggest a good clothing shop for women? I forgot to bring my mother a present." Sarah smiled in delight at his request.

"Right you are, sir. There are a few ladies' apparel establishments on Winter Street. My wife's mother is partial to Madame Renée's Emporium."

"That'll do just fine." Carson closed the hatch. "Sarah, what's your dress size?" He drew a bulging purse from his inside jacket pocket. "We can't register a uniformed powder boy at Moore's."

"Darling, how gallant!" She swooned mischieviously, then became serious. "Carson, I don't want to be without you."

"We'll see each other—but we shouldn't be seen together. You know how the navy is. I'll lose my commission or be transferred."

Sarah nodded and leaned her head on his shoulder.

"Any favorite color or style?" Carson asked.

"Buy what looks best to you—something lively. I like yellows. Happy, light colors."

"Yellow it is."

"Or white with yellow stripes, or polka dots." After a moment she added tentatively, "I could buy a long wig, red or something. Then we could be seen together."

The smile Carson gave her was the answer she'd hoped for. "Good idea. Here." He peeled off a ten-dollar note and pressed it into her hand. "You'll need money anyway."

"I still have some left from my pay." Sarah reached down into her pumps and proudly unfolded a dollar bill, displayed it front and back. "I'm good with money. I saved it in case we got shipwrecked. We could at least buy food."

"And you gave your mother the rest . . . Don't ever change, my love." He kissed her tenderly and the bill fell out of her hand.

"They had wigs, too!" Carson fumbled with the twine, then ripped the box open and shook out the contents on Sarah's lap. "Here, might as well put it on."

"Oh, it's beautiful, and not too red." She turned it slowly, then lifted it and set it squarely over her short bob.

"Sorry, I should have bought a mirror." Carson slumped back. "Much better for an up-and-coming officer to be seen with a pretty girl than with a boy."

"Now close your eyes." Sarah demurely unbuttoned her trousers and laid out the dress. "Ooooh, it's just like I've seen the fancy ladies wear in Baltimore. It must have cost—"

He put one hand over her mouth and opened his eyes. She was quiet as he slipped her jumper over her head and kissed her naked breast. He made an animal noise as she sighed deeply, his hand inside her dungarees . . .

"Peggy Moore's just up ahead!"

The cockneyed shout tumbled Sarah into action, leaving Carson dazed. Sarah stepped daintily out of the coach.

"I'll come by at six tomorrow." Carson kissed her lightly and got back in as the coachman looked around perplexedly and scratched under his leather tricorne.

Kahlini's burnished copper skin glistened in the candlelight of the Exchange Coffee House. She projected the aura of an exotic goddess as she sat in a leather-covered wing chair studded with silver buttons. To her side, William Green was engrossed in a notice he'd found attached to the wine list:

> Captain Hull, finding his friends in Boston have been good enough to give him more credit in escaping the British squadron off New York than he ought to claim, takes this opportunity of requesting them to bestow a great part of their good wishes on Lieutenant Morris, the other brave officers and the crew under his command for their very great exertions and prompt attention to orders while the enemy was in chase. Captain Hull has great pleasure in saying that notwithstanding the length of the chase, and the officers and crew being deprived of sleep and allowed but little refreshment during the time, not a murmur was heard to escape them.

"I adore this gown. Is it from Canton, Billy?" Kahlini brushed her cheek with a satin-frilled sleeve.

"What? No . . . Singapore, my pet, er, Princess."

"You are far away, no?"

"I was, but I'm back again and you're the only thing in my life . . ." Green moved closer to the almond-eyed beauty. "May I order you a pineapple with rum?"

"You grow pineapple in Boston?" Her teeth shone white with her broad smile.

"No, but we're working on a new method of shipping perishable foods by manufacturing ice on board, and as an experiment we bought a test machine invented by an Englishman, one Sir John Leslie, two years ago. The principle is a vacuum pump combined with a sulphuric acid container. It only made two pounds of ice in an hour, but that was enough to keep one crate of pineapples on ice for the whole trip. I had several sent over here earlier from the *Hindu.* We're still working the ice machine aboard."

"You're so smart, Billy. Always finding new businesses."

"I wish the *Hindu* could have brought back some sandalwood."

"You did not offer my uncle enough percentage like Mr. Winship. Kamehameha is also smart man. You may order for me American apple pie. Spirits make me silly." Kahlini looked up and smiled as Lieutenant DeWitt passed the table. "Such dashing men, the American officers."

"Now, now, Princess . . ." The silver-haired magnate put his ringed hand on hers. "Jewels and gold are not enough for Kahlini, I see."

She leaned closer to him, unknowingly exposing her ripe breasts. Carson DeWitt, on his way out, stumbled into another man who had stopped for a view of the ebony-tressed beauty's anatomy. Kahlini, at first puzzled, suddenly understood and quickly sat back, embarrassing the lieutenant.

"You bought me this gown, you old devil." She pinched Green's mutton-chopped cheeks with her cerise-tipped fingers. "I think it is your plan for excitement. I forget, because in my islands breasts are not covered."

"They will be—soon, or I won't have any crew to sail my boats back." Green nodded as a waitress set down their order.

"She is pretty, or maybe I am not used to blond people." Kahlini surveyed her pie before attacking it as her escort dug into his half-pineapple.

"You liked the blond lieutenant too?" Green did not look up from his dish.

"You notice everything."

"If I didn't I wouldn't be here with you." His hand strayed under the table, found her knee. "You know, I told the boys yesterday that I was in town because the *Betsey* and *Hindu* had come in."

"Such a liar," she giggled.

He drew closer, hand moving over her knee and whispered, "I'll have my coach pick you up at ten. You'll come to my pied-à-terre, a small mansion on a cliff overlooking the ocean. We can be alone, except for the servants. A person of your family can't stay in that cramped little—"

"But I like my little room!" She slapped his hand as it moved up from her knee without changing her above-table demeanor.

"We *will* get together one of these days before you go to New York."

"Maybe I come this week, yes."

"You'll have lunch with me on Wednesday."

"I wait outside your office, yes."

Malika Tombs was smartly turned out in shiny black tarpaulin hat, red striped shirt, blue bell-mouthed trousers, short blue jacket with six large brass buttons, black pumps and a black silk kerchief square-knotted at the neck. But he still felt like a Mohawk deep inside, and Magnus DeWitt knew it.

"The Mohawks are disappointed, I am disappointed, and the redcoat officer will be disappointed." Magnus craned and peered over the high-backed inglenook bench. Good, only privateers and cutthroats in this tavern. It was hot. He pushed open a leaded window; its stained glass crown and sceptre cast ruby and amber patterns on the gnawed-up tabletop. He slung his jacket onto the bench post and opened his vest, then pushed his bottle of rum across the table. "Pour what you will, Malika."

Malika stared at the bottle.

"Don't be afraid. You won't get like your father with one drink. Here, I'll pour you a little one. You don't have to drink it; you can just sniff at it. After that sea chase . . ."

Malika bent to the tumbler, then snapped back bolt upright, mouth twitching and broad nostrils quivering. He took off his shiny brimmed hat and sniffed again. This time he picked up the glass and guzzled the warm liquid in one swallow. "I take one more, please."

"Tell me what happened off New Jersey," Magnus said as he poured.

"Captain Hull too smart for British. Also boat very fast when we have good wind. I try to stop kedging by cutting the rope before they use it."

"And?"

"I don't know. Rope should have broke. British boats very close behind us for long time in calm, two days almost in cannon range. British 18s not as good as 24s."

"That's yet another problem, the range. We've got to find a way. If Hull's ship wins an engagement with an equal ship, you and I are sunk. There will be no gold for us, and no trip to England."

"And no red cape for Malika. I still be free

if British capture us?" Malika drank his second rum.

"If you're alive, yes."

"Then it better we have no battle."

Magnus drummed his squat fingers on the edge of a pewter plate and squirmed as he wracked his brain for a plan. "Number one, the ship's hull is practically unbreachable—"

"Is what?"

"Cannot be holed by shot."

"All boats can be holed with good cannon." The Indian poured another drink for himself.

"I might as well tell you all. Certain merchants like myself stand to lose a lot if this war continues. The war will continue if the rebels—I mean the Americans—have something to stir them up. Something like an important sea victory. And the *Constitution* may accomplish just that because it can't be holed. We found out that her planks—of ironwood, and God only knows where they found hornbeam of such size for planks—were bent without steaming them! And steam weakens wood fibre. It was an experiment by the builder and hasn't been tested in battle, but an old shipwright told us that an 18 was secretly fired at a backed-up test section, built the same as the *Constitution*—and the ball, fired at a hundred yards' distance, bounced off! The process of bending without steam is so time-consuming and expensive that it hasn't been done again since."

"Then how to sink?" Malika asked.

"A boat doesn't have to sink or be shot up to be defeated." Magnus paused to think, then suddenly grimaced in pain. "Damn this affliction!" He kicked a shoe off under the table.

"You still have devil in foot?"

The old man glared at him. "I know—great wise Mohawk chief say, 'Eat too much, devil eat you!'"

"Malika have enough to drink already. My father was drink dead by devil."

"Malika, the *Constitution* can be defeated by drink!"

The Indian shook his black-haired head. "All whisky locked up with rifles."

"How many gallons of fresh water in each cask below?"

"Twenty."

DeWitt's hooded eyes narrowed. "Malika, you are going to poison the drinking water!"

"Maybe Malika will not!"

"Do you realize what you're saying? You're throwing away a chance to become a great chief, with riches, a commission in the British army, a fancy uniform . . ."

"I am afraid that second time is not lucky. Muck risk."

"What do you want *now*?" DeWitt was fidgety. But he'd known the Indian long enough to know that he too had his price.

* * *

131

Department of the Navy
United States of America
Washington, D.C.

July 28, 1812

NAVAL ORDERS

To Isaac Hull, Captain, U.S.S. *Constitution*,
By order of the President of the United
States. Said ship, crew and commander
shall remain in the Port of Boston for an
indefinite period during which said ship
shall be kept in ready condition effecting
such maintenance and repairs as are necessary in advance of a transference of command, further orders of which are in
progress.

Paul Hamilton,
Sec. Navy
James Madison

Secretary Hamilton, no relation to the late
Alexander, signed the orders, closed them and
affixed his wax seal. He then slid the envelope
into a leather packet of official communications.
Shuffling his papers, the secretary from South
Carolina fingered a personal note from the president and re-read a portion:

". . . and it befits such experience as Bainbridge has that he be given command of the
frigate *Constitution* at the first available opportunity. Please convey my congratulations to
Captain Hull for his brilliant maneuver against

superior enemy forces and for affecting the safety of his ship. You will advise him of the next available command. I am of the opinion that a 36-rated frigate would suit his station . . ."

Hamilton set a match to the note and dropped it flaming into his fireplace where it burned black and crumpled into dust behind the logs. It was almost five o'clock and there was the party at the Russian ambassador's house; considering the state of commerce, it was an occasion of great moment. He picked up the leather packet, then set it back down on his desk. Time enough tomorrow; he'd have his assistant handle the packet sometime in the morning. Tonight, he'd promised his wife to be home early. The only important message was the letter to Captain Hull and there was plenty of time for that. The Boston naval agent had requested additional funds for the deployment of provisioning funds. The *Constitution* could not leave Boston without such appropriation, and any man in town knew that it meant weeks of waiting.

"This is my friend Lieutenant DeWitt. He's to meet a lady friend here soon, and I want you to give them best table in the house. But now we have a drink, no? Then I have to go."

"Very happy to meet you, Lieutenant." Denise Julien curtsied daintily, then slipped behind a counter where she handed a swabbing cloth to the chagrined barkeep apprentice. She held two stemmed glasses and set them lightly down as the boy finished cleaning the counter. "What will it be, gentlemen?"

"Cognac for me." Claude Chassagne slapped a coin on the cherrywood, startling the apprentice.

"No, *no*, Claude!" Denise pushed back a strand of her graying hair. "For memories, first one is on the house." She selected a liqueur from a locker and poured a small amount into an aperitif glass.

Denise held her glass high. "To the kitchen . . ."

"To the kitchen," Chassagne toasted solemnly.

"To the kitchen," Carson echoed.

Denise lifted her apron to her eye and dabbed quickly. "Please excuse me, I have work." The frail woman slipped by and into a corridor.

"Now I explain the toast to the kitchen," Claude said in his heavily accented English. "It is not the kitchen that she go to now. Poor woman, her husband died six years ago. Jean Baptiste Julien made his restaurant, Julien's Restorator, famous for soup. Jean was called the Prince of Soups by everybody. Anyhow, I met Denise in Paris many years ago. Then she married Jean Baptiste and they worked for Georges Jacques Danton. He was famous man and leader of *Cordeliers*. Denise and Jean cooked for his friends too. Then came the Revolution. Danton and his friends all—" Chassagne made a slicing gesture at his throat.

"Guillotined." Carson blanched.

"Monsieur Robespierre did in his friend, Danton, to save himself, then he was executed too. Good! Anyway, when the 'committee' found us three, they asked if we were friends of Danton. 'No,' say Julien. 'Then who do you drink to?' Julien raised his glass of wine and said, 'To the kitchen.' Committee say, 'We drink to kitchen too,' and they went away with good soup Julien made for them. We didn't want to take any chances that the crazy fanatics would change their minds, so Claude helped put them on a boat to America. Now when we toast, it's for kitchen that maybe saved three necks."

"And then you joined the French navy?"

"Another way to save my neck. I like America; they have no guillotines. Maybe I'll try to stay here."

"Our navy is very satisfied with your ability. Captain Hull thinks you'll have no trouble getting a commission after a year or two. You might become naval liaison with France, who knows?" Carson tried to cover his concern over Sarah's lateness.

"Thank you, but pretty soon this seadog wants to have a family, and that means getting a nice farm or plantation somewhere. Maybe in your south when this war is over. I have some friends in New Orleans. I'll go see them, find a nice French girl whose father owns a plantation."

Just then Carson saw Sarah enter the restaurant. He slipped off his stool to meet her.

"She come, I go," Chassagne said.

"Better you meet her than she sees a handsome

man running away from me!" Carson joked.

"Now, wait a minute. I'm French, but not *that* French."

"Sarah, I was worried," Carson said, taking her hand in his and facing the Frenchman. "Sarah, this is Lieutenant Claude Chassagne, formerly of the French navy—and temporarily an able seaman on our boat."

"Now starting, as you say, from chicken scratch." Claude picked up her hand and kissed it. *"Enchanté, madamoiselle."*

"Quel coup de main, monsieur."

"Un coup d'essai, ma cherie."

"Now, just a minute, I don't mind a little hand-kissing, but all that secret talk—" Carson took them by the elbows and escorted them into the dining room.

"No, my friends," Chassagne protested. "I have a previous engagement for supper and I really have to go. I've enjoyed meeting you, Sarah. I'm sure we'll meet again. Carson . . ." Claude gripped the American's arm. *"Au revoir, mon petit mouette."* He spun his hat on one finger and backed graciously from the room.

"Did Claude call you his little mouse?" Carson asked.

Sarah took Carson's hand as they were led to a cozy corner table. They sat down under a framed chart of *The Town of Boston in New England* by Captain John Bonner, 1722, showing wharfs, rope walks, burial grounds and ships in the harbor.

"Do you suppose he recognized me?" Sarah

asked. "The way he stared at first . . . and then to call me his little seagull . . ."

"Don't worry your pretty head, my love. I have a feeling we can trust Claude. Now let's get some good food into you. Navy chow is not meant for growing young ladies."

"I'll wait for you *forever*, Carson DeWitt."

"That's silly. I mean in war you can't plan."

"Do you love me, Carson?"

"Of course, there's never been anyone . . ."

"Then leave the navy and we'll go away, maybe west, and start a new life. You can leave after a year and nobody would blame you. It's an unpopular war. Even unnecessary, according to some people I've met."

"Boston is not America. Have you forgotten Baltimore already?" Carson poured himself another brandy and drank swiftly, his expression perturbed.

"Are you mad at something? Unhappy with me?"

"God, no, Sarah. But I'm not a quitter. Damn, what's the use."

She leaned toward him, candlelight flickering in her violet eyes, and clasped her hands under his. He gripped them firmly. "Sarah, I promise, when this is over . . . Will you marry me *then*?"

"But suppose it takes a long time, like the Thirty Years War?"

"It won't, this is the nineteenth century," he scoffed.

"Carson, there *is* something wrong."

"It's not us, my love." He counted out the tip.

"Then what is it?"

Carson toyed with the coins. "We can't get funds to provision the boat. The Boston naval agent rejected Captain Hull's request. He said he was already in debt with the suppliers and can't afford to send out another man-of-war."

"I should be happy—but I can't be, unless you are." Sarah watched him gravely, then reached out and touched his hand. "There's a lady staying at Peggy Moore's. She's from the Sandwich Islands, very beautiful and very nice. She told me of a Boston merchant who is anxious to finance privateers . . ."

Carson smiled at the suggestion as he stood up to escort her to the door. "Perhaps I could get the captain to run up the Jolly Roger as our colors."

"And you could wear a black eye-patch."

"And a big bushy mustachio," Carson said, holding the door for Sarah.

"I don't like mustachios. They tickle too much."

"How do you know?" He kissed her on the forehead.

A quarter hour later, they climbed the stairs to the second floor of her boarding house. "Are you sure," Sarah cooed as Carson bolted her door behind them, "that you didn't know about the back stairway before you brought me here?"

Carson pulled the drapes shut and turned the sperm oil lamp up to its brightest as Sarah sat on the four-poster bed. He slipped his trousers and drawers off, standing next to the lamp, an arm's length from the demure young girl. Lids low, Sarah hung her auburn wig on the bedpost and wiggled out of her yellow and white dress. She sat on the edge of the quilted bedcover, waiting, expecting strong hands to lay her back and divest her of her laced drawers. Eyes closed, she waited for her lover. She felt her hands in his and waited expectantly to be bedded on her back. But it was not to be. He gently pushed her back on the bed. Something warm was given to her coldish hands, something she dared not look upon. It was offered at her lips and she resisted. It was offered again and she accepted, lips parting, brain reeling, as she felt his strong hands on the nape of her neck. Suddenly she opened her eyes and swallowed the intruder, biting and gnawing until she became aware of his groans. She crawled out from under Carson and he rolled over onto his back. She sat on her haunches, watching him, studying him. She caressed his erection, then trailed it against her skin, drawing it slowly toward the throbbing between her legs.

July 29

THE GOLD-BORDERED black sign ran the entire width of the red brick building's façade: WILLIAM GREEN & CO, INC. Three narrow windows above, two windows and a centered entrance below. The panelled front door, deep sea green, was flanked by black wrought-iron balustrades, embedded in white marble steps and topped with spherical brass finials. On the top step a mud-scraper lay bolted and clean as Carson and Hull ascended, decked out in their frock coats and gold-scabbarded swords. When the brass dolphin door-knocker was answered, an aproned clerk took the captain's calling card and bid the two officers wait in the foyer.

Moments later he beckoned from the curved stairway.

"Lieutenant, please wait here." Captain Hull left his plumed hat with DeWitt and tramped upstairs to the firm's offices.

Carson balanced both hats on a rack, picked up a copy of *The Boston Globe* and stretched his legs out from the deacon's bench, shutting out the mercantile bustle and riffling through the daily for news of the war. Had anything happened while *Constitution* was at sea? The Tuesday edition had carried an account of the three-day chase which he'd clipped and proudly mailed home.

Carson got no further than the first page. The lack of sleep over the past weeks had caught up with him.

"Forty-four thousand pounds of bread—1784 dollars. 27,200 pounds of beef—1752 dollars. 10,900 pounds of pork—1526 dollars. 1500 gallons of spirits—960 dollars!" William Green took off his spectacles and shook his head. "Captain Hull, as a businessman I need collateral. Seventeen thousand dollars would send one of my merchantmen to Canton with a six-fold profit upon return. If Colonel Binney can't get such funds—"

"He will, you know how Washington can be." Hull's fingers twitched nervously behind his chair.

"When will the colonel see me?"

"He's left for Washington already!"

"I see . . ." Green set his glasses back on and

looked at the sum total once more before leaning back on his leather-covered rocker. "Water?"
He poured from a pewter pitcher. "What happens if you lose an engagement, if you lose the
ship? Off to Halifax like *that*," he said, his fingers snapping sharply. "You were lucky once.
But the odds are against a second such escape."

"But we *will* win in an equal encounter."

"That's like a merchant saying he'll profit in
a port he hasn't been to."

"You only have my word, and my signature."

"And either is good from a Maine man . . ."
Green played refracted sunlight through his
bifocals and onto the sheet of figures. "Captain
Hull . . ." The graying elder made a pitched roof
of his slim fingers, his sapphire ring a glowing
chimney. "I'm in this for profit and some say I'm
successful. If I am it's because I have not fi-
nanced many schemes as nebulous as the one you
propose. Should I back you, I would require
affidavits, letters of intention by the owner and
so on. It's the same procedure whether the in-
vestment be real estate, produce—or your frigate.
I assume you have official documents or orders
regarding your purpose, your destination, its
duration. Please understand, this is a business
formality. The owner of your ship is the American government, I take it—no liens or claims. I
must see something in writing before I can even
consider such an outlay of funds. No matter
what my political and personal views are, I am
bound by my investors to use caution in invest-
ing their money, if not mine!"

"I'm afraid the orders have not yet arrived."

"And if you tarry here you chance being bottled up?"

"Sir Broke's squadron could do worse . . ."

"As indeed they already have. If I were him, I'd want immediate satisfaction for your mortifying action. London will not take his blunder lightly." Green tapped his spectacles on the provisions listing. "I'll have to think this over carefully, Captain. Though I'm as patriotic as the next fellow, this year does not promise good. Expect my reply to be sent to your ship by this time tomorrow."

"Oh, excuse me!" Kahlini stepped agilely over Carson's sprawled legs. He awoke with a start, newspaper slipping from his lap. She bent over to pick up the paper but regained her posture, clasping a gloved hand to her bosom. Her fingers searched the frilled neckline and drew it in tighter.

"It's my fault," he apologized, recognizing her as the voluptuous lady he'd seen at the Exchange Coffee House two evenings earlier.

Boots thumped down the steps, then striped blue trousers and a saber as the captain descended.

"You're finished already?" Carson asked.

"I suppose."

When Carson retrieved the hats, Kahlini ascended the stairs.

"Who was *that*?" Hull sniffed perfumed air.

"She didn't say."

"The lady had quite a nice *Guerriere!*" Hull joked.

"Then I missed it." Carson opened the door eagerly. "How did it go, sir?"

"Looks bad. Green wants to see official orders. But even if I had 'em, I suspect he's just putting off his decision to make it less painful for us. He's to send word tomorrow."

"Perhaps they'll come by the morning rider." They walked briskly along Ship Street, under the sprits and yards of Boston's mercantile fleet, while watched from a window above by intrigued Polynesian eyes.

"Who were those American officers, the two who came out of your offices as I arrived?" Kahlini unfolded her vermillion parasol and hooked her arm over her escort's.

"I'm sorry, it took more time than I'd expected. Captain Hull of the frigate *Constitution* stopped in. Perhaps he had an aide with him."

"My, my," Kahlini said coyly. "Is the navy going to make you an admiral with a grand uniform?" They strolled up Charter Street, stopping and admiring the wares in shop windows.

"Strictly business, between the government and William Green, financier. It seems Boston's illustrious man-o-war needs money."

"What an exquisite tea set!" Kahlini pressed against a shop window, her flame-red taffeta dress bright in the sunlight. Inside, a stout old man looked up from polishing a silver pitcher and smiled at her, beckoning her in. Green tipped his cane hat and begged leave.

"He's a legend. We were lucky to see him as he's usually at his copperworks some distance from Boston. Every schoolboy knows his name."

Kahlini read the engraved door-plate:

MR. PAUL REVERE,
Silversmith

"He was one of the so-called Mohawks in the Boston Tea Party." They continued strolling.

"Are you going to give them the money?" Kahlini asked after a time.

"Give who the money?" Green's hand slipped lower on her back as they cut through an alley.

"The American officers and their poor boat!"

"I don't think so."

"I think you should."

"Why?" Green halted, confronting her face to face.

"Do you really want me to see your *pied-à-terre?*"

"Hmmm . . ." The entrepreneur had a preoccupied air as he led Kahlini across State Street.

"Yes, or no? I mean it!"

Green said nothing. His mind was figuring profits and losses, and imagining the secrets of a body he had desired for ten years. He'd first met Kahlini when she was barely pubescent, when he had arranged his trade agreements with Hawaii a decade earlier through her father, John Young, who had visited the islands with Captain

Metcalf. Here she was, now an educated woman of almost twenty-one years. It was time. If 17,000 dollars was the price, he'd kill two birds with it. At sixty years of age, she might well be the last feather in his cap.

He followed Kahlini dutifully into the Exchange Coffee House, acknowledging greetings and hand waves right and left.

It was ebb tide when the big frigate warped out from its dock, helmsman under orders of the branch pilot. Topsails and spanker were loosened and inner jib raised. From Back Bay, from East Boston and Cohasset, Sunday bells called the faithful to worship.

Sarah Lewis was the last to leave Clarke's Wharf. There was a tear in her eye as she waved to Carson, who waved back from the broad stern under the colors.

They'd spent all of Saturday together, and he'd left her at six, only two hours earlier. It was now nine as the ship picked up way and swung past a group of moored merchantmen. Thursday and Friday had been very hectic; she'd meant to tell him, but he was so involved and happy with his duties. Loading provisions, all those crates and casks that so miraculously appeared one morning. Then she almost told him on Saturday, but she didn't want to burden him or to spoil their last day. It would have seemed contrived, a trick, and he would have left in confusion, a dangerous way to go to war.

Now the large flag was streaming out from

the spanker vane and she couldn't see him any-more. She could hardly make out the ship's name or the gilded American eagle below the stern gallery windows as the *Constitution* passed the parapets of Fort Independence and headed east with the channel.

Warm summer southerlies billowed the t'gal-lants as *Constitution* bore through the Roads and disappeared behind Deer Island's verdant hill. Only the raked, bare royal masts and gallants with pole pennants streaming were visible, mov-ing swiftly northeast against a blinding sun.

Sarah walked slowly along the deserted Sun-day wharf. The shops, warehouses and sail lofts that lined the dock's north edge were closed and quiet. Gone were the sightseer's wonders of the previous day: the "sapient dog," the dancing polar bear with his fiddling master, the prankish urchins. . . . She suddenly quickened her gait, picking up her yellow and white skirts and run-ning along Ship Street and up Charter Street toward Christ Church, where gentlemen were helping their ladies out of private carriages, where Carson had found the public coach and taken her to Moore's after buying her the dress she was wearing.

She had a dollar left and searched for a car-riage to hire. Carson had bought her a ticket to Baltimore on the afternoon stage but there was still time to see the ship, to watch it from a high place. She'd had more money but spent it for a birthday present. Carson had had no choice but to accept it as he went up the gangway. He'd stopped at the top, then motioned a kiss to her. She'd had him promise to open the ribboned package on the nineteenth and hoped that the present, which she'd sneaked away to buy while he was sleeping, would be useful to a man at sea as well as on shore.

"Please take me to the hill, where I can see far out past the harbor." Sarah climbed into the open carriage and unfolded her lucky dollar for the benefit of the driver.

"Beacon Hill it is." The rig went trotting up Middle Street and over the canal, veering left on Hanover and up on the Valley Hill road. She strained her eyes to the south, over the shops and houses, but could see neither the harbor approaches nor the ship. Higher and higher they went and the driver drew his reins and swung the carriage around. "This is as far as the road goes, ma'am. Is that there what you're lookin' for?" He pointed at a sail that was slowly disappearing beyond the Winthrop Highlands, north of Boston.

Sarah jumped from the cab, tearing her precious dress. Sobbing, she threw her dollar into the carriage and ran toward a jagged hill overlooking Beacon.

"Miss, that's no place for . . ."

But she didn't hear him, didn't care. All that mattered was that she see, until the boat had reached the horizon, until she'd cried herself out. Tripping, half crawling, she reached the barren summit and climbed up on a huge granite outcropping. It seemed to be the top of the world. She looked toward the northeast and there it was.

Alone, like her.

Tearing her store-bought auburn tresses off, she flung them into the wind-tossed trees far below, shaking her small fist at the distant sail. "Carson, I wanted to tell you but I couldn't . . . You're going to be a father . . . Please come back to me. Please . . ."

Sarah slumped down on her knees, sobbing. The wind rose and murmured about the ledge and through the woods. She listened and tried to hear its words. As a child, as a young girl on Baltimore's sandy shores, the wind had often spoken to her. This time there were no words, only a wail.

Now the sail was dipping beyond the edge of the world. How long had she been here? Minutes? Hours? She had no sense of time anymore. Nothing mattered anymore. Sarah inched to the brink of the ledge and looked down once more.

Carson was gone.

"Damnation, lady! You almost went over!" A powerful hand gripped her arm. "Can't go no higher, and it'd do ye no good anyway. That ship is plumb gone." The carriage driver helped Sarah down from the rock.

"Good thing ye had change comin', young lady, or I mightna have followed you up here. Are you wantin' a ride back?"

"But I don't have enough."

"I'm goin' back anyway, ain't I?"

"In that case, thank you, I will."

The driver waited, hiding a chiseled inscription on the grey rock from her view. Then he followed her down from the steep hill and the rock that was marked as MOUNT WHOREDOM.

"Yes, Dranik, come in." Captain Hull tidied up the papers on the table in his day cabin. "Take a seat," he said, motioning the bosun's mate toward the armchair opposite him, across the polished cherrywood table.

"Sorry to disturb you, sir." Dranik moved his chair carefully and set his hands with cap on his lap.

"Since when do I not have time for the man who knows this ship better than anyone aboard? Nine years, is it?"

"Served with Commodore Preble, sir."

"Dranik, never in my four years have we had occasion to speak privately. I consider this an honor—for me. You've done your job well."

"Nice of you to say so, sir."

"Now, what can *I* do for *you*?" Hull leaned back attentively.

"There's no problem, I hope, sir. It's just that —well, now that we're at war, and I've been a citizen for some years of our great country . . ."

"Go on," Hull softly urged.

"I've done some thinkin', sir, and there seems to be no need for using a name that ain't my given one. I made up Dranik when I signed up, being afraid, after I jumped His Majesty's ship off Cuba, that if I was ever on a ship boarded by the British . . . But now, seeing as I've a proper

family and I mean to stay in this navy if ye'll
have me . . ."

"What is your given name, Bosun?" There was
a trace of smile that quickly was extinguished.

"Kevin Kinnaird, sir."

"A fine Scots name." Hull commented.

"Would it be too much trouble to set it right?
The twins are about to start their schoolin'.
We've got a little place near Scituate."

"Boy and girl?"

"How'd ye know, sir?"

"I didn't. I just hoped for the sake of your
wife."

"Right ye are. Meg's already a help around
our place. And John wants to go to sea like his
father."

"Maybe we can send him to the new academy."

"I'd best be wastin' no more o' yer time, sir."

"Nonsense. Jack, what were the circumstances
of your leaving? You can tell me; it won't leave
this cabin."

The bosun closed his eyes. "A press gang
'persuaded' me into the British navy in the first
place—when I was under the influence, you
might say. Then there was a man aboard the
H.M.S. *Carnatick*, a two-decker 74 I had the
misfortune to serve on. We were in the West
Indies laying off Cuba . . ."

"Were you aboard during the *Baltimore* inci-
dent?"

"It was because of me and several of my
friends having swum to shore that Captain Luce

---

boarded Captain Phillips's boat. We used inflated sheep bladders to float us in at night when the *Carnatick* rounded Cape Varadero."

"Captain Phillips lost five men impressed, three merchants from his convoy and his commission for striking his colors without resisting. An infamous event since our Congress had issued orders against engagement with the British lest it injure trade. I remember it well."

"I am truly sorry for the events I caused. But this man, a bosun's mate at the time, gave us a brutal flogging that was not at all deserved. Many of the crew knew of the escape plan and abetted in their way but thought it foolhardy and dangerous. It was only when I swore to kill the bosun's mate, Bartholemew Creech, that I went with the plan. It would have been him or me—and probably me. A mountain of a brute he was and I'd have been forced to some kind of treachery to best him, something that was against my grain."

"You did the only thing you could, Dra— Kinnaird. I'll talk to the purser about restoring your name; you'll have to work it out with the men. I think Kinnaird will fit your brogue better than Dranik."

"Captain, there's one more thing . . ."

"Another good story, I hope."

"I'm not sure, sir."

"Why?"

"The coasters spoke about *Guerriere* being about."

"What of it?"

"The man I vowed to do in is her bosun!"

"Then, Kinnaird, we have yet another reason to defeat her."

9 *August*

It's been a week since I last saw my lovely Sarah, waving joyously from the wharf. How I miss her, how it hurts to leave the girl. Perhaps . . . No, she really didn't want me to desert my ship. No, better this way. Better not to marry, even though I desire it. God grant that she is safely back to Baltimore.

Captain and I are quite amazed at Mr. Green. He is a true and rare patriot for a Bostonian. He made us believe all was lost, but a miracle occurred overnight. What made it happen we shall never know. We might now have been trapped in port as happened to Captain Stewart in the Chesapeake after we left Norfolk. We are a fortunate ship.

Sometimes I think I know our captain, and at other times he seems so distant. I've heard about "loneliness of command." At thirty-nine, he must indeed have experienced it, especially as the eldest bachelor frigate commander by far. Or are the ship and all of us aboard his family?

After standing east from Boston for two days, we ran the Maine coast and ducked into the Bay of Fundy. There was nothing worthwhile off North Head, the British probably having been warned of our intention by fast-riding loyalists from New Hampshire or southern Maine. Then southeast around Cape Sable's reefs to Nova

Scotia. Off Cape Race we communicated with a brig that confirmed the notions rampant in Boston: another American vessel has been burnt by H.M.S. Spartan, which sailed in concert with Guerriere.

Many of our crew had been paid off at Clarke's Wharf, and I was lucky to have had recruiting help from the local agents. Our replacements were more experienced than those we lost. A new naval directive allowed us special landsmen, including a professor of mathematics, a Finn by the name of Arvo Uuro, to calculate from Mr. Bowditch's tables. Midshipman Lovett and the professor are already inseparable, working their mysterious sums and logarithms till all hours. Bosun's Mate Kinnaird is not quite as happy over the professor's presence. He claimed to me in private that the reason for our ship's previous survival has been the absence of a jinx. In his words, "The only amulet worse than a woman aboard ship is a Finn, regardless of gender," Mr. Kinnaird seems to be getting more Scots by the day.

Thanks to the purchase of extra powder and shot due to Mr. Green's generosity, our gun crews have been practicing daily since Boston. Twenty-five gallons from the grog-tub and a few rounds at a rock or a barrel target have done wonders for the crew's morale and well-being. Our last land-observed position was fixed from Whipple Point and we are now proceeding under moderate airs toward Cape Sable, which

is but ninety sea miles from the Royal Navy
bastion at Halifax.

15 August

During the past week we took a small British
brig from St. John's, bound for Halifax. Too little
to send back as prize, we removed the crew and
burnt her. Next, we took the schooner *Adiona*
and did the same. Her cargo of spruce and
pine for ship timbers made quite a lively fire . . .
a proper answer to the British newspaper that
had recently referred to Constitution as a "pile of
spruce, tied together." So far, this war has been
one of wit and words.

This morning, shortly after daybreak, our topman spotted four sail in the haze. After a chase
we closed and found them to be merchants
escorted by a small British man-of-war, *Avenger*.
She set fire to the brig in tow, cast loose and
ran. The other vessels proved to be a British
brig, just taken with an American prize crew
aboard and about to be retaken by *Avenger*,
and the American brig *Adeline*, captured while
enroute from Liverpool to Boston. (What strange
schemes afoot; certainly news of war had
reached England before *Adeline's* departure!)
The captain took out the British prize master,
put on our own and sent her to Portland with a
message for Commodore Preble's widow from
one of "his boys."

Intelligence from the captured British prize
crew has Broke's squadron on the Grand Banks,

a day's sail from us. Captain Hull is prudent in turning south, not wanting an encore to last month's grueling chase. Our mathematics people and navigation officer have agreed on a clever course to Bermuda.

Other shipboard skirmishes: Seaman Crowninshield, black sheep nephew of an illustrious Salem mercantile family, has run true to form. I suspect he's lost at playing cards and become destitute once more. He showed me a handbill indicating that Will Cuffee, one of our several Africans, is a runaway slave with a bounty of sixty dollars on his head. The spoilt young man proposed that the purser advance him thirty and he promised to give the balance to ship's fund or any needy cause. Not wishing to burden the captain I gave my first threatening order: that unless he gave up gaming and forgot his claim against Cuffee, he would instantly be transferred to Lieutenant Hale's contingent of marines as a specialist in the art of boarding and close-fighting. The gambler handed me his evidence with no further ado and I tore it to little pieces before him.

Shortly thereafter, Will Cuffee, the helmsman's mate, came to me. He was deathly afraid he'd be put in irons but offered to surrender so as not to embarrass me since I'd recruited him . . .

"It be true, sir. I am the 'Mingo' of Mr. Crowninshield's poster." *The African's glistening black head dropped to his massive chest.*

"Will . . ." *I pointed to the paper scraps on the*

wardroom writing table. "Please do me a favor."
He looked up aghast. "Take that stuff and throw
it overboard." I feigned being busy at my desk
*while watching him keenly. Cuffee pushed the
*paper scraps around, then fitted them one to an-
*other till he saw the obvious. Never before had
*I seen a grin that said so much. He shuffled the
*scraps together and snapped to attention with a
sharp "Thank you, sir."

*Hardly had he gotten out the door when I
called to him, "Make sure you cast to lew'ard!"

"Captain, I am sorry to have detained your
good ship, but I have an urgent message—if you
will be so good as to include it with your register
at the New York Customhouse after you arrive."
Captain James Richard Dacres handed a note to
Captain Fash of the merchantman *John Adams*
with a cargo from Liverpool. "Since our coun-
tries are still in occasional mutual commerce, and
your letters are in order, you are free to go. Had
your boat been a larger prize I might have been
obliged to take it into Halifax, but as it is . . ."
The American graciously accepted the terms
and cracked on extra sail and energy for his de-
liverence. In two days the following would be
deposited for public notice:

Captain James Richard Dacres, commander of His Brittanic Majesty's frigate *Guerriere* of forty-four guns, presents his compliments to Commodore Rodgers of the

United States frigate *President*, and will be very happy to meet him, or any other frigate of equal force to the *President*, off Sandy Hook, for the purpose of having a few minutes' tête-à-tête.

17 August

Sighted a large brig at dusk. Chased and brought her to. She was the American privateer, Decatur, 14. Once aboard, her captain explained he had taken us for a British frigate, considering the waters and our lack of colors. In frantic flight, he'd jettisoned all but two of her guns to lighten ship for speed. Having no extra guns, Captain Hull advised him to proceed far offshore to Charleston—which, coincidentally, was her port of hail—in order to evade the mounting blockade.

Decatur's captain recounted having outrun a large British frigate the day before; it was headed north. This was good news since it indicated that Constitution is faster than the enemy man-of-war. Invaluable information for maneuvering, should an engagement be in the offing.

Sarah's present tempts me so, but I shall be true to her wishes and wait until a minute after midnight before I open the mysterious package. Why is it that a woman often manages birthdates better than a man?

August 18

GOOD JOB, McINTYRE." Captain Dacres squinted up at the fore-t'gallant as it loosened and stretched before the southerly wind. He braced himself, hand on the fore royal stay and feet planted apart on the port bowsprit grating forward of the crew's head which had been covered with canvas for the occasion.

Midshipman McIntyre was justly proud that he had finished the job a day before port. It was not the sort of thing that could be accomplished while the boat was loading and refitting. After a week of driving the sailmakers, it was done. The fourteen-year-old apprentice officer read it softly to himself, six words in two lines across the fighting sail, each crimson letter tall as Bart Creech himself:

THIS IS NOT
THE LITTLE BELT

"The Yankee upstarts should have no trouble seeing that," Dacres said. He preceded his phalanx of lieutenants aft to the quarterdeck, stopping to sniff near the galley smokepipe. "Ah, my favorite." He marched on as his subordinates relished the aroma of a roasting pig being basted for wardroom dinner.

" 'E always walks to lew'ard 'o the pipe," leading seaman Jamie Baker observed through the belfrey as the procession passed. "And all we get is salt horse and weevil biscuits."

"I say Dacres is askin' for trouble with that sign of his." Rigger Moffat snubbed a canvas line taut on the pinnace's bow.

"And I hope he gets 'is share," Baker snarled. "The bastard and 'is 'igh-falutin' cronies are going to the entertainment now, all dressed and swaggering as if they were at a music hall."

"God have mercy on poor Daniel Tripe."

"Now ye know Dan is not guilty—"

"Quiet, Creech is about!"

"Proceed!" Dacres called down from the poop.

"Aye, sir." Bosun Creech took over the quarterdeck. "Henrick, call up the scoundrel. Jukes, make ready for a gauntlet. Stand by the band . . ." Creech slashed his whip threateningly at a group of boys as they dragged a hatch grating from under the poop stairs. "We ain't got all day, damn ye." He prodded them briskly as they lashed a wooden tub to the grating and secured a short plank as a thwart.

Bosun's Mate Henrick set another group of boys to tying two hundred three-yarn nettles; short, knotted ropes, one for each of the ship's company. Creech flayed an ominous black cat-o'-nine-tails at a gun carriage as the master-at-arms appeared on deck with his charge in irons. The red-coated marine's saber prodded the seaman forward, the latter shielding his eyes from the bright sun with bloody shackled wrists. He staggered blindly ahead as the drum and fife struck up the dreary "Rogue's March," summoning the entire crew, off watch and on, to the top deck where they took stations port and starboard all the way to the foremast. The boys ran amongst them, distributing a rope nettle to each. Every man in the crew must either cut the accused once or be suspect of implication in the misdeed. They waited, glum and quiet.

Another signal and the master-at-arms unlocked the wrist shackles and shoved the prisoner onto the sledge, where two mates hauled him atop and into the tub, tying his arms to the grating and forcing his back to be bared. Jukes ripped off the man's foul shirt and stepped back as Creech strode forward and towered over the unfortunate victim. The giant flexed his arm muscles proudly, then took off his high black hat and shortcoat and handed them to Jukes.

Creech measured the radius of his swing, then

raised the whip high and came down with all his might, leering at the result. A blood-curdling scream accompanied the lash, sending shivers through the men from quarterdeck to head and stern. The second lash brought on a moan, as did the next ten.

The whip passed to the mates, each of whom added six more lashes to the pulpy streaked back of Daniel Tripe. The last of the thirty-six slashes was followed by silence as the mates rubbed the running blood from their fingers.

Four boys dragged the sledge forward along the deck between two rows of crewmen, fifty inboard and fifty by the guns. Such was the "gauntlet." They struck with diminishing intensity toward the bow—away from Creech's bloodshot eyes and the ship's officers on the poop. But the bosun ran down the port side and waited at the bow, fingering his bull-whip for a swipe at anyone who shirked duty or command.

"Just what did the culprit make off with?" young McIntyre asked haughtily of the helmsman.

Wizened Harris Watfield humored the boy as he steadied the helm. "They say, *sir*, the poor sod was caught in Lieutenant Tovey's cabin, going through the man's gear. It was Mr. Creech who caught him red-handed."

"What did he steal? Answer my question."

"A precious gold watch is missing."

"Then the prisoner was obviously guilty. And the watch . . . it was recovered?"

"No, that's why the severity of the sentence.

Tripe denied the charges and had not the least idea where the watch was."

"Well, helmsman, some people will do *anything* for gain." Midshipman Ewen McIntyre marched through the cordon of starboard hands, fingers tightening about their nettle-whips for want of spanking a child.

"I say, Captain, if my watch isn't found will Tripe be allowed off ship at Halifax?" Conversation halted as the wardroom stewards set crystal wine goblets before the officers. The master-at-arms appeared and handed two bottles of claret to a steward who bent to open them.

"How does it look, Sergeant?" Dacres hailed the marine.

"The spirit locker will make it another week, sir."

"We'll have enough for a party tomorrow?"

"Aye, sir." He left, easing the door closed.

"To answer your question, Tovey, there's no proof except for the bosun's word—which I am bound to take at sea. But once we're ashore it will be decided by a court-martial if you still prefer changes. A fifty-pound loss is no trivial matter. Ten to twenty years' sentence is not uncommon, though I think it might be difficult to prove a case without more evidence."

"Can't Tripe be searched before letting him ashore?"

"I'll put you in charge of that, Lieutenant, but we can't be searching the whole crew . . . in case someone else has it."

"Someone else?" Tovey gripped his arm chair.

"Precisely. Now if I were to steal a watch and I didn't want it found in my possession I would enlist an accomplice."

"Then you think Tripe guilty."

"I think the watch is still on the boat, but I don't believe that Tripe would go through such agony if he knew where it was. Unless . . ."

"Unless what, Captain?" Surgeon Claibourne asked.

"Unless, Doctor, the gauntlet were the *least* painful option." The other five at the table exchanged glances, each thinking of Bart Creech. There was no doubt that the man performed his job efficiently. More than that, none of them wanted to know.

"I move we drink our nightly toasts." Lieutenant Joyce held his glass toward the ceiling lamp.

"To the King," all sang in unison.

"And now the day's toast. What is the day? Tuesday?" Six glasses were raised again as Joyce quickly scanned a card next to his butter plate.

S. *Absent Friends*
M. *Our Ships at Sea*
T. *Our Men*
W. *Ourselves*
T. *A Bloody War or a Sickly Season*
F. *A Willing Foe and Sea Room*
S. *Sweethearts and Wives*

"To our men," he whispered righteously.

"To our men," the swaying room resounded.

August 19, Midwatch

THE SHIP'S BELL, mounted in the gallows between the *Constitution*'s deck boats, rang eight times, ten-year-old powder boy Tommy Ganly dampening the sound with a cloth as he'd been taught to do during sleeping hours. He turned the sand glass and climbed sleepily into his canvas hammock slung between two carronades. Dawn blushed faintly as the dog star glimmered on the zenith.

Midships below, on the dark long-gun deck, Malika Tombs rocked the filler plug from the top of the scuttlebutt barrel which lay on its side on a raised cradle. The head spigot had been removed at nine the night before and a cork tamped in. The Indian listened, ear to the staves.

The barrel was filled for the day's supply. At reveille the marine guard would take his station, and at noon the grog tub would be filled with rum. But now Malika was alone. The plug came loose and he nervously turned out the stopper from a small apothecary's bottle. Only an occasional snore from the berthing deck below and a snort or bleat from the livestock manger forward broke the peace of night.

He heard the powder fizzle into the vatted water and picked up the filler plug, then recoiled as a shaft of light sprang down the stairs. A lantern beam swung through the darkness.

"Hold on there . . ." The light came closer.

Terrified, Malika dropped the bottle and ran from the voice but someone leaped at him, momentarily stunning him and pinning him to the deck. A light blazed near his head and he looked up at Will Cuffee's dark face.

Will studied the strange powder that speckled the pine plank next to his whale oil lantern. "I saw you putting something into the scuttlebutt, from this bottle . . ."

"Will," Malika entreated on his back, "I can give you much gold if you say nothing. We will stand together," he whispered, "against those who enslave our people. Here, I have gold in my pocket . . ."

Hearing footfalls from above, Cuffee relaxed his hold and the Indian drew his knife slowly from his boot. The African saw the glint of metal and he rammed his knee into the stomach below him. As Malika squirmed in pain and dropped his knife, the powerful slave clasped his fists and delivered a sledgehammer blow, striking the Indian behind the right ear. Malika groaned and slumped limp.

Cuffee tipped the twenty-gallon barrel off its cradle and propped it so the contents would run out through the fill hole. Then he put the bottle in his pocket, flung the knife through an open gun port and heaved the Indian over his shoulder. Cuffee went down past the berthing deck and into the cable locker. There, he bound Malika, hands and feet. The Indian groaned as he gained consciousness, so Cuffee stuffed hemp into his mouth and tied a strand to gag him.

"Who is it?" Carson responded to a knock on the door to his tiny cabin, feeling in the dark for the birthday present Sarah had given him. He pressed a trigger and a spark leapt from flint to pan, igniting a candle.

"Lieutenant, this be Will Cuffee. There's trouble on the gun deck."

Carson slipped into his trousers, grabbed his spring-bayonet pistol and extinguished the candle. Cuffee led him up the companionway and forward to the disarrayed scuttlebutt.

"I saw a man pour something into the barrel from this," Cuffee said, handing Carson the apothecary bottle. The lieutenant sniffed at its neck, then replaced the ground glass stopper and touched his index finger to the wet deck.

"Bitter," he said, spitting out the taste. "You're right, Will. Lucky for all of us that you came down here. There's enough poison in that water to put half our crew in sick bay. Clever rogue . . . Whoever it was knew that the water ration mixed with rum would be drunk first without anyone tasting the poison. Stay here, Will, I'll get the mate to clean this up and rig up a new scuttle—and leave all the explaining to me. I don't want *anyone* to know until I've seen the captain. We don't need a panic."

"Aye, aye, sir. I understand."

"Did you recognize the man who did it?"

Carson lay awake. He would have to put a report into writing before seeing the captain after morning call. Malika Tombs could be left where he was for the time being so that no one would know what had happened. A thing like this could damage morale, hinder the crew's efficiency, make them afraid to eat or drink for fear of poison. Napoleon said that his army marches on its stomach. The same could easily be said of the navy. He lit his "birthday candle," as Sarah's sweet letter had termed the brass contraption. ". . . I'm sorry it's not new," she'd written, "but we should save." *We should*? Carson felt a pang of guilt.

He turned the empty bottle around slowly, examining each facet and detail. There was a torn label on one side. He held it up to the candle. Small, precise handwriting had been washed off, only an initial flourish and a crossed *t* remaining. Obviously the apothecary's imprint and address had been torn off because the print was insoluble. But there was still a faint impression. Closer to the flame, Carson noticed something as he looked through the bottle, label translucently lit. The handwriting was backwards: a name! Cold sweat formed on his blond brow. His gut knew before he did: a name he recognized from blotting paper . . . *ttiWeD M*. He spelled it letter for letter. It was his uncle's name. M for Magnus. . . .

The knowledge burned into his brain, throbbing, coruscating and screaming. Time. He would need time. Best now to keep it from Hull for a day or two. It was impossible to believe that Tombs had acted purely on his own behalf. But to believe that the plot had been instigated by Magnus . . . True, Magnus was an old Tory. And Carson had heard the rumors that his uncle had become slightly irrational in his later years. But only a madman would conceive such a scheme. There must be a mistake, an explanation.

He dressed and went up to breathe ocean air. The red eastern glow said "sailor take warning" and he flung the wretched bottle as far as he could into the breeze-rippled sea.

August 19, Morning

THE BOSUN'S PIPE pierced the dreams of three hundred shrouded bodies hanging in the hammocks along the darkened berth-deck. High above the sloughing sea, the harsh first rays of sun glistened down on the sails.

The light sleepers and the eager leapt at first trill, neatly bundling and lashing their duck hammocks, rushing topside and stowing them in spar deck nets, while the laggards dragged and yet others curled back to sleep. Kevin Kinnaird skitted from one sleeper to the next and whipped his starter rope to the soft round bottoms of the hammocks. As the sun caught the royals, all were mustered and piped to morning tasks, scrubbing down anything that could be reached. Below, a perplexed Kinnaird examined the empty hammock.

Eight bells heralded breakfast, where the talk over deck messcloths concerned the maintop Mohawk who'd missed his daybreak station.

"Sail, ho . . ."

Mauls stopped in mid-air, curved steel needles paused in canvas seams, and Surgeon Biggs quickly covered up his distilling apparatus in the medicine locker.

"Where away," First Lieutenant Charles Morris called aloft as Bosun Sam Paynter and Lieutenant DeWitt came up from the gun deck. Officers and crew surged to the port waist and gunnels; Paynter and a mate started up the main ratlings for a look as the answer was passed on: "Hull down, east by southeast. A fair-sized rig . . . She's making for Halifax by her tack."

Isaac Hull inhaled and buttoned his tight waistband on the run. The cabin steward helped him into his uniform coat and Morris handed him the glass.

"Seems she's flying colors . . ." The captain winced.

"Going to a party perhaps!" Morris bantered.

"I don't think we're invited," Hull said, handing the glass back and walking toward the quarterdeck. "Let's take no chances, Lieutenant."

"Aye, sir." Morris signalled Alwyn and Paynter. The deck and ratlings suddenly swarmed with life, mates calling into hatchways and stairs as the *Constitution* cleared for action.

The sailhandlers, who also manned the top-deck carronades, hauled up the studding'sls and *Constitution*, wings sprouted, leaned with the mounting northeaster, cutwater splashing and copper bottom showing to weather over grey seas. Topmen went aloft and bent second guys to the main spars and lowered the lighter top yards. Quartermasters and mates set up relieving tackle and strung hammock nets over the spar deck.

Below, carpenters broke out felt-edged shot plugs and stacked them in two sizes corresponding to the 18- and 32-pounders used on British frigates. Because of greater velocity, long guns tended to pierce small holes in wood whereas a carronade of equal bore made larger, splintered breeches.

The master-at-arms unlocked the armory down by the keel and stationed a marine to distribute rifles and pistols. The gunner, Robert Anderson, assigned his mates to the magazine while the ship's corporal manned the light room, a tight cubicle faced with a double-glazed window through which shone a dozen bright and swaying lanterns, illuminating the adjacent magazine and powder filling room.

Men were put in passages and stairs to pass empty and filled boxes horizontally and vertically. The marine contingent, gaudy in blue, white and gold, broke in three sections and assembled on the waist and decks where they prepared their rifles.

In the galley, turned war-room, the crew's cook stoked up his huge cast-iron stove under its sheet-iron canopy while the armorer rigged a metal sling of chain and bar with which to heat round shot, if called for—the galley being between two long 24s and forward of a shot rack.

The surgeon and his two mates prepared an area near the main companionway in the cockpit below the gun deck to receive the wounded. Armstrong unwrapped greased cloths from crude steel saws and chisels while Yeates rubbed salt pork on the instruments to remove rust spots. They cut cotton cloths into strips and hung them on cords around a heavy oak table, arranged lanterns overhead and tubs of brine for separated limbs. Biggs was alone in his forward lair, copying notes from a surgery manual.

Jacob Conegys and the other sailmaker's mates quickly fashioned canvas bags which were sent to the filling room to be packed with gunpowder and iron nails before being fused and set into deck scuttles. In the event of close combat, these "bombs" would be ready to be cast onto the enemy's deck. Earthen vessels filled with rancid slops and decomposing livestock entrails were uncapped and topped up with rapeseed and sperm oils and held ready to be hung from the main-yard end, where they could be set aflame and swung over the adversary's teeming deck to spout intolerable stench and acrid smoke over the defenders.

At quarter of three, the stranger's intention to engage became apparent, and quartermasters uncovered the hammock racks as the bosun called "Up all hammocks." Gun crews passed four hundred rolled and lashed hammocks like so many rolled napkins with rope rings into the double nettings to cover the quarterdeck, waist and ends, protecting gunners and officers from the enemy's topmast sharpshooters.

"What do you make of her now, Lieutenant?"

"She bears a message on the fore t'gallant . . ." Morris refocused the glass as *Constitution* heeled to a sudden gust, spars moaning to the filling nor'easter. From his weather perch Alwyn trumpeted forward and the flying jib was slackened and brailed while the main sheet trimmed taut to the port chess-tree and the studdings were taken in.

Morris read slowly, compensating for the beam reach angle of heel: "This is not the . . . *Little Belt* . . ."

"So, it's not a party we go to, but a challenge, eh? She seems to be *Shannon* class, but why *alone*?" Captain Hull fastened his jacket buttons and set his black silk hat firmly on his head. "The stranger seems to be shortening sail drastically. I think she means to lie and wait. How do you see it?"

"Make for her, sir!"

"Clear the decks, Lieutenant!"

"Aye, sir, and we'll get some gauge while we're at it."

* * *

Lieutenant DeWitt rushed to his foredeck station, recalling the newspaper article his friend Commodore Bainbridge had read him in St. Petersburg six months earlier . . .

". . . American frigate of forty-four guns, *President* . . . engaged the British sloop *Little Belt*, eighteen guns . . ." Carson had not been very proud of the uneven contest, some reports indicating that Commodore Rodgers had fired first and had eventually recognized his feeble enemy's size and armament before holing him again in the darkness. A court of inquiry in Halifax corroborated Captain Bingham's contention that he had not been the aggressor on the basis of testimony from two deserters from Rodgers's frigate. The American navy had supported Rodgers while the Tories abused him as a warmonger—one year before war was actually declared. The British frigate *Constitution* faced now was evidently bent on revenge.

While the drum beat the crew to stations, Carson made rounds of his sector, which included all the guns forward of the main hatch; four carronade 32s on the spar deck, two bow chasers and eight long 24s on the gun deck. Lieutenant Hoffman was in charge of the stern and quarterdeck while Lieutenant Shubrick was responsible for the waist. Carson stopped at the carronade nearest the starboard bower anchor as Tommy Ganly and two other powder monkeys heaved buckets of ash and sand on the white decks, spreading the mixture evenly around the foredeck ordnance.

Quarter-gunner Timothy Hazzard stripped his red and white striped shirt off and shouted: "Men, get your backs clear before ye forget . . ." The eight foredeck gun crews, seven to a piece, stripped bare from their waists save for the black silk neckerchiefs and hats for those of thinning hair. Gunner's regulations stated that a body wound would fester worse through the lint of a shirt than without, and a shirt would also impede proper surgical dressings.

Seaman George Truett drew swirls in the grey ashes with his barefoot toe around the aft carriage wheel of "Demon," as his 32 had been named. He set his seaboots near the gunnel along with those of his mates and hefted his handspike before laying it down with the other tools beside his gun. Double-shotted with rough grape and solid ball, Demon waited, coldly poised among her attendants: sponge rod, powder horn, crow and priming wires, all laid out in neat order. Powder monkeys—hardly more than truant schoolboys—stood by to each side, protectively holding their leather cartridge buckets and admiring the strong men at the guns, men who were older brothers and teachers to them.

Captain William B. Orne was escorted to the *Guerriere*'s quarterdeck, first out past the helm to open deck and thence up the port stairs to the raised deck, a feature not included in American men-of-war. Orne, a Marblehead sailor whose brig had been taken by Dacres a few days earlier, marveled at the comforts of continental naval warfare. Helm and sea quarter-deck protected by another deck . . . remnant of earlier wars when crews were expendable, when the privileged were too privileged. *Guerriere*, formerly a French warship, was even more grandiose than its counterparts of the British navy. It had lavishly ornate billhead and trail-boards, and baroque quarter-galleries and companionways.

Orne trudged forward to the beckoning hand of his captor, thankful for being spared the demise of his brother Joseph in the Red Sea at the hands of less gallant seafarers.

"Captain Orne . . ." The gangly Britisher, sleeves a trifle short, led the American to the taffrail. "My word as to your safety is still in effect. But would you be so kind as to lend me your opinion of that brash sail?"

Orne took the spyglass and observed the closing stranger. "Without doubt, Captain, it is an American frigate."

"She comes down too boldly for an American." Dacres paced nervously. "But the better her captain behaves, the more credit we shall gain by taking him!" He faced his officers. "Lieutenant Joyce, I'd like to prepare a welcome for the intruder. We'll have time for tea while we put red before the bull's eyes."

A bright red pennant was hauled to each of the sky poles as the handlers backed the main tops'l, bringing the 38-gun frigate to an abrupt halt among the pulsing swells.

"Captain Orne," Dacres addressed the Massachusetts man politely, "as I suppose you do not wish to fight against your own countrymen, you are at liberty to retire below the waterline and join your ten compatriots. We have no need of complications during a battle."

Dacres ran his sword loose in its scabbard several times as his solemn drums beat to quarters. Vice Admiral James R. Dacres, conqueror of Curacao, would have been up to the occasion, as would his uncle, a famous captain in the Dardanelles campaign. They would settle for nothing less than victory over such a rascal opponent. Victory even for a ship built by France in a sudden emergency, with unseasoned timber that was now decaying . . . For a ship that only a year earlier had been dubbed by an eminent British naval biographer as "a worn-out frigate."

"'E's runnin' up *three* flags, the braggart." Seaman Nicolas Baker was still safe, known to no one aboard as Lucy Brewer. She hauled a royal spar under the pinnace and lashed it. She adjusted her black neckerchief—a broader cloth than worn by others—over a bare, hairless chest. Nicolas hadn't counted on an *engagement* in which festering lint would deprive her of her disguise. It had been difficult enough. Six months of hiding the fact that one was physically not a man, covering up as others pissed freely with the wind off the bow, the swims, the horseplay on the berth decks after duty . . . But a gravel voice had helped. So had a back that was stronger than that of any one of a score of "men" she could name, not counting the eighty boys and stewards. There was even an officer or two that she knew she could best if it came down to it.

Small breasted and tomboy wiry, she'd grown up as Lucy Brewer of the Charleston tidal flats and shipped as a "cabin boy" on coasters. Then, in Baltimore, she'd met Sarah Lewis and the two girls had come up with the scheme to stow away aboard the frigate as men. Now she was part of the navy, perhaps the first woman ever. She'd learned from her three brothers who were now in the Indies trade . . . ropes, tides, storms and survival. She didn't think of herself as a woman, although there'd been signs on the current cruise. She was sixteen now and it was beginning to show, especially when stripped to the waist. Time to ask for a transfer below or aloft.

Only six months earlier, in Charleston, she'd been oblivious to the thought and sight of men's bodies, having spent so much time at sea with her brothers. She'd worried that her attachment to Sarah was, as people might whisper, "unnatural." Now she knew all was right with her. First it was the Frenchman, Claude, at the examination before she sneaked out of sick bay. Then it was Albert Pisano, the carpenter's mate . . . She'd near swooned when last she saw suntanned Albert's sleepy erection. Nicolas yearned for that day she'd be payed off next

June . . . to return to Charleston before she either went berserk with passion or succumbed to certain temptations.

"Nicolas!" Tommy Ganly's high-pitched cry stopped her at the relieving tackle near Demon, the carronade. The boy, excited, was also frightened, and it took more than a man to sense the difference. Nicolas held her thumb in a "up" gesture and Tommy smiled his thanks.

The marines were turned out in uniform wearing blue coats with brown leather collars, white pantaloons, and shiny plumed shakoes over flour-whitened pigtails. Seven marines gathered at the foremast; like-numbered groups gathered at main and mizzen. Six in each group carried loaded rifles and one a bag of powder and shot. Looking like toy soldiers, they climbed up the ratlings and through the lubber holes to the "fighting tops," the platforms some sixty feet above the spar deck.

Six midshipmen and their topmen went up six ratlings after the leathernecks, as the marines were called, and stationed themselves on cross-trees for sail-handling chores. Nicolas, welcoming her jumper back, could climb like a cat and she scampered to station for the fore t'gallant yard as eight bells rang out a hundred feet below. She gave thanks that others were available to replace the missing Mohawk at his place, some forty feet higher yet. The wind had risen to a moderate gale of almost forty knots and the grey spuming sea seemed to reach up with white fingers as the frigate pitched and yawed toward the crouched opponent. Far below, long 24s bristled from the hull like black legs on a seagoing centipede.

Nicolas braced herself within the topmast shrouds and catstay with the others of her level and awaited commands to reduce or multiply sail. On all points the yards and trees were speckled with crawling and hanging figures.

"We're comin' up fast . . ."

"Just over a mile I make it . . ."

"Looks like a match for us, the braggart," Nicolas shouted into the whistling wind. "Look, he's wearin' round."

" 'E's firin' . . ."

"A broadside!" The topmen swung behind the twelve-inch doubled mast juncture at the futtock hoop as flicks of orange flame and puffs of white smoke erupted from the yellow stripe on the black hull.

"Short . . . 'e missed," screamed Ben Miller as frothy plumes danced on wave crests two boat lengths off the port bow.

"Now he's comin' about for another broadside."

"No, his bow chasers . . ."

A small hole appeared in the sail below their feet, then another which ripped a jagged opening and cut a royal halyard, leaving it slashing wildly from the foretop.

"Damn, this is real war!" Ben clung tightly to the mast, a knot of bodies close around him.

A gunner, Moses Smith, would write later:

Before all hands could be called, there was a general rush on deck. Word passed like lightning from man to man, and all who could be spared came flocking up. From spar to gun and berth decks, every man was roused and on his feet. All eyes were turned in the direction of the strange sail, and quick as ever our studding sails were out and we fairly bounded over the billows as we gave her a rap full and spread her tall winds to the gale.

The stranger hauled his wind, and laid to for us. It was evident that he was an English man-of-war and all ready for action.

As we came up she began to fire, trying to rake us. But we continued our course, tacking and half-tacking, avoiding being raked. We came so near on one tack that an 18-pound shot came through us under the larboard knight-head, striking just abaft the breech of the gun to which I belonged. The splinters flew in all directions, but no one was hurt. We immediately picked up the shot and put it in the mouth of one of our two bowchaser 18s, sending it home again with our respects.

Another stray shot hit our foremast, cutting one of the hoops in two. But the mast was not otherwise injured, and the slight damage was soon repaired.

Captain Hull regarded the scene calmly but with resolution. "Men, now do your duty. Your officers cannot have command over you now. Each of you must do all in your power for your country."

A second broadside rumbled from the Britisher. Then there was a whistling over the hammocks. A commotion and shouts broke the ship's silence at the first carronade starboard station. The black tin galley pipe had been partially shot away near its base, smoke issuing from the breach and spreading below the hammock parapet, causing much uncomfort to those nearby.

But the greater concern was for the gunner who lay dismembered on deck—with part of him searing on the galley pipe. He lay perfectly still, scarlet seeping from his open wounds and mixing with grey ashes on the white deck.

Young George Truett was the first.

Gaunt and anxious, they glared toward the quarterdeck, entreating, questioning and ready to flame their matches.

"May I have leave, sir—"

"Answer with long Tom, Lieutenant."

Morris shrugged, disappointed that it wasn't to be a broadside, and passed on the command. Sailing Master Alwyn took his cue and put the helm over lightly so the long gun could bear past the bowsprit.

"Prick and prime," the gun captain barked. A handler stuck a wire down the breech vent and pierced the powder cartridge, then poured horn powder into the vent and atop the grooved pan.

"Lay on aprons . . . Point your gun . . . Level

your gun . . ." The layer jammed a wooden wedge under the breech as he sighted *Guerriere*'s mast-top. At eight hundred yards, a shot aimed at the tops would travel a trajectory ending at the hull if the timing was right. The layer sighted again, then signaled that he was zeroed in. Alwyn, at the helm, kept her straight on the southwest lubber line. The spikemen moved clear with their wooden levers, as the frigate's bow dipped and rose rhythmically toward His Majesty's ship.

"Blow on your match . . . Aprons off . . ." The layer, on one knee, turned his head inboard and reached his glowing rope toward the pan while the gun captain raised his arm in cadence with the bow's rise and fall.

"One . . . two . . . fire!" He called the command as the bow rose and the pan flash preceded long Tom's thunder. The two-ton cannon recoiled abruptly and rolled its length backwards until stopped by the heavy breeching rope, report echoing forward with the wind as all near hands strained over the headrails to observe the shot's effect.

None to be seen, the gun was made ready again. The powder boy, his leather buckets empty, disappeared down the galley hatch.

Lieutenant Morris gripped tightly on the mizzen pinrail as George Truett's dismembered form was heaved through the vacant carronade port and the deck washed down, the water running pink in the white scuppers. "Permission for broadside, sir . . ."

"Not yet, Morris. Strike the main course. We're coming up."

"Aye, sir." He called to Alwyn and soon the largest sail was goose-winged on the main yards and all fore and aft sail had been brailled save the main jib, sixteen-foot stars and stripes streaming forward from the spanker boom.

Evading the anxious looks of his crew, Hull studied the waiting frigate. "What ship do you make it to be?"

"We've seen him before, sir."

"Precisely. Her head has a French accent." Captain Hull paced the quarterdeck as a shot embedded itself in the mizzen mast, where his head had been a moment before. The *Guerriere*'s fire had begun to tell, chunking into the American's hull on the starboard and richochetting from the spars. The line of young powder monkeys huddled fearfully while the gunners murmured restively about duty and idiocy, each shot adding to the tension.

Six bells announced five by the clock and shortly thereafter a moan mounted as enemy grape struck the mizzentop, parting a halyard and loosening the proud, starred blue flag. Without a word an Irish lad by name of Dan Hogan scampered to the foretop in the face of deadly grape and lashed the flag in place.

Morris looked mournfully at his commander and was told, "Not yet, Lieutenant. Soon."

Constitution charged at *Guerriere*'s port quarter but the Britisher wore northeast in a sudden spurt, avoiding an American bow shot and bringing its port guns to bear. Alwyn countered by veering to starboard and the fifteen sequential shots fell harmlessly to port of the American. Puffs rose from *Guerriere's* stern as she crossed and ran with the wind, which had veered through north to northwest. There was a sharp crackling in *Constitution's* top hamper and a main spar dangled and tumbled into the sea.

Closing at better than ten knots under fighting sail, Captain Hull recalled an action off Santo Domingo during the quasi-war with France when he, as sailing master of the ship he now commanded, had executed a similar fast approach that resulted in cutting a privateer out of a convoy. He had enjoyed the subsequent acclaim; now, fourteen years later, he had another chance to prove that a good commander need not come from the political and social circles. Perhaps his last chance. A friend had posted him advance notice of his impending change of command. He'd commanded *Constitution* for a long time, six years, and there was talk that a younger man might do better in war. Here was the test. He knew that if he did not return victorious, he would be cashiered for having left Boston without orders. No orders meant to stay where you were. . . .

The timing was perfect! *Guerriere's* gunners would be loading at this very instant. That was reason enough for coming up on her port, from which the last broadside had been fired scarcely a minute earlier.

"You shall now have as close as you please, Mr. Alwyn . . . Lay 'er alongside!"

A cheer went up from the crew as the ship swerved to starboard and bore down at the enemy's bow.

Moving twice as fast as her adversary, the American, approached from *Guerriere*'s blind quarter, stern chasers frantically trying to bear, and suddenly, squaring her sails, put helm to port in an unexpected burst of speed and pulled up parallel, no more than half a pistol-shot away from the quarry. As the gilt, snarling cat-heads on her bow passed the enemy's quarter gallery, the stout American captain shouted at the top of his lungs:

"Now, boys . . . Pour it into them!" He gestured with such exultation and vehemence that his tight white naval breeches split clear down the back, from waistband to knee.

The crew cheered loudly as twenty-five guns were flashed at the command to fire, ringing out from stem to stern on both decks as *Constitution* ran alongside. Three hundred and sixty pounds of double-shotted grape and round smashed into the thinner-skinned Britisher, starting at the stern and moving progressively forward. Such was the impact of massed carronade and long gun that splinters flew to *Guerriere*'s topmasts, her entire starboard side shattered and weakened, with two score killed and wounded. As the American drew past, the enemy's main yard dropped into its slings and the mizzenmast staggered and careened aft, flinging its marines and topmen far into the gale-swept sea and crushing the counter amidst screams and an ineffectual round of return fire, most of which went high, tearing the American rigging.

"Damn," shouted a British marine watching 18-pound shot strike *Constitution*'s hull and bounce off. "Her sides are made of iron!"

The sailing master backed a t'gallant and held the ship back for a second broadside. Lieutenant DeWitt, like the others, ran from gun to gun, cheering the layers to shoot for the waterline.

Guerriere's mizzen was slung over her starboard quarter, trailing in the sea and fighting her helm. The English hacked and dragged at the mizzen to no avail as their ship wallowed slowly in circles, taking round after round as the Americans now fired at will. Blood ran from *Guerriere*'s scuppers and stained her sides; crimson ran from her gold and white figurehead, a mythical goddess of war and wisdom, wearing a goatskin breastplate and carrying a lance and olive branch.

Hull brought his ship around under the enemy's bow and poured two raking broadsides of grapeshot that swept her decks from sprit to taffrail, mowing down the men at their guns. Almost clear, a sudden swell tossed *Guerriere*'s bow over Hull's quarterdeck and her bowsprit fouled tight in the latter's mizzen. Both ships waltzed round and around in the sloshing seaway, locked in a wooden embrace, hopelessly tangled in shrouds, stays and spars, the Britisher's sixty-foot bowsprit looming clear across and over, a boarding bridge with footropes.

Almost simultaneously, bugles blared from each ship: sharp, curdling calls for boarders. Pikes were stripped from their racks, cutlasses drawn and pistols passed. The deck marines took square positions on higher decks and topmen zeroed in on the boarding junctures. The rolling, heavy seas tore at the tangled frigates. Geysers spouted from between the ships, long guns gouging paint and wood as the two vessels crashed against each other's hulls.

Jake Conegys and his mates came up with their stink pots and nail bombs. The carpenters bent to secure pre-cut oaken parapets pierced for small arms against the ratlings. The master at arms distributed a box of flintlocks, followed by a boy with a sack of powder horns and shot. Again and again the bugles shrieked, and soon the American's deck was armed with eager, clamoring crewmen. Though similar in size and armament, the boats were disproportionate in complement, *Constitution* manned by 468 to Dacre's 263.

"Outnumbered," observed the British captain. He had his bugler call retreat, though some of his forces were already on the sprit ropes over the adversary.

"Defensive stations," his lieutenants ordered.

"Boarders away!"

Captain Hull pulled his swallowtail coat over his torn pants just as Lieutenant Morris, brandishing his sword, leapt up on the rail and made for the British spar and its defenders. He was closely followed by the lieutenant of marine and the sailing master. Carson DeWitt leveled his pistol and fired at a Britisher who was about to slash at Morris. The man fell to the sea moments before the two ships rolled into each other.

"Follow me, men!" Marine Lieutenant Bruce Hale crawled up on the gigantic spar and brandished his sword and pistol. A tremendous fusilade of massed musketry crackled from the enemy quarterdeck. Hale's pistol discharged as he was felled by a Brown Bess one-inch ball between his eyes.

Morris crumpled onto the boom, grasping at his stomach, while Alwyn was spun off the spar, a shot in his shoulder. Hull, aghast at the carnage, started to climb to the nets but was restrained by a hand clutching his sword arm. In a rage, he confronted the seaman who dared stop him going to the aid of his next-in-command. Bosun's Mate Kevin Kinnaird coolly pointed to the captain's bright epaulettes. "We need you, sir."

Kinnaird, taking the situation in hand, scampered to the boom, pistol cocked at the mammoth of a man in British regalia who was scrambling toward the wounded Morris with a murderous pike held high. Kinnaird grabbed Morris and hauled him from the pike's scathing swipe—only to find his eyes locked into the bloodshot leer of Bartholemew Creech. The bosun poised his weapon for the kill. He aimed carefully and pulled the trigger at Creech, who stood not six feet away. A flash—and no discharge.

Once more "the executioner" screamed and charged. Kinnaird flung his weapon, striking Creech hard on his mouth and knocking him off balance into the breach between the two ships' hulls. Creech caught hold of a long 24's hot black muzzle, but just then a swell ground the ships together, with Creech mashed between *Constitution*'s iron and *Guerriere*'s planking. A rush of sea water washed the remains away.

Lieutenant Shubrick, trying to lash the swaying bowsprit down for another boarding attempt, gave up for want of a strong enough rope and retreated behind the parapets with gunfire volleying about him. Morris, declining to go to the cockpit for surgery, held a hand to his bloody wound and encouraged his men as before.

"Where's DeWitt?" Hull scurried about as the bowsprit creaked and slid, ripping and twanging the strained rigging.

"There!" Claude Chassagne leaned far over the rail, gunfire pitting the wood beside him. The wiry Frenchman grabbed a loose stay and swung over the side, sliding down to the recessed head deck where the dazed officer lay among other wounded.

"Covering fire," Morris shouted, gripping his stomach. The Americans' fire converged on the enemy foredeck, cutting down a "lobster" musket squad and keeping the enemy away from the stove-in area below *Guerriere*'s grated catwalk.

"Sorry I have to tie you, but we'll both go up together . . ." Chassagne bent a timber hitch under Carson's bloody arms and dragged him out from under the corpse of a British marine lieutenant. He yanked Carson's bayonet pistol out of the redcoat's side.

"Okay." He tugged on the rope and guided Carson's limp body over the trailboards, then swung himself out as the crew hauled briskly. "Hurry, she's goin' . . ." A gigantic swell tore at the fettered frigate as rifle and small arms fire spurted from *Constitution*'s rail and gun ports. Many stout arms pulled the dangling Americans through a carronade port as the gun was drawn back. Chassagne crawled over the gun tackle as DeWitt was carried below.

"The lieutenant," Chassagne gasped, "he killed two Englishmen who tried to hang a barrel of gunpowder to our hull. I cut the rope with this and the barrel fell." He snapped the bayonet back on Carson's pistol. "Here, it belongs to the lieutenant." He handed the pistol to a powder boy.

"Fire! Fire!" The ship's bell clanged as black, acrid smoke poured from *Constitution*'s port stern gallery windows. The pumps were manned and soon a bucket brigade was sloshing water aft and down the companionway where Lieutenant Hoffman's gunners were fighting the blaze in

Captain Hull's aftercabin. *Guerriere* had found an Achilles' heel, their shot couldn't penetrate the American non-steamed planking, but it could pierce window glass. One of their bow carronades, hardly two yards away because of the current that laid the enemy alongside, was firing furiously, blasting shot and flaming cloth wads into the cabin. Hoffman and his men were in great danger, ducking the barrages while trying to keep the flames under control and away from the ammunition scuttles that led down to the aft gunpowder stores.

Bosun's Mate Chassagne, in the absence of key wounded and occupied officers, sprinted up to the port counter where he climbed into the davited quarterboat and blew on a gunmatch. Touching it to the fuse of one of Conegy's canvas nail bombs, he counted as the fuse sizzled to within an inch of the bag, then stood up and flung it down on *Guerriere*'s canted deck. The explosion that followed demolished the harrassing gun and blew out the gunnel, splinters and nails cutting down the enemy crew and narrowly missing the Frenchman himself. Shouts of jubilation rang out as the smoke stopped billowing and the *Constitution*'s crew turned back to the battle at hand.

High in the mizzen fighting top, leatherneck Corporal Blake Hampton cocked a Pennsylvania long rifle, a frontier version of the celebrated German *Yaeger*. Hampton swung his piece left and right at the enemy's gorey deck and lined up at a surprise spot of color, a blue, white and gold form against the nets, crouched behind the mizzen stump.

"That turkey ain't got much meat on it, but I like his comb. Real purty . . ." The corporal carefully squeezed off a shot and Dacres slumped into the nets.

Three decks below the waterline, Will Cuffee passed cartridges from the magazine filling room to the waiting powder boys, who stuffed them two at a time into their leather buckets and climbed up the steep orlop deck ladder. The negro's powerful muscles glistened in the glare of the many hanging lanterns behind the window of the oakum-sealed light room. How easy, he thought; Malika Tombs could have blown up the ship by getting to the ammunition. If the Indian hadn't feared a bullet from the guard . . . The guard! Gone! Will brushed the grey gunpowder from his hands and slipped aft, into the cable locker.

The Indian was still there, eyes now open and glazed, though his body was still warm. Dead? Yes. The Indian had been thrown, no doubt with the broadside from *Guerriere*, and had received a fatal blow on the head. Cuffee closed Malika's eyes and untied him, then carried the body up through the maelstrom of rushing, shouting men to the berth deck where the surgeon and his mates worked feverishly on the wounded. The negro laid Malika out next to several other wounded. Bloody-aproned Biggs took no notice of the addition as he sawed through a thigh bone and plopped the shattered lower leg into a brine tub.

The frigates, still reeling in the swells and gusts, suddenly rolled in contrary directions and amid a crashing and creaking they wrenched apart. The slacking of *Guerriere*'s forestays upon parting put such strain on her foremast that it crackled sharply at the base and tumbled over, carrying the main after it and catapulting the surviving topmen screaming into the turbulent waters. Hull, on John Alwyn's platform, drew his ship off for repairs. It was about half past six o'clock. The action following his first broadside had taken but forty minutes in reducing the invincible British man-of-war to a shapeless, rolling hulk.

The *Guerriere* wallowed like a gutted fish, tattered sails shrouded over rigid bodies, ropes tangled with limbs and broken spars. A shred of topsail flapped from the crushed railhead.

Third Lieutenant Read, the prize officer, approached the sorry frigate in a pitching quarterboat. After much maneuvering, the prize launch made fast and Read presented himself and his message to the bandaged commander.

"Captain Hull sends his compliments, sir, and wishes to know if you have struck your flag."

Dacres, wincing from a back wound, regarded the colors lashed to the shattered stump of his mizzen and dryly responded, "All our masts are gone . . . I think, on the whole, you may say we have struck our flag . . ."

"We *may* say, sir? Is that your reply?" Read started for the gangway.

"All right, Lieutenant, my ship is taking water fast and most of our guns are out of action." He motioned glumly to a midshipman to unlash the flag. "Your commander is Isaac Hull?"

"Yes, sir."

Dacres remembered he'd made a wager with Hull some years earlier, over wine in Paris. It was done in jest, neither officer believing that he might actually collect after an engagement. Yes, there had been a possibility of war then, but the odds against the two men meeting in battle were absurd. Or so it had seemed. "Lieutenant, I shall come to your ship in my own gig shortly."

Before descending the gangway, Read asked, "Would you like the assistance of a surgeon in caring for your wounded?"

Dacres looked surprised. "I should suppose you have business enough aboard your own ship for your medical officers."

"Oh, no!" replied Read. "We have only seven wounded, and they've been dressed for some time."

Dacres was astounded, for on his decks lay twenty-three dead or mortally wounded men, while the surgeons were doing their best to alleviate the sufferings of fifty-six wounded. The ship looked like a charnel house. In addition, there were a dozen men unaccounted for.

"Tell Captain Hull I need his help."

Dacres buried his face in his hands as the prize officer left.

Captain Orne, freed by the outcome, came up on deck.

"How have our situations changed!" Dacres greeted him. "You are now free and I am a prisoner."

Later, Orne would describe the scene to the *Constitution*'s officers. "At about half-past seven, I went on deck and there beheld a scene that would be difficult to describe. As *Guerriere* had no masts nor sails to steady her, she rolled like a log in the sea's trough. The men were employed in throwing the dead overboard and the decks were covered with blood. Gun tackles were loose and some guns were surging from one side of the ship to the other. A crowd of petty officers and seamen had broken out some liquor and were intoxicated. What with the groans of the dying, the noise and confusion of the enraged survivors, the ship was a perfect hell. . . ."

All hands set to work in removing the wounded from the sinking man-of-war. In the midst of this rough-water transfer, a sail on the darkening horizon roused the drummers to beat once more and the exhausted crew manned battle stations again. Fortunately, the other ship veered away.

Captain Dacres, in Hull's charred cabin, un-

buckled his sword and set it on the table alongside *Guerriere*'s log and assorted records he'd
turned over, records that he deemed non-military
and valuable for the well-being of his officers
and men in captivity.

Hull pushed the sword back. "No, Captain, I'll
not take a sword from someone who knows so
well how to use one. But I *will* trouble you for
your hat!"

By midnight, with the seas still running, the
transfer had been accomplished. Torches were
put to the battered hulk by the last launch, while
both victor and vanquished watched the hungry
blaze. The fiery glow seemed to be the symbol
of a new age, the recognition of America as a
world naval power.

Dacres watched dejectedly as a cox'n went
below with his ship's torn colors. He closed his
eyes as the flames burst out of *Guerriere*'s berth
deck portholes, just above the magazine. A
bright flash lit the onlookers' faces, some glum,
some joyous as the once-proud frigate disinte-
grated in a chain of thunderous explosions.

The hulk smoldered and glowed crimson, an
alien sun in the east of night, as *Constitution*
crowded on her studdings and headed west,
watching for Polaris off her starboard beam as
the clouds thinned and stars broke through.

"This is the last of 'em." Jacob Conegys
palmed his needle through the burnt canvas
shroud and knotted the cord at the mummy's
neck. Six battered bodies had gone over the side,

each accompanied by a short line from the scriptures as read by Elias Lovett in a nasal twang, his midshipman's hat covering his breast. Lovett read on as the sailmaker felt for the body's nose, squeezed the canvas over it and pierced the nose, drawing the needle through, this being done with bodies that exhibit little or no evidence of injury.

"The Mohawk's very dead." Jacob snipped the cord and moved away as the American flag was draped over the form and a split 32-pound shot was tied to the ankles.

"We therefore commit this body to the deep . . ."

The grating was tilted and the body slid feet first from under the colors. Many of the gathered crew murmured and crossed their hearts. Will Cuffee sang out a soft hallelujah as he fought the helm steady.

". . . to be turned into corruption, looking for the resurrection of the body, when the sea shall give up her dead, and the life of the world to come. . . ."

September 6

A FTER A PARTICULARLY *grueling ten days of beating against weather and tending to the numerous wounded of both sides, we at last lay off Boston Light and sent in our launch to deliver messages and arrange for dockage at Charleston Navy Yard.*

On 30 August, one week ago, the sabbath silence of this Puritan metropolis burst into excitement as the news passed through its streets that Constitution was in the outer harbor with British prisoners aboard. After being escorted in by myriad buntinged skiffs and small sail, with surrounding vessels dipping their flags in salutation, we made our way to the wharf where a volun-

tary artillery company was assembled. As our ship came up, they fired a national salute, which we returned.

Captain Hull was escorted to quarters in the city and he passed through streets alive with flags and pennants and lined with people in Sunday best. Smiling ladies waved from balconies and windows; men of all professions and stations shouted huzzahs to this war's first hero. That night a banquet was held for the ship's officers. Over six hundred sat down to feast.

Our captain's victory, we soon found, had rescued the nation from the disastrous news, just received within the week, that the entire northwest army of our United States had been surrendered to the British forces, abetted by the six Indian nations, at Detroit on August 13. The brigadier general who capitulated, against the intelligence of line officers, was William Hull, Governor of Michigan Territory and uncle of our captain! Even today, couriers still arrive with new accounts of the debacle in which our army had given in to inferior forces, "affecting so foul a stain on our national honour," as the Boston Patriot put it. It was a saddening shock for Captain Hull to be told that effigies of his aged uncle were being burnt in the cities.

The loss of two thousand militia and regulars and a great quantity of ordnance and stores seems to make our ocean victory pale. It is but small consolation that Essex, of 32 guns, answered a challenge from H.M.S. Alert, a sloop of

20, and captured the small foe on the same day as the above-stated end of our much vaunted Canadian invasion.

The great city of New York voted our captain a gold box and freedom of the city, as well as purchasing exquisitely made ceremonial swords for our officers. Mine sits before me now, as I write in the gleam of my one other proud possession, Sarah's flintlock waking candle, on the eve of boarding a coach for home.

Hull is quite busy these days. He sat—or rather stood—for an oil portrait to be hung in the Governor's Room of New York's City Hall. He was also sketched in profile for a gold medal to be struck by the Congress in his honor.

The city of Philadelphia voted to design and execute an elegant silver plate depicting the battle, one for presentation to the captain and a similar one for Lieutenant Morris. As to the officers and men, aside from numerous appearances at public functions we are to divide fifty-thousand dollars in prize money as voted by the Congress, down to the youngest powder monkey!

I am happy to learn that Captain Hull has at last met a lady of beauty and distinction. His demeanor, always delightful, has changed yet for the better. There being rumors of marital intention, we all wish him well with his lady and with his new assignment as Commander of Harbor Defences, Port of New York.

My injuries are healed after some days at the naval hospital, and the scars may be visible only to my future bride.

Tumultuous days in New York are over. I pack tonight for my furlough and shall not return till after the ship is repaired and refitted. My work in recruiting replacements for our many paid-off men will be negligible as we now have a reputation for luck and victory. Already the avalanche of volunteers is descending and we should be well manned by our next orders.

I was pleasantly surprised to find that the ship had been transferred to my old friend, William Bainbridge, who has now become a true commodore. Very few of us comprehend why Captain Hull was replaced after such an enviable record, but then he assured us that it was also his wish. Last night we had supper with Bainbridge. He was jubilant at the prospect of leaving his position as commander of the Charleston Navy Yard and going to sea with us "veterans." All in all, the officers liked him, but I share Chassagne's impression that, compared to Hull, he may prove "stiff." Chassagne, by dint of his heroism in the engagement and Morris's misfortune, is once again admitted to a wardroom, now as a fifth lieutenant. Sailing Master Alwyn is now first officer, and yours truly has moved up to third, with Hoffman being re-assigned elsewhere. Lieutenant Morris will be promoted to captain and transfer to the Department of the Navy after he recuperates from his wounds. At least we shall have a friend in high places!

Of course I did not comment upon Claude's assessment of Bainbridge, but he does seem to have changed since our adventures in Russia and

Finland only nine months ago. Perhaps he was reborn with a uniform. Or is it I who have changed? There seems an invisible gulf between us—as if we had never met, much less almost died together . . . I assume he has paid his accounts with my father . . . We wished each other health and went our ways.

"So you did manage it, Isaac!" Commodore Bainbridge ogled Hull's sparkling commemorative sword, jauntily swinging as they walked along the heights of Brueklyn, under the ramparts of Fort Hamilton.

"I've always been a sailor, Bill, and after six years I knew her every move and fault. It would have been shameful not to have tried."

"Especially after that chase." Bainbridge acknowledged the smile of a parasoled young lady by tipping his plumed hat. "Or was that intended for the conqueror?"

"Come now, William, *I've* never had a way with the ladies." He patted his stomach dejectedly. "How do you keep your waist?"

"Eighteen months in a Moroccan jail did wonders."

"Ah, but you also have such perseverance. I shall probably succumb to the pastries and puddings of shore duty." Hull led the commodore up a stone stairway to elm-edged parade grounds.

"How did you find out about the orders?" Bainbridge asked.

"I don't expect that *you* would divulge such a secret."

"True, true, Isaac."

"William, I know how much you want a chance, after being plagued with such ill-fortune. I was lucky, and it's my devout wish that the ship will enhance your success as it did mine. You're getting a more experienced crew than I had; it seems everyone wants to serve aboard a winner. Now I shall be content to command a stone ship or two. See that ruin of a fort—on Hendrick's Reef?" Hull pointed his scabbarded sword at the narrows below. "That's old Fort Diamond. We're going to enlarge it and put seventy-five heavy guns on it. With Fort Wadsworth, across the stream, we'll muster more metal than Brock's entire fleet. He won't dare come into New York Harbor."

"Isaac, you could have been court-martialed."

"If I'd lost I would have been shot. If you'll excuse the pun, the nation had enough Hull in my sorry uncle. What would you have done in my place?"

"I'd have been gun-shy from my past failures. God grant me a chance for restitution—an enemy frigate out of squadron."

"You can do me one year better, being only thirty-eight," Captain Hull chuckled.

"I hope I'm not too rusty." Bainbridge propped one booted foot on a rampart. "Too bad about Lieutenant Morris."

"You'll have some fine officers. Alwyn is quite capable."

"They seemed so young . . ."

"Don't let that fool you."

"Perhaps you're right, Isaac. Thanks for relinquishing command without making waves."

"I didn't have much choice!"

"True, true . . ."

"In all seriousness, William, you know it's not only our tangent sights that made the difference in that battle . . ." They waited until a passing guard was out of earshot.

"Are you referring to the plank tests?" Bainbridge grinned smugly. "Why do you think I wanted this ship!"

Hull's prominent jaw dropped. "But only the president and the actual commander are supposed to know. We have all been sworn to secrecy!"

"Madison and I are good friends."

On Carson's last night in his New York hotel, his uncle came to pay his respects. Carson had put the Malika Tombs affair to the back of his mind, having neither the time nor the heart to pursue the matter. But now he told Magnus about the poison bottle with his name on the label, and he listened with growing shock to the old man's reaction. Magnus did not confirm or deny complicity in the scheme, but rather tried to persuade his nephew of the futility of resisting the British, especially with the prospect of British regulars streaming from the peninsula campaign to make yet quicker work of the "miserable American armies." Magnus implored him to invest his interest in the DeWitt enterprises with his own.

"Carson, you're a fool to disregard my generous offer. I have it in confidence that by the New Year, Admiral Warren will have blockaded the entire seacoast from Maine to the Gulf of Mexico."

"But there's already been a change of mood in Boston—the bastion of your royalist merchants. There was none of the derision of our navy that existed prior to the engagement with *Guerriere*. Even the staunchest Tory businessmen were on hand at the wharf. This time I saw no posters advocating separatism."

"The victory was only a flash in the pan. *Guerriere* was a worn-out frigate; her masts were rotten. We must also not forget your boat's disguise!"

"Disguise?"

"The American 44s are ships-of-the-line in disguise. Originally designed as two-deckers, one was razed before building."

"But as a razee, we shouldn't be as fast as a frigate!"

"Bah." Magnus emptied the brandy bottle into his coffee.

"The victory has given our navy support," Carson replied proudly.

His uncle made no reply. Carson noticed that Magnus's gout had not improved any as the old man grunted, shifting his afflicted foot under the serving table. Magnus suddenly set his cup down with a clink and said harshly, "You will, of course, say nothing about this ridiculous bottle of chloride to your father!"

Carson's head reeled. He had said the bottle contained poison, but had not specifically mentioned chloride, which was both rare and expensive. So Magnus had indeed masterminded the plot. . . .

Carson assured Magnus that he'd said nothing of the affair and kept up conversation until a plan had emerged. Nobody had seen Magnus enter the room. Magnus was dangerous, a changed man. He wouldn't even have stooped to such an evil plot when he was a Tory spymaster during the American Revolution. Was he involved now as a businessman or as an actual British agent? In either case he might be armed.

The rotund face was being stuffed with sugary cakes. The wig was in need of soap, and there were greasy stains on his waistcoat . . . Magnus was no longer a DeWitt. He was more like a caricature out of Rowlandson's bawdy cartoons. He sat complacently reading the *Boston Patriot*'s accounts of the Detroit disaster.

"He'll most probably be shot, that imbecile general of your northwest army. They're all so incompetent, unprofessional. Your government is in a frenzy. Soon the Great Lakes will be ours!"

"Ours?" Carson realized that the older man did not regard his nephew as any more than an irresponsible juvenile sporting a toy uniform. Carson was determined to press the issue, but not without preparations.

"I see we've finished one bottle. Let's replenish the brandy. I shall join you in a toast, Uncle Magnus."

His uncle snorted and pushed his cup across the table without looking up as Carson foraged through his Boston bag. After pouring more coffee and brandy, Carson settled into his chair, bayonet pistol snug beside him, and toasted the ladies, whoever and wherever they be.

"Magnus . . ." He purposely left out *uncle*, and the older man, startled, lowered the newspaper.

"How did you know about the chloride in the bottle?"

Magnus slowly took off his reading glasses and folded them. His smile turned into a frown as he slipped the glasses inside his coat and was suddenly confronted with the muzzle of Carson's weapon. His eyes blinked as the flint snapped back and the barrel leveled not a foot from his nose. Magnus's fingers moved, grappling under his coat. Carson pushed a trip lever on the pistol and the nine-inch razor-edged bayonet sprang out, narrowly missing the old man's nose as he snapped his head back in fright. His trembling hands shot up, palms forward and empty.

Prodding his cheek with the bayonet, Carson reached over and drew out a tiny cannon-barreled muff pistol of London trademark. Beads of glistening sweat ran from Magnus's forehead to the corners of his mouth, where he nervously licked at them with a whitened tongue.

"I'm sorry, Uncle Magnus." Carson pried the

miniature flint from its lock and replaced the pistol inside his coat.

"What do you intend to do?" Magnus asked, his eyes on the bayonet blade.

"Let this be a lesson—*Major* DeWitt. I don't know what you're up to, but I assure you that I've made a full report of my observations—to which I will add today's revelation. The report is already available to the proper authorities, and will be released for investigation in such case as you give us further reason. You're lucky that I hold our family's honor equivalent to that of my country at this time—for this *one* occasion." Carson rose and motioned Magnus to the door with his pistol.

"Get out, before I change my mind and turn you in."

Magnus left without a word as Carson slammed the door.

"Fool!" Magnus bellowed from the hallway. "You should have done me in when you had the chance!"

"Mother!" Sarah sprang up the stairs, then remembered her "condition" and walked primly into the cluttered room. "Look, a letter from Carson. I told you so, I knew he would write." She danced a short jig by the door as her mother measured a window for new drapes. "He says he's going to visit us after the next cruise. And that he's been promoted to third lieutenant. And that he loves his birthday gift—wrote this letter by its light!"

"Did he write of his intentions?"

"Mother, you know I've yet to tell him."

"Regardless, he should still be responsible . . ."

"But only one more cruise. The last one took less than a month." Sarah kissed the letter. "He wrote a whole line of kisses on the bottom. See?"

"What happens if he goes to China?" Mrs. Lewis climbed down from the stepladder and folded a length of flowered cotton.

"China?" Sarah blanched. "That would take months—"

"A year, my child, with no dallying and all fair winds."

"But that . . . he couldn't. I just know."

"You just tell that to the secretary of the navy." Mrs. Lewis went downstairs, mumbling to herself.

Sarah sat on her bed in a back gable and felt her stomach. Soon, they said, she would feel life inside her. But it didn't feel big enough for a baby to be inside, a baby that was due in January, only four months away.

Should she write him and tell him? He'd included his address at Hastings-on-Hudson. No, she couldn't! It would sound so cold in a letter, and it might seem like a trick. No, it would be wrong to burden him during his furlough at home. And his family . . . how would it look to them? Sarah lay face down, sobbing into the pillow before she fell asleep.

The front page of the *Baltimore Patriot* was pinned to the wall beside her. GLORIOUS VICTORY

AT SEA, rang the banner. Below, in the accompanying article, a penciled arrow pointed to the name of her promised one.

St. Michael's tower bell rang eight over Marblehead Neck. It was the same bell that had announced the Declaration of Independence almost fifty years before, when it had cracked and had to be mended by Paul Revere.

Lieutenant Chassagne turned up the sperm oil lamp.

"You can't go on the ship again," he said, massaging the small of Lucy Brewer's pale back. "I won't have it."

"You're just afraid of all the other men."

"Lieutenant Chassagne is afraid of nothing, man nor beast." He kneaded Lucy's thigh so hard that she groaned. "Maybe I won't let you go this time, eh?"

"And have me lose my prize money! Claude, I like you very much, but I like money too. So I'm finishing my enlistment."

"Okay, Lucy, but if I see anything going on with any of the other men I—" Claude zipped a finger across his neck.

"Doctor Guillotine!"

"That's me, thank you. Now turn around . . ."

"Whoa, Casanova, not so hard!"

"But I am passionate about your body. Maybe I'll show you the secrets of French acrobats now, no?"

"No . . . Claude, do you remember Sarah Lewis?"

"The *other* clown."

"She wrote me—she's pregnant!"

"I congratulate the boy friend."

"Promise to keep a secret?"

"I promise on my father's grave."

"And your mother's?"

"She'll live a long time yet."

"If you tell anyone, I'll say that you made homosexual advances on Nicolas Baker and I'll run away."

"I give up; you win!"

"It's Lieutenant DeWitt!"

"I thought as much. But doesn't this mean trouble?"

"No, they love each other. Sarah wrote me about it."

"It's possible . . ." He kissed her ankles and nuzzled between her shins, spreading them.

"That's far enough, *chéri*. You promised."

"So I did." Claude gallantly handed Lucy her drawers as he flopped back on the bed. Fiddle music wafted through their second floor window from a tavern up Hooper Street.

"Sarah is coming to stay with me in two weeks. You'll have to stay somewhere else for a while. You understand he doesn't know."

"So that's why he didn't say anything."

"He agreed to marry her after the next cruise."

"When is the baby due?"

"January."

"If we leave, say, end of October—" The shirtless Frenchman counted on his fingers. "She has two, maybe three months."

"We'll be back in port by Christmas . . ."

"Why, we can have Christmas at sea. Jesus won't care!" Claude crossed himself and raised his silver cross to his lips.

"You're joking again."

"Put on your dress, Lucy. The music is calling."

October 21

THE SHIP IS READY! *New sail, all stays and shrouds tarred and stations filled. Two curious-looking crates arrived today with orders to be put under 24-hour armed guard below decks; they were heavy and we're all anxious about their contents. My guess is ordnance, possibly swivel guns.*

This is the last liberty week and Commodore Bainbridge is due from New York with orders. Upon his return this Friday, he expects the ship in perfect sailing trim. It seems that the men cannot do it well enough for his taste, though in my estimation they have done a better job than for Captain Hull. Two of our crew have been tried for mutiny and discharged for refusing to do work they deemed superfluous. Even I had to placate my "compatriot" for overstaying my furlough of a month because of my father's illness, so I "doubled up" in watch duty for the remainder of this month.

News of the land war is still bad. Our militia under Colonel Winfield Scott has been surrendered at Queenston Heights on the border near Niagara. The British forces were aided by Indians from the Six Nations. Small consolation that General Brock, the captor of Captain Hull's uncle, was mortally wounded in the battle. Our western and southern war-hawks are now quiet about the prospects for their vaunted easy invasion of Canada. The experienced British regulars from Spain have strengthened the Canadian front.

Captain Decatur has just left harbor in the United States, *our sister ship, in company with* Argus, *a sloop of 20 guns, leaving* Hornet *in port. We should most certainly sail within a fortnight.*

"Yes?"

"Sorry to disturb you, Lieutenant, but there's a lady to see you." The marine rolled his eyes skyward and handed Carson a small envelope.

DeWitt slipped out a card; it was William Green's. "Thank you, Corporal. Bring the lady aboard. I'll see her in the captain's day-cabin." Carson handed the guard a key.

"Aye, sir."

Cursing his cravat, which habitually resisted a neat knot, DeWitt stumbled up the steep companionway and went aft, thankful that most of the officers and crew were ashore. The after cabin still smelled of smoke, though all the paneling, furniture and draperies had been replaced.

A strikingly attractive woman stood by the sideboard mirror. She wore a robe of emerald velvet that shimmered under the cabin skylight. Her matching cap was topped by a curly white ostrich plume, in contrast with her long, ebony hair. Her skin was smooth and bronzed, setting off her flashing eyes. A white ermine stole lay casually over the captain's chair.

"Hello." She studied him frankly as she fingered the furnishings.

"Lieutenant DeWitt at your service. Miss . . ."

"That *would* be nice," she whispered.

"Pardon?" Carson flushed in embarrassment, not sure he'd heard correctly.

"I'm Kahlini Metcalf. We've met on two occasions but never been introduced."

"Won't you please sit down, Miss Metcalf." Carson slid the other chair around the table. She picked up the ermine stole and sat attentively, leaving Carson no alternative but to sit in the captain's chair, rather too close for comfort. The smell of battle smoke had given way to musky perfume. The lieutenant was already fearing that the scent would linger and bring down Bainbridge's wrath.

"Very pleasant perfume," Carson tried.

"Thank you, Lieutenant. It is made by the Sandwich Islanders—my people—from the whale sperm."

"The spermaceti whale, of course, Miss Metcalf . . ." A clatter of tools on the deck above checked the subject. Hands appeared on the skylight and the rasp of holystones on spruce started up like a forest of gigantic locusts.

"Commodore Bainbridge will be here on Friday. May I give him your message?" Carson got up and set a notepaper box on the table. To her amusement, he moved his chair away.

"I came to see *you*, Lieutenant, since Captain Hull is no longer in command . . ." Kahlini drew her chair closer to him. He toyed with his pencil, making intricate doodles on the notepaper. The exotic lady breathed perfumed fire upon him for what seemed a short eternity.

"Is your ship in need of anything? I speak for Mr. Green, and I'm sure he will listen to me . . . *again*."

"Again?" Carson finally looked up.

"Why do you think he gave the captain 17,000 dollars' credit?"

"Then we are in your debt, Miss Metcalf. Indeed, so is the entire nation . . ."

"I didn't do it for your nation." Kahlini stood and leaned over DeWitt. "He's away on business. We can have dinner. We can talk . . . Can I call you Carson? I read your name in the newspaper."

"Can I stop you?"

"Smart boy . . ." She relaxed.

"Look, Miss Metcalf—"

"Kahlini!"

"Kahlini . . ." Carson shook off his blush. "I think we could have a fine time . . ."

"Yes, Carson?"

"But I'm already promised to a woman I dearly love. Her name is Sarah, and she lives in Baltimore."

Kahlini gave him an astonished look that he could not at first interpret. When she finally spoke, it was with a warm smile. "*Makai.* I mean very good, beautiful Lieutenant DeWitt, that you are good to your woman. I am only sad that I am not the woman you have promise to." Kahlini kissed Carson lightly on his forehead. "The Americans I have met, the Germans, the English—all the same, so powerful in commerce and politics. I try to like them, but they make me feel like cargo to buy and sell . . . May I be your friend? Please, I need an honest friend like in my islands."

Carson took her hand and nodded. He led her up to the spar deck and they stood near the gangway. "Perhaps if we had met earlier . . ."

"Tell your commodore that the provisions will be supplied." She winked at Carson as the holystone detail passed by.

"Please convey our thanks to Mr. Green." Carson assisted the woman down the gangway. Once at the bottom, she whirled and walked briskly through the clutter of crates and barrels and disappeared in the crowd on Long Wharf.

*　*　*

"Excuse me!" Kahlini found herself blocked by a somewhat dishevelled but pretty young lady wearing a yellow dress under a seaman's coat.

"Let me pass! What is the meaning of this?" Kahlini sidestepped, but to no avail.

"He's mine!" The girl stood squarely in front of her.

"I've met you before . . . at Miss Moore's place."

"You were with him," the girl said, a look of misery on her face as tears started to her eyes.

"Were you watching?"

"I just arrived from Baltimore . . . Oh, I should have—"

"You are Sarah?"

"But how . . ." Sarah wiped her eyes with her sleeve.

Kahlini took her by the arm and walked. "Sarah, it's not what you think. I must admit that I tried, but he would have none of me. We have a mutual friend who's done business with his captain. I was foolish enough to visit the lieutenant under a pretense of business. The lieutenant had no idea I was coming. He told me he was promised to a girl named Sarah. You are very lucky to have a man like that."

"Forgive me, I'm just upset . . ."

"Call me Kahlini. Now, child, please go back to him."

Sarah stared at the Polynesian beauty, then looked at her own clothing. Tears welled and she felt ashamed, unfit. She picked up her skirts and valise and began to walk, blinking at the sun. Away from the waterfront.

Moonlight poured through the window, moving fir branch patterns on the wall over Lucy's bed. Two figures were all but lost under a mountain of patchwork quilts.

"Are you awake?"

"I can never sleep more than four hours at a time. Ship's watch does that."

Sarah lay on her back. "Lucy, I just have to do something. I can't bear being so near yet not being with him . . . just watching him on deck. What can I do?"

"For one thing, mothers should get more sleep. I think you should send him a note. We're due to sail next Monday or Tuesday, according to Claude. You still have a few days to arrange a meeting. Use this room. We've rented it for the rest of next week anyway. I'll put on Nicky Baker's uniform today and drop off your letter."

"But if I see him, I'll have to tell him . . ."

"On you it doesn't show."

"Not with clothes on."

"Turn out the light."

"I can't write. It would look as if I'm blackmailing him. I'd just as well be a street-walker from Fells Point. And the new commodore would be angry with him."

"*If* he found out."

"What do you mean?"

"Nothing. Nothing at all."

221

"Lucy, do you think you'll be back before . . ."

"Claude said that all admirals plan campaigns in the tropics for winter. Besides, he found out that Bainbridge had a new, unlined uniform jacket made while he was in New York."

"Oh!" Sarah turned round and pounded the pillow.

"I'm sorry." Lucy reached over to console her.

"It's not your fault," Sarah sniffled. "I guess there's only one thing I can do. Wait."

"At least you know he's been true. Even that was worth coming all the way from Baltimore to find out. Perhaps you can stay with the Polynesian lady for a while, in case the cruise is short. Orders can change."

"You're right, Lucy. She is so nice."

"And she's rich. You'll get the best of care."

"Doctor Biggs?"

The voice startled him. He jumped aside, putting his experiment between him and the voice. Charcoal flared up in the brick stove and cast an eerie light in the room. "What do you mean, breaking in. How dare you?"

"I've been watching you." The voice was boyish. "Do you know how to test your . . . liquid for proof?"

"I don't know what you're talking about!"

"I've been hiding in your stores for almost three days. I saw you put the rye mash on a keg of corn sprout."

"It's just a medical experiment."

"Are you ill?" Sarah came forward, dressed as a boy.

"Of course not. Get out before I call the sergeant at arms."

"If you're not ill, why did you drink the spirits? I saw you drink a pint."

Biggs shrunk back, deflated and quiet.

"Go call the sergeant," Sarah went on. "I'll tell him about your *still*."

"You're crazy! What do you want of me?"

"Do you recall Seaman Wilson? Lemuel Wilson?"

"Oh my God! Not again!" The surgeon staggered against his work table, clinking some tubes and retorts.

"I want you to let me stay here, hide me."

"It won't work. I have two assistants, you know. They'll find out. They have access here."

"Then I'll tell the sergeant that you lured me to your cabin in Boston and got me drunk on your moonshine, and that's how I got aboard. Bainbridge would not take it kindly."

"You wouldn't!"

"What have I to lose?"

Biggs ran a hand through his meager hair.

"Tell your mates that I'm a steward, that you requested one for cleaning and laundry, and that I'll bunk here at night. I'll stay out of your way, wash things, tidy up. You'll see."

"I have no choice." Amos Biggs crumpled weakly in his chair.

November 12

"CAPTAIN EDWARD KERR of His Majesty's ship *Acaste*." An African announced the officers to Colonel de Andrades, commandant of the military garrison of Porto Praya, Cape Verde Islands.

"Welcome, Englishmen. I saw your beautiful ships come in. What can we help you with?"

Lieutenant Chassagne, dressed in a British naval uniform, translated from the Portuguese as Carson DeWitt, similarly attired, kept his hand on his sword hilt.

"Tell the colonel we will pay for water and take a look at the island's livestock." Bainbridge, in a lavishly embellished British captain's uniform, took a letter from his pocket and handed

224

it to the colonel. "Ask him if he would kindly keep this for Captain Yeo of the frigate *Southampton*, due to stop off soon." The envelope was unsealed, suggesting unimportant matter.

"Yes, he'll present the letter to Captain Yeo," Chassagne said after listening to the commandant's response.

Colonel de Andrades led the officers out onto his battlement terrace. Carson winked at Chassagne as the colonel proudly demonstrated his four-inch Dolland achromatic telescope to Bainbridge. They looked at *Constitution* and *Hornet*, flying huge British ensigns as curious small craft clustered around in the harbor.

Captain Porter's *Essex* was nowhere to be seen at this remote island group, four hundred miles off the west coast of northern Africa, the first of several rendezvous points agreed upon before the 32-gun frigate left the Chesapeake to join Bainbridge in a hunt for British East Indiamen along the tradewind routes of the southern oceans.

After filling with fresh water, *Constitution* and *Hornet* sailed southwest, across the Atlantic narrows to the Portuguese island of Fernando de Noronha, a distance of sixteen hundred miles. They had logged almost five thousand since leaving Boston. The fast passage was due in large part to excellent lunar observations based on Bowditch's revised navigation figures. The combination of *Essex* being held up while awaiting supplies in the Chesapeake, and of a navigational advantage that gained one day for every five was to prove vital in the fortunes of all three of the ships concerned—and cause death within a year for one of the captains.

The two ships crossed the equator five hundred miles northeast of Brazil's shoulder, just west of the tiny island of San Pedro on December 9. For most of the crew, it was the first time.

> In latitude oo-oo and longitude 29.5, let it be known to all Mermaids, Sea Serpents, Whales, Sharks, Porpoises, Dolphins, Skates, Eels, Suckers, Lobsters, Crabs, Pollywogs, and other living things of the sea, that *Nicolas Baker* has been found worthy to be numbered as one of our trusty shellbacks, and has been gathered to our fold, and duly initiated into the Solemn Mysteries of the Ancient Order of the Deep.

Nicolas read the scroll which had been prepared for her, as representative for her mess, considering that to initiate four hundred crewmen would not meet with the commodore's approval. She crossed her fingers that her shirt could be kept on. It was the unknown that she dreaded. Sooner or later, by accident, her secret would be found out. Or would it?

The bosun and his mates had spent hours making wigs and beards of tow and spun yarn; Jacob Conegys and the sail gang had sewn showy undergarments for the good-looking young man who would play Amphitrite, Nep-

tune's wife. Nicolas was glad the part had gone
to a fair topman. Gunner John Dilkes was named
as Neptune because he hid his age so well.

A day after "Davey Jones came aboard," the
bosun reported to the commodore that Neptunus
Rex was alongside to pay respects and receive
tribute from those of his subjects who had not
yet paid their debts to his domain. Neptune and
his wife were feted on the foc'sle by his courtiers
and the officers, while men in bear costumes
harrassed the ship's company. On his elaborate
throne, Neptune, somewhat the worse from ac-
cepting a pint of the captain's private stock, was
leering at the young man in pinks and whites.

One by one, the shellbacks were brought forth
by the bears, shaved by the ship's barber with
a large wooden razor and a bucket of flour paste.
Then their chairs were tipped, dumping the
initiates backwards into a large tub of very salty
water.

Of the officers, Carson had drawn the short
straw—to the delight of Sarah, who watched
from behind a deck launch. Even the commodore joined in with cheers—much to everyone's
surprise. More punishments had been recorded
in the ship's log for the month of November
than in any one year of the ship's ten in active
commission.

12 December
*This morning we dropped anchor in Fer-
nando de Noronha's small harbor, 175 miles
from the coast of Brazil. Hardly more than a*

rock, it is some eight miles long and a mile wide, surrounded by a few uninhabited reefs. There is one conical peak, probably of volcanic origin, and were it not for the island's function as a penal colony, it would be a most comfortable place, trade winds keeping the temperature between 75 and 78 all year long. There is little excitement among the crew about going ashore since the population of about two thousand is all male, mostly criminals, and a military garrison of one hundred fifty.

With the British colors flying, as in Cape Verde, we again went ashore in disguise and had an audience with the Portuguese commandant, who did not know about "our war with the upstart Americans." As before, we left a letter for Captain Porter, alias Captain Yeo. Our letter, in sympathetic ink, contained instructions that Captain Porter should not wait for us to return but proceed south around the Horn and raid English merchantmen in the Pacific, of which many have been observed, plying their routes in safety.

The sympathetic ink we used is quite ingenious, a product of our East Indies commerce. In the margins of the letter is written a second, invisible message in rice-water, which reappears in strong sepia upon being lightly washed with iodine.

Tomorrow we shall go into Bahia to communicate with the American consulate. Perhaps there is news of the war.

14 December

Seeing an English sloop-of-war in the harbor, our commodore sent in Captain Lawrence with Hornet, *and we lay outside in the event of a trap. It turned out to be* Bonne Citoyenne, *18 guns and a perfect match for* Hornet. *Lawrence challenged Captain Greene to make for open sea and engage, but Greene declined. He carried a million pounds in gold and silver, destined in part for payments to American merchantmen in London, and he did not want to put it in jeopardy. Lawrence and his crew, delighted at such a prize, took up a blockade position. We are all wary at such a declaration; the enemy is fond of such gambits.*

> *"Hark the herald angels si-ing,*
> *Glo-ry to the new-born king . . ."*

Four hundred voices rang out to the accompaniment of the ship's full complement of ten musicians under a full moon as gentle southerlies wafted the hymn into the lush rain-forest above *Constitution*'s anchorage. The frigate swung slowly on her bower, her crew forgetting for one evening the smell of smoke and tar, the care of cannon and the fear of blood. On the wide beaches of Todos los Santos the devout and the savage listened, looking in awe at the dark form silhouetted on a shimmering tropical sea.

Nicolas Baker and short-haired Lemuel Wilson knelt and watched Tommy Ganley unwrap his present as Lieutenant Chassagne stood proudly by. The ten-year-old face beamed as it beheld a scale model of the captain's gig.

"Now everything is okay . . . *boys*," Chassagne emphasized for the benefit of nearby pipe-smokers. "I'd better go up now and wish the crew a Merry Christmas."

Midshipman Archibald Hamilton thundered into Washington, his horse steaming and snorting along the marshy roads of the desolate new seat of government. This was his fourth horse for the trip. He had started in New London during a snowstorm, and stopped at Yonkers, Trenton and Wilmington, crossing three rivers on the way by barge and ice. One saddlebag contained the tattered colors of a defeated British frigate, *Macedonian*. After sending the *Macedonian* to Newport in Rhode Island, Captain Stephen Decatur had given Hamilton despatches and accounts of the victory to carry to a grand naval ball that was being held in honor of previous exploits. The captured colors of *Guerriere* and *Alert* were on display in the banquet hall where President Madison and his vivacious wife Dolly were presiding.

Young Hamilton was filled with tales to tell, having recounted and rehearsed his stories on the long ride. He would tell of the British captain—a sundowner and flogger, who was offended at surrendering to Decatur because the American had not been properly dressed for the occasion. And about capturing an entire eight-man French band which had elected to stay aboard its captor, the frigate *United States*.

The revelry was at its height as Hamilton dismounted in front of the president's house. The ladies were turned out in dazzling coiffures and the men were resplendent in dress uniforms and diplomatic attire. A thousand wax candles glittered over the colorful scene.

All at once, during a stately minuet, murmurs mounted near the hall's entrance, spreading from group to group, first in whispers, then in shouts. News had come of yet another great naval victory over his Majesty's invincibles.

Word was brought to Secretary Hamilton, who directed that the bearer of such despatches be at once admitted. Amid cheers and applause the young midshipman entered the bright hall and presented Decatur's papers to his father. Young Hamilton turned from his parents and sisters to receive the congratulations of the president's party and the assembled naval officers. He opened his bag and drew out the captured flag and laid it out before them. Dolly Madison, it is said, draped the flag about her shoulders, adding to the humor and delight of the evening.

The orchestra struck up "Hail Columbia" and toasts were proffered—to one another, to the holiday season, and to the illustrious American captains.

Four thousand miles away, below the equator, a different party was about to begin.

December 28

AFTER ADVISING MASTER Commandant Lawrence of the proximity of a British ship-of-the-line, the *Montague*, Bainbridge hauled anchor and left Bahia at daybreak. The destination was Cabo Frio, just north of Rio de Janeiro. It was to be the last rendezvous place with *Essex*. The morning was blindingly bright and clear, the water calm, with a light offshore breeze carrying exotic jungle fragrances over the waking boat.

Shortly after nine, two sails were spotted by the topmen. They were bound south, showing white against the gently rolling green hills and the hazy grey plateau of Diamontina. They appeared to be heading for Rio. The next leg—if they were Indiamen—was across to Good Hope and around Africa.

It wasn't long before the smaller ship beat in to shore and the larger put its helm over and bore toward *Constitution*.

"They don't answer our signals, sir. Nor do we understand theirs." Lieutenant Corneck called the flags down.

"I say there, Captain; surely we are not to engage. Your ship is hardly prepared for such . . ." Lieutenant-General Hyslop fingered his baton nervously. "The viceroy expects me and my staff—that is, we're already behind schedule."

"Sir," Captain Henry Lambert coolly addressed the superior army officer. "I must ask you to leave the quarterdeck."

"This is preposterous, Captain. The office of governor-general of Bombay takes precedence over sea squabbles."

"We are at war, sir, and you are my passenger. We are at sea and I am in command."

"Very well, Lambert." The elderly general marched haughtily to the companionway.

"Clear the decks, Lieutenant. I think they're making for us as well."

"Aye, sir . . . Their courses are furling."

"If it's a Yankee frigate, we'll show him a surprise. One thing I'll say for the French . . . They know how to build boats for light airs!"

Java, née *Renommée*, had been captured and refitted by the Royal Navy a year earlier. A first-class frigate of 44 guns, she'd been named for the island Britain had wrested from the French. The English had re-rated her for 38 guns, though she actually carried 49 to *Constitution*'s 52 and her broadside shot weighed 288 pounds compared to the American's 327. Her complement of 426 men was 24 fewer than *Constitution*'s, although she also carried 100 passengers, many of whom took part in the engagement. As to displacement, *Java* was a third lighter, and smaller by several yards in length.

Java was not primarily a warrior, and had not expected a confrontation on this commercial voyage. She carried a cargo of sheet copper for ships that were being built in India, and had captured a small American brig, the *William*, which she'd just jettisoned to shore under a prize crew.

Commodore Bainbridge drew the stranger seaward until the two ships were alone on the vast circle of placid ocean. Midshipman Lovett entered the ship's position at 13 degrees, 6 minutes south latitude by 38 west longitude, about thirty miles southeast of Bahia—too far from the island for the *Java* to retreat easily for repairs or stores.

By noon, telescopes of both ships had picked out each other's colors and they'd beat to quarters. *Java* hauled down her national ensigns and left a jack flying on the bowsprit, an eccentric move for a man-of-war. Bainbridge, after observing the flag, a scarlet cross of St. George on a blue field, ran on a parallel tack, standing off about one mile. At two o'clock, the British frigate put her helm over and went for *Constitution*, intent on a rake. The latter wore round and fired a 24 across the enemy's polychromed figurehead, asking for the ensigns to be reset. The British 18s answered with a broadside that fell short.

Constitution had the advantage at distance; her thirty 24-pounder long guns could puncture a 22-inch oak hull at 1000 yards. British and French frigates of *Java* size had hulls of less than 15 inches. Within an hour, most of her cross spars had been shot away as Bainbridge stood away from her heavy carronades. At this moderate distance, the American guns proved devastating. Out of pure chance, ten out of the score of *Java*'s midshipmen were killed or wounded by the initial cannonading. Since guns were supervised by these ranks, it followed that her firing efficiency suffered accordingly and allowed the American guns to nullify a maneuvering disadvantage which Lambert had counted upon.

Sulphurous clouds of black smoke rose high into the maintops of *Constitution* as she reached in the lee of the Englishman. Marine sharpshooters on the fighting platforms picked out moving targets through the occasional voids between hammock nettings and swirling cannon smoke while midshipmen on the fore and mizzen tops figured trajectories for Bainbridge's secret weapons, the stubby, four-inch brass howitzers lashed to deadeyes on the trestle trees. The blasts of these unorthodox weapons punctuated the cannon rumble and tremored through the masts to the very keel they were stepped into.

Bainbridge screamed and reached for his leg. An enemy musket ball had grazed his shin. The commodore hobbled back of the mizzenmast, out of line with the enemy's topmast musket marines, when suddenly a splintering crash drove him to the deck. A sharp pain in his thigh and a shower of wood. The helmsman was down and both wheels were gone. Ignoring his wounds, the commodore called for midshipmen to man jury stations as the frigate's head, rudder free, turned helplessly into the northeast breeze. *Java,* sensing the kill, came about for a rake to her adversary's bow. A shout came through the deck grating:

"Standing by on jury rudder . . ."

"Hard aport," bellowed Bainbridge as the sailing master hauled in on port.

"Hard aport . . ." the command was repeated at several stations below, from the gun deck to the berth deck and finally to the men who hauled on the relieving tackle, easing the port rudder post forward.

Lambert, surprised, was left behind and had to settle for another parallel run. As the *Java* came up on the American's starboard, the newfangled brass tangent sights of John Dilke's battery were perfectly set. The two 32-pound carronades, along with one 24, recoiled into their breechings as they fired, immediately followed by the thunder of the gun deck group below.

Clouds of caustic smoke billowed back through the ports, stinging the gunners' eyes and blackening their sweaty bare backs.

Java fell back as the smoke blew to leeward and a great cheer went up as her bowsprit crumpled at the cap. Dangling by bobstays and shrouded by the cross of St. George, the bowsprit swung into the bow wake alongside her stem. The bluntnosed frigate wore to starboard, her helm unsteady.

John Alwyn, who'd replaced Morris as first lieutenant, took over the quarterdeck as the commodore went below to have his wounds dressed. Having come up through the sailing master route, as had Captain Hull, Alwyn was quick to capitalize. *Constitution* sprang ahead under increased sail to gain a raking position but the Englishman's headway was such that he rammed his bowsprit stump over the American's starboard quarter, fouling in the mizzen stays.

Captain Lambert knew he was done for unless he could board. *Java* nudged in tight as British bugles screamed for "boarders away." Captain Lambert, cutlass glinting, scrambled up onto the head gratings, followed by his faithful with pikes and pistols as the bosun's mates prodded the shirkers forward with starting ropes and speaking trumpets. The valiant among them raised a cheer designed to intimidate the enemy. But the Americans, having been stung once by *Guerriere*, were not to be fooled. A reception committee was well braced in the yards and tops.

Lambert was among the first to fall. He lay on the ash-strewn deck, eyes glazed, with a ball in his spine. It had come down from the tops, shattering his clavicle and sluicing a lung. He tried to cry out, but the legs ran by him, back to his ship. The boarding attempt had failed.

A gust filled *Constitution*'s forecourse and wrenched her free of the intruder. She leapt ahead, came round the enemy's bow and delivered the first rake of the contest. Two by two, above and under, each starboard gun spewed its grape and solid ball as it came to bear on the broad black bow, raking the spardeck from stem to stern, cutting down entire gun crews and catapulting carronades from their carriages, whipping cables and splintering pin rails, launches and hatches. Even the ship's bell was torn, knelling as it fell from its belfry to roll against the bloody dead.

A crackling of spruce and the foremast wavered and careened madly down on the foc'sle, breaking through two decks amid the shrieks of crushed gunners and falling topmen. The struggling and the dazed and the tangled fell to the warm ocean which, blossoming with red froth, announced another enemy—one with fins. Hardly had the foremast been cleared when the main topmast, weakened by parted stays forward, came crashing down, helped to leeward by the breeze and some well-timed cutlass slashes. The topsail and yard dragged over the engaged side and caught fire from the flaming wads of the remaining active guns.

Now totally out of control, *Java* was at the mercy of the American gunners under Ezekiel Darling. They picked their targets unerringly, shooting away the spanker boom and gaff, holing at will between wind and water, even through the copper bottom as the battered hull listed. A shot parted the transom davit tackle, loosing the bow of the captain's gig so it swung to and fro by the stern, just above the water and the hectic grasps of doomed swimmers.

Lieutenant Henry Ducie Chads, acting captain, watched the American wear away to repair its rigging and marvelled that the ship had not lost a single spar. She'd even carried royals into the fight! What kind of frigate is that? the bloody gun crews asked. Our shot is of no great effect, observed the officers. First *Guerriere*, and now us?

"Sir, there's trouble below." Midshipman Lovett accosted the commodore as he observed the enemy through his glass.

"When is there *not* trouble below?" Bainbridge sneered. "Ah," he exclaimed as a cheer rose through the boat. *Java*'s mizzen, her last mast, had collapsed overboard.

Lovett repeated his statement, adding that it was of a sensitive nature.

"Sensitive?" barked the commodore. "Explain yourself."

"A woman, sir—she's wounded, and about to have a baby!"

"What?" Bainbridge turned crimson and gritted his teeth.

"She's in labor, sir. Surgeon said it was premature. He thought it discreet to bring her to the flagship cabin, sir."

"How on earth . . ."

"She'd gone to a carronade station to take the place of young Ganley, a powder boy who was hit, sir."

"I won't have it. I won't have a woman or a baby—" Bainbridge jammed his telescope into Lovett's stomach and limped toward the aft companionway. "Parker," he growled at the first lieutenant, "take over, and call me when repairs are made." He went below, past the cockpit wounded station, noting at least a score of bandaged men on the cornhusk mattresses. Lieutenant Alwyn, badly wounded, was being attended to by the surgeon's mate.

"How is he?"

The mate shook his head.

Sucking in his breath, Bainbridge entered the aft daycabin. "Biggs, what's the meaning of this?" His powerful frame shook with rage. "Who is responsible for this—*woman* on board?"

"I didn't know, sir. We thought he . . . she was a powder boy when Lieutenant Chassagne brought her down. I think she'll pull through; she took some grape in the shoulder. But she's had a bad shock. Delirious. Doesn't want to live."

Sarah lay in the guest commander's bunk, in a private room, aft and to port of the day cabin.

Her wound had been cleaned and dressed; she lay under a sheet, mumbling incoherently.

Bainbridge paced, then looked in at the bunk and paced again. "How on earth . . . Don't you examine crewmen before they're signed up?"

"I believe she was a stowaway, sir." Biggs closed her door.

"There's going to be an inquiry, sure as shooting. I'll not be responsible for this idiocy." Bainbridge started to leave when DeWitt Carson rushed in, followed by a young seaman.

"Where is she?"

"And pray, Lieutenant," the commodore demanded, "what business is this of yours?"

Without answering, Carson went into the aftercabin. His voice carried out to the others. "Sarah, my love . . . I just found out. Why didn't you tell me? Never mind, nothing matters now except that I love you and everything's going to be all right . . ."

She opened her eyes slowly. "I'm sorry for what I've done."

Carson kissed her on the forehead and she smiled. "Nothing to be sorry about." Carson looked back at Commodore Bainbridge, then stood and approached him. "Sir, can I talk to you—alone?" He shut the aftercabin door. Bainbridge, with five children of his own, felt a tinge of sympathy but didn't show it.

"Sir," Carson said, taking Seaman Baker by the arm, "Baker here, has had some experience with—" Carson gestured aft.

"Biggs!" Bainbridge turned to the surgeon with an inquiring look.

"I'm not very well prepared for this."

"Very well." Bainbridge motioned Baker aft to Sarah. Surgeon Biggs went with the seaman.

"Now what do you have to say about this, DeWitt? I have exactly one minute. This isn't Boston, you know!"

"You won't have to court-martial anyone—or even hold an inquiry." Carson stripped off his lieutenant's gold epaulettes.

"Then you admit it. Very well, DeWitt. I don't want to be involved, nor do I want my ship to be involved in such folly."

"Nor do I want to spoil your victory."

"You'll assume full responsibility?"

"My word as an officer."

The tall commodore pulled at his cheek whiskers. "DeWitt, there's one thing wrong with you, aside from this fiasco."

"Sir?"

"You don't know how to lie. Sometimes a little twist is necessary. Put back your rank until Boston; we want everything to look right. The woman—and her baby, if need be—will stay in the flagship cabin, and I'll post a marine."

"That won't be necessary!" Carson said sharply.

"Well taken . . . but I want one thing understood. Nobody need know about this, that the quarterdeck was involved."

"I understand, sir."

"Very well. And I'll handle Biggs. That *this*

had to happen at this time . . ." Bainbridge slapped the breech of one of the day cabin long Toms and blustered out.

As *Constitution* headed for its adversary to deliver the coup de grâce, a splendid banquet was being attended by Captains Hull and Decatur at Gilson's City Hotel in New York, four thousand miles away, provided by the mayor, Clinton, and other officials. Five hundred important gentlemen sat down to the occasion. One eyewitness described the hall as decorated like a marine palace, walls festooned with ship's masts and Christmas holly, and flying all the world's pennants. Each table had its own barrel of beer and featured a miniature model frigate as a centerpiece. On the dais, near the table of President Madison, who had just rushed up from Washington, was a large grassed-in area, in the middle of which was a pool of water, made to look like a lake, with trees and houses around it. A yard-long model of *Constitution* lay upon the lake. As a backdrop, a full-size frigate's mainsail hung from a spar suspended before the wall.

Decatur and Hull sat on either side of the president as the gathering, tipping their tankards, made the hall resound with toasts, the last being "To our navy." With three huzzahs the mainsail furled up, revealing a room-high transparent screen painting. Torches backlit the diorama which illustrated in garish color the trio of great naval victories during the past year,

including that of Captain Jones's *Wasp*. Jones
was absent and at sea.

Many a tankard was lifted before the evening
was done. Children danced, carrying large al-
phabet letters strung with holly that spelled out
the names of the three victorious captains as
the orchestra struck up "Yankee Doodle Dandy."
The celebration was capped by an Irish clown,
Mr. MacFarland, who sang a comic song written for the occasion. Its refrain went:

> *No more 'o your blatherin' nonsense,*
> *'bout Nelsons of old Johnny Bull.*
> *I'll sing ye a song by my conscience,*
> *'bout Jones and Decatur and Hull!*

31 December
My son was born shortly after Java *struck her
colors, thanks to Seaman Baker. Our surgeon
seemed dazed by it all, as if drunk, though I can
imagine the strain a battle puts upon him.*

*I reassured Sarah that we'll be married after
I resign my commission in Boston. This placated
her and she's finally sleeping soundly. I am in-
debted to the surgeon for his concern with her
wound. And to Seaman Baker, who, I have just
found out from Lieutenant Chassagne, is especially well suited for taking care of infants. That
French rascal has been having a time under all
our noses! If Bainbridge knew he had yet
another woman aboard, one who has been un-
detected for a year, he would no doubt walk*

*the plank himself out of embarrassment. But I
gave my word. There'll be no scandal for the
ship, or for my son and future wife. My agree-
ment with the commodore includes two main
points: one, that I carry on my duties as before
until port; two, that I give no sign of my con-
nection with Sarah, or that her pregnancy was
in any way connected with the quarterdeck.
Even now, certain crewmen are suspect and it
is of great interest at the scuttlebutt.*

*I have explained all to her and we have
arranged that Baker convey daily letters between us. Sarah is already suggesting names for
our son, whom I've only seen twice. I favor her
father's name, with my father's as middle.
Thomas Schuyler. With fair winds we should
make Boston in six weeks. I can hardly wait for
this limbo to be over.*

*Java, having been holed below the waterline,
is in danger of sinking and so she's not a worthy
prize. All of her small boats and three of ours
were destroyed in the battle, and it has taken
almost two days to transfer her five hundred
men, including over one hundred wounded.
Their surgeon is very expert, a graduate of excellent schools in Glasgow. Were it not for this
charade I would have him look at Sarah and
the baby.*

*The frigate carried a large passenger detach-
ment destined for East Indian service, including
the newly appointed governor-general of Bombay, an irascible professional soldier who insists
that we let him off immediately. Our crew is*

eager to oblige. Many of the passenger detachment are naval personnel. They lost thirteen of their number in aiding their countrymen. Captain Lambert lies below, mortally wounded, in the wardroom, while our own John Alwyn, who assumed temporary command while the commodore had his wounds dressed, is in grave condition and not expected to survive. We found on deck a letter by a Lieutenant Corneck to a friend, accidentally dropped, which listed his losses as 65 killed and 170 wounded.

It was a sorry thing to blow up the frigate this afternoon, especially without salvaging its cargo of sheet copper destined for building ships in India. But we had no time to risk transfer; nor had we any room, with a thousand men aboard.

Repairs have been made, including a new though ungainly wheel, courtesy of the vanquished. We shall proceed into Bahia and grant our prisoners parole, the understanding being that they shall not take part in any battle against our forces until exchanged according to the rules of war. Rules? At times war seems a ridiculous game played by admirals and generals who have unknowingly replaced tin soldiers with flesh and blood.

1813

January 7

THE BRITISH FRIGATE *Macedonian* rode at
anchor in New York Harbor, having come
down through Long Island Sound on New
Year's Day. "She comes with the compliments
of the season from Old Neptune," commented a
newspaper. Barges and skiffs offered rides for
the curious to inspect the prize taken by Captain Decatur and his frigate *United States* three
months earlier in the Sargasso Sea, 500 miles
west of the Canary Islands.

One of the sightseers on that blustery afternoon wore heavy fur boots to protect his afflicted
foot from the cold and the spray of the oars.
While others cheered and laughed, he alone
cursed under his breath as the skiff rounded the

once-proud hull, pocked with shot holes and rigged with splintered spars and yards. The prize commander, Lieutenant Allen, waved at the boatload of gawkers from the transom rail.

Magnus DeWitt spat in return.

Over three hundred "Jackies" from the foc'sle of Decatur's ship were landed at dusk on the Battery pier and marched in formation to a hotel to the rousing tunes of the captured French band from *Macedonian*. The happy bluejackets were in their shore-leave finery: glazed black canvas hats with broad, stiff brims streaming long black silk ribbons, snappy blue jackets loosely buttoned over red-striped waistcoats, and bell-mouthed dungarees flapping over shiny black pumps. They strode two by two among the ringing cheers from the crowd-lined narrow streets, confetti falling from the windows and balconies above as they made their way to City Hotel for a sumptuous banquet.

The dinner over, the tars were marched into a theater where they sat in the reserved orchestra section by the pit. A program had been prepared for the seafarers, and more than one glazed hat was seen to skim over the heads of a rowdy audience.

17 February

We arrived in Boston on the fifteenth to a blaze of fanfare, artillery salutes and banquet invitations. My resignation was tendered as a simple letter to Secretary Hamilton, with a copy for the commodore should he need it. My "indiscretion" had all but been forgotten in the tumultuous celebration, one which Bainbridge delighted in as he was swept from place to place in fancy carriages. The hubbub allowed us to purchase proper clothing and go with Claude and Lucy-Nicky to Salem where we were married, with their blessings as Thomas Schuyler's new godparents.

Last evening was spent in extreme luxury after a raucous celebration was given in our honor by Kahlini Metcalf in her merchant friend's elaborate waterfront mansion. Sarah and I were treated to breakfast in our rooms and a coach at the door.

As I write here, in the comfort of an inn at Hartford, I am sad not to be part of the victorious homecoming after a year's service aboard. My choice, however, was the only one I could make and I feel in my heart that God has given me two victories instead of one.

Not much given to church-type religion, I look at my wife and son and pray that my family will accept us. And I shudder at the thought of my uncle's last words lest he try to disrupt our happiness.

"You have made a fine choice, my son. Only two days and Sarah has become part of the family." Schuyler DeWitt coughed, pale and drawn beyond his years, and Carson drew another blanket over him. "I'm so happy at how Sarah gets on with Cathy. They're almost like sisters, being the same age."

"Father, I'm sorry I had to resign."

"There's no shame after your part in two great battles, and your resignation was voluntary." Schuyler propped himself up. "I think I'm getting better. Our house has taken on its old happiness since you brought home Sarah and little Tom. Do you realize that I'm a grandfather? I swear I feel well enough for a brandy. By George, I'll have one tonight."

"How is Mary Clinton . . . and her family?" Carson slid a wing chair closer to his father and sat down.

"The girl's got enough suitors—and well she should with all her family's money," Schuyler added. "Frankly, son, I think you've done much better." The elder man winked.

"Thanks, father. She *is* lovely—and smart. She knows French and mathematics."

"Good, maybe Sarah can keep our books."

Carson hesitated before he spoke. "Has Magnus been around?"

"Why do you ask?"

"I saw him in New York, after *Guerriere*; he came to my rooms. The reason I ask is that he acted . . . strangely. Is there something wrong with him?"

"That could well be." Schuyler lowered his voice. "Something in him seemed to crack when his wife, Joanna, left him. He's seemed more and more like a stranger since then. No one could have been more surprised than I was when I learned that he's run through his holdings in our business. Magnus got involved with Aaron Burr a few years ago. Our auditor only recently found out that huge sums of DeWitt stock had been given over to Colonel Burr. Your uncle bought himself a gunboat flotilla at Marietta in the Ohio Territory. We suspect that Burr offered him a position or land in the Louisianas."

"The same scheme that ruined Blennerhasset?"

"Yes. Nothing came of it; the flotilla and stores were seized by federal troops. Magnus, broke, tried to borrow from me. I refused. Jefferson's embargo had hit us all hard. You were stationed at New York Navy Yard when Magnus barged into this house. He ranted about assassinating the president, hiring naval officers including Decatur and Stewart, and capturing New Orleans as the capitol of his western empire. I humored him but to no avail. He was like a madman. His deterioration over the past five years has been the talk of the valley . . ." Schuyler shook his greying head sadly and looked out of the frost-edged window at the snowy palisades.

"I had no idea it was that bad."

"You're old enough to know. And considering everything, I am old enough to tell you. Magnus has sunk to the lowest depths." Schuyler muffled a cough with his hand and stared forlornly into space.

"Have you heard from him?"

"His creditors say he's gone to the northwest and suggest that he's cast his lot with the British at Detroit."

"It follows." Carson said thoughtfully.

"How so?"

"Magnus said he knew Admiral Cockburn. He's next in command to Admiral Warren in Halifax . . ."

"I see. Do you suppose he took a command, being a major?"

"Magnus functions better in mufti, doesn't he?"

"As a spy?" Carson's father blanched.

"The next thing to it, an agent for hire."

In the silence that followed, Schuyler's somber face suddenly brightened. "By the way, we have news. There's a chance that Caleb is alive."

Carson gaped at his father in astonishment and clasped his hand. "Tell me, quick!"

"There have been reports about an Indian brave who rides with the Iroquois in Ontario. His hair is blond and he speaks English as well as the language of the Muskoka tribe."

"Father, there's a notice posted at town hall," Carson said excitedly. "Commodore Chauncey at Sacket's Harbor is calling for volunteers and shipbuilders for the lakes. He needs carpenters and smiths—and the pay is good. At least I can handle an adze."

"My son, you've hardly arrived here. Stay with your wife and my grandson for a while. You've done your part. If Caleb is alive, he's survived for over ten years in the wilderness among those savages, and it would be better to wait til the thaw anyway."

"I'll wait one month, Father, to make sure you get well. In the meantime there's much work to do around the house—especially a new fence for the north pasture. It'll be good practice."

March 23

THREE LARGE SLEDGES, each with snorting six-horse teams, came whooping out of the snow forest to the clearing at Belle Valley and careened past the general store on the old French road to Presque Island. Flags flying, the first sledge flung loose snow at the curious towns-folk who had left the warmth of their homes to see the cause of their dogs' yapping.

"How far to Erie?" one of the twenty huddled men cried out as the last sledge passed.

"Five miles, 'bout." The store proprietor held up five fingers in answer as red-faced children and dogs ran after the caravan of rollicking arti-sans. The men on the sledges were oblivious to the cold, thanks to a barrel of "social lubricant."

* * *

"Where's the *city*?" bellowed a blacksmith as his sledge slowed down at a roadsign that proclaimed Erie, population 200. There were roads under the snow, intersecting one another in monotonous square symmetry; but only a few buildings were to be seen at the far north of the white clearing, their chimney smoke winding up into the waning winter sun.

Jud Hansen, one of the sledge drivers, spoke up. "The city was laid out twenty years ago by army engineers. It'll take time to put houses on all the streets," he explained.

The procession glided past three long, desolate barracks set at an odd angle to the uniform grid. "Built 'em that way so as to get better sun in the windows . . ." Jud snapped his reins and pulled up on a bluff overlooking the white inland sea. "That's the peninsula," he said, pointing his mitten. "The French named it Presque Isle. And down there on the beach are the frames for two brigs. Up harbor you can just make out the gunboats off Cascade Creek. And that there blockhouse was built by Mad Anthony Wayne, the Revolutionary War hero and injun-fighter."

Turning around, Jud headed for the ominous grey barracks, where a detail of teamsters had gathered to tend the exhausted horses. Carson DeWitt, in frontier leather and fur, shouldered his adze, hefted his suitcase and slid off the sledge. The bandsmen hauled out their instruments and followed the drivers into headquarters barracks, while the artisans tried out their land legs and resisted the efforts of a marine corporal to line them up. "C'mon now, men, let's get some order here."

"Welcome to the great city of Erie," a naval captain called out, struggling into his greatcoat as he sprinted toward the group. "I'm Captain Dobbins. This place may look like the end of the world to you big city people, but don't let that fool you. We've got more food and liquor here than any base in the country." Dobbins stayed the cheers. "Now I expect you're all very tired. It's no easy trip, I know. I've done it."

"Yea," mumbled Corcoran, hammer in hand, "but I'll bet ye didn't have to sleep in stables, with yer gold stripes."

Dobbins continued, "The sergeant at arms will show you your quarters and see to your comforts. Tomorrow, after we get you organized into work platoons, some of you may want to arrange for your own lodging. There's a fine hotel up the street, and a few private houses to let. One more thing before I give you to the sergeant: Don't be alarmed at our heavy guard. We don't expect an invasion, but there may be agents about who would like to put a torch to our boats. If there be any among you who have military experience, please see me tomorrow, after reveille.

"Incidentally, as civilians, you are not being shanghaied into the service. I am merely naval liaison. Your boss will be a very fine shipwright, Noah Brown. Thank you."

"He's not so bad," Carson said to Corcoran.

"It ain't that he's bad, DeWitt. It's just that he's got gold stripes and that makes him different from us. We drink beer and he's got brandy."

Carson didn't argue.

25 March

To my beloved wife:

At last I find time to write—as if I wouldn't post this on the first mail coach! How is my bride and our son? I'll bet he takes after you, and lucky for him! I trust my father is even better than when I left. And mother—I hope she's been happy.

The weather here has been milder than I expected. That is, when the wind is not off the frozen lake, in which case I put your beautiful knit sweater under my coats.

A few extra dollars found me a room in the best of Erie's two hotels after I was told it was filled. The officer in charge of this base, Captain Dobbins, is a fine man and we get along. He insists that I meet Master Commandant Perry when he arrives this week and give him my first-hand accounts of the Atlantic war.

Good news! I've been promoted. Instead of "ordinary seaman" I am now also responsible for certain night-watches in return for extra pay and privileges. A deciding factor was that my trusty pistol is one of the few on base that has a bag of shot. I'm glad I didn't bring your candle contraption because I'd worry too much about some-

one stealing it. Indeed, it is so unique that it might be exchanged by a Shawnee for an entire province in the Michigan Territory.

The trip was tedious. There were days when we made only a few miles because of snowdrifts. Accommodations in Scranton were excellent, but the rest of Pennsylvania is a wilderness, at least in the north, and some barns were better than others. I never realized how precious privacy is until being quartered with snoring men all in one room. I was spoiled by my little cubicle on the frigate.

We've received notice that Captain Lawrence and his Hornet have captured two brigs, Resolute and Peacock. Dobbins and I had a drink on that!

My first days as axe-wielder were hectic. No sooner are the trees felled than they are brought to me for cutting into knees, beams and planks. If one can judge by the use of green wood, our flotilla does not expect a long war! With this positive thought I leave you until the next mail coach on Monday. Alone as I am, Captain Dobbins has let me borrow his copy of Hakluyt's Foure Notable Voyages made by Certayne French Captaynes into Florida. The author, I'm told, is a favorite of Commandant Perry.

I look forward to being with you before autumn.

Your loving husband,
Carson

Carson glanced at his wall calendar. Sunday, the eighteenth of April, already a week past Easter! The eighteenth! The anniversary of the beginning of the Revolution! Now, thirty-eight years later, the British were at it again, threatening this time from Canada by way of the lakes with overpowering fleets and regulars from the Napoleonic wars. He picked up Sarah's letter again and read in part:

. . . my brother will survive. Constellation *took a position behind Craney Island and fought off Admiral Cockburn and his huge fleet. The British burnt and sacked Havre de Grace "to chastise the savages." I'm so worried about my mother and pray that the British do not land in Baltimore next. Cockburn is pillaging the Chesapeake, arming negroes against their masters and carrying off livestock. Soon the blockade will strangle the entire east coast. Your father's business is suffering but he manages to keep his humor. Catherine is a dear and she has a boy friend—a handsome Irish lad, Tyrone Dolan. And your mother is knitting socks for you.*

Thomas Schuyler eats like a horse. You'd hardly recognize him, he's grown so. My darling, our thoughts are with you.

> *Your affectionate wife,*
> *Sarah DeWitt DeWitt DeWitt, DeWitt!*

18 April
To my dear wife:
Crocuses are already pushing through the

261

grass. I miss you with each new sign of spring, a season we have yet to share.

We planked our first gunboat yesterday and I'm beginning to believe we can have a fleet ready by June. She'll be called Porcupine. I've learned a new trade by her, and should the blockade persist, we can survive by building riverboats.

Commandant Perry still amazes me. I don't believe he ever sleeps! One day he's in Pittsburg casting anchors and the next he's in Buffalo cajoling cannon from naval stores. It costs a dollar a pound to haul a 12-incher 100 miles over the swamp and ice from Black Rock Depot, and the gun weighs 1800 pounds! The British fleet blockades the Oswego, cutting off supplies from our industrial cities and making overland haulage necessary.

We've many ships building but no sailcloth as yet. Messages have been sent to Philadelphia as well as New York. Iron is scarce and Perry has sent men to scour the towns for rod and bar with which to fasten our carronade mounts. We are fortunate in having enough blacksmiths, however. Caulkers we have in plenty, but no oakum.

As far as operations are concerned, I am not at liberty to discuss more than I have. I'm so glad you—

Carson set the letter down. He would finish it later . . . or he might rewrite it. Was it too depressing? Was the futility getting to him, the prospect of an invasion? No; he couldn't alarm his family. Nor would he write of the problems that counted.

Many of the new rifles were inoperable. Some locks had no contact with the pan, others had locks that were set covering the pan, while some had not even had touch holes drilled, such was the hurry and the greed for profit! One could hardly imagine how the Americans would fare with weapons that were more dangerous to them than to the enemy.

So acute was the fear of invasion that many townspeople had gathered their belongings and gone to the interior. As a ruse to make the American forces appear stronger to British scouts, Captain Forster marched and then counter-marched his small contingent of militia every day. At least the inoperative rifles *looked* real.

To prevent enemy agents from setting the ships on fire, Perry had added 200 armed men to the yard's defense and built two more block-houses at strategic points. In addition, he had advised public houses and inns to report any strangers to him. Carson could almost envision Magnus DeWitt charging down to the beach, torch held high.

Glancing at his open copy of Hakluyt's *Voyages*, Carson turned his thoughts to Perry. The man was an enigma; he'd never known anyone with so much drive and energy. Corcoran had told him that Perry's first command, the swift schooner *Revenge*, had been wrecked in passage around Watch Hill, the Commandant's home

waters. Perry had been exonerated and the
blame put on the hired pilot, who conceded a
navigational error of some miles. Two years
later, Perry was in command of a squadron of
wretched gunboats guarding the harbor of Newport. He'd been overlooked for new commands
while others of lesser talent and experience
were reaping glory on the ocean. Then he
took a job no one else wanted, and was determined to make it as important as any in the fleet.
Carson thought of Bainbridge, who had lost a
frigate by bad navigation, but had still prevailed
and got another. Yes, he admired the commandant—and yearned to be of help. But as an
assistant shipwright, how could he hope to offer
any real aid?

The ice had broken early, giving impetus to
the workers below the Cascade bluffs. During
the first week in May, three of the smaller boats
were launched. On the twenty-fourth, both
brigs slid down their ways, but Perry was not
present. He had left the day before in a rowing
cutter to join Commodore Chauncey in an
attack upon Fort George, at the mouth of the
Niagara River ninety miles to the east. Driven
by the prospect of commanding a marine detachment, Perry fought the chop of Lake Erie
all night, arriving in Buffalo the next day.

Fort George surrendered, Fort Erie was evac-
uated in flames and the British fell back along
the entire river, with Perry distinguishing himself as a shore warrior. Not one to pass up an

opportunity, he commandeered five vessels that had been bottled up by Canadian guns and brought them to Erie, loaded with stores from the Black Rock Navy Yard. Two hundred militia helped his crew shoulder ropes on the shore and pull the boats for six days against a contrary current until open water was reached. The men were further aided by a "stiff-horn breeze"—cattle yoked to cables. The sloops mounted only one gun each, but were nonetheless welcomed at Cascade Creek.

Disease plagued the base. Over one-fifth of all the crews and workers were laid up with lake fever, the military term for cholera. Perry himself was often treated for recurring malaria. He wrote letter after letter to Chauncey, begging for men to man his boats so that he could engage the enemy fleet of six sail just off the bar of their harbor.

Word was received in mid-July of the tragedy off Boston Light. Captain Lawrence had been killed in a murderous duel between evenly matched frigates, the first victory for Britain. Captain Broke of *Shannon* was injured for life, a cutlass slash exposing his brain. The *Chesapeake* was taken to Halifax. Lawrence, whose previous ship, *Hornet*, had sailed to Brazil with *Constitution*, uttered the most famous phrase in naval annals as he died: Don't give up the ship. A pall descended on the nation and Secretary Hamilton ordered that Perry's flagship be called after the slain captain.

Perry's fleet was ready. There were occasional

loose ends which were surmounted ingeniously. In one instance, a five-inch-thick anchor rope could not be delivered through the forest because there was no wagon strong enough and large enough. Perry solved the problem by having each man of a large company shoulder two yards of it, one behind the other like a half-mile-long snake.

On July 21, Barclay's fleet was becalmed off Erie and Perry went out with three gunboats. One of his shots hit *Queen Charlotte*'s mizzen before a breeze came up and the British left.

Lest his luck change, Perry impetuously decided to take the initiative. On the first day of August, a Sunday, he ran up a square blue flag emblazoned with Lawrence's words and moved his squadron to the harbor mouth, intending to cross the protective sand bar at first light the next day.

On the same evening, Captain Robert H. Barclay, empty red sleeve pinned to his dress jacket, raised his sherry in response to a toast tendered him by the citizens of Port Dover, a small town directly across the lake above Long Point. "On behalf of His Majesty's Erie Squadron, I thank the major and the people of Port Dover for this exquisite feast and for the hospitality you have shown us during our stay. A month ago, Captain Finnis reconnoitered the enemy's base and returned. I wish to quell rumors that he *fled* when threatened by Perry's gunboats. Pshaw! Two little toys with a gun or two against his squadron! Were it not for this

invitation we might already have sailed, but I
expect to find the Yankee brigs hard and fast on
the bar at Erie when I return, in which event
it will be but a small job to destroy them. Here
is an instance in which a battle will be won
through scientific methods. Lieutenant Bird of
the Royal Hydrographic Service will explain."

"Thank you, Captain." The ascetic red-coated
officer sprang to his spindly legs to address the
gathering. "As you may be aware, England is in
the vanguard of natural sciences—unlike certain
other *backward* nations." He waited for snickers
to subside. "Lake Erie is landlocked, and is by
far the shallowest of all the Great Lakes. A
combination of factors has acted upon Erie's
eccentricities, effecting a lowering of its water
level this year by some five feet. One factor is
the lack of rainfall and snow run-off this year.
Another is the preponderence of southerly
winds, which has served to 'push' some of the
water toward Port Dover—and away from
Presque Isle Bay. As Captain Barclay pointed
out, Captain Finnis only wanted to be sure the
Yankee brigs were still behind the sandbar, a
place they had picked to be safe from our deeper
draught vessels. It was a sound idea, for if we'd
had ingress, our ships would simply have
pounded the brigs to pieces while they were
still being planked on the beach. We will all
take great pleasure in seeing Perry's expression
when he finds out the bar has only four feet of
water over it rather than nine—which is about
what his brigs draw." The table of officers ap-

plauded and was joined by the townspeople.

Across the lake, hardly thirty miles distant, General Mead, after being piped aboard *Lawrence* with a 32-gun salute, had left with assurances he would post 1500 men near Perry's base in case of a British invasion. As Barclay and his officers reveled, Perry took his fleet to a cove near the harbor channel, intent on crossing the bar at dawn.

"Mr. DeWitt, perhaps we ought to try out those 'camels' of yours." Commandant Perry surveyed the dismal scene. His flagship was fast on the sandbar. All her guns were propped on the beach to lighten ship, but there was no response to kedging or hauling. *Niagara* stood by, keel touching bottom while the lighter boats, across the bar, put their broadsides in defensive position. Perry and Carson walked dejectedly along the beach.

"I saw the system used in St. Petersburg, which has a very shallow entrance channel. Most large boats tie up at Kronstadt Island and bring their cargo in by barges."

"We've got to get out soon. I don't think we can arrange any more banquets for Captain Barclay."

"Do you think he wants to engage before *Detroit* is ready?"

"You may be right, DeWitt. Her hull is twelve inches thick compared to *Lawrence*'s two . . ."

"And twenty more long guns will give him the edge."

"But his ordnance is mixed. By the way, De Witt, I admire your courage in enlisting as a seaman."

"I had no choice. Besides, I wanted to see if the boats I helped build can float."

"I have some idea what you ran into, DeWitt. Commodores and admirals can be very difficult."

"Maybe the lake will be lucky for both of us. Are you serious about the camels, sir?"

"How long will they take to be ready?"

"There's enough rough framing and planking left over," DeWitt calculated mentally. "With a hundred men working round the clock—two days, sir."

"I'll get them to Noah today, including the ship's carpenters. And I'd like you to supervise for me."

"Aye, aye, sir." Carson set his rimmed hat at a rakish angle and Perry called for the pinnace to row them back to Erie.

The twenty-ton inverted barges curved snug to both sides of *Lawrence*. Heavy ropes were strung from them under the *Lawrence*'s keel as spars were put through the gun ports and lashed tight, resting on the "camels'" flat spruce backs. At Perry's order, vents were opened and the eight-foot-high barges sunk down to the sand-bar. Cables were tightened and blocks set on the "camels'" backs, which were just above the surface, bearing up on the spars. The vents were nailed shut and caulked with lead. All the base's pumps were manned on work barges that crowded round the 110-foot brig like suckling pigs. Slowly, the 500-ton flagship rose, first listing, then corrected by equalization of the buoyancy to either side.

Cables were run from the bow to hauling crews on the beach, to small boats, and through pivot anchors for warping round the bar's high spots. Kedges were set and a winch crew leaned into the heavy capstan bars aboard the brig. At a third "heave-ho" a swell rolled in and the ship shifted slightly. More blocks were added and the cables under the keel tautened. The company waited for another swell, then hauled once more and the stern swung free.

While gunners stood ready, their timber-propped long twelves pointed seaward from the peninsular beach, the *Niagara* was similarly floated over the sandbar. *Lawrence's* guns were refitted outside the bar, each carronade swinging gingerly over the gunnels by yard tackle to be settled into its carriage and bolted.

"Sail ho!" The long shout from a blockhouse was repeated by *Lawrence's* topmen, who could see over the forested dunes of Presque Isle. A short-lived joy gave way to fear as the men realized that *Niagara's* cannon were still on the beach. The crew worked frantically to put the second brig into readiness as Barclay's sail grew larger and larger, now to starboard of the beach promontory.

Perry's luck held. The light breeze veered and swung his anchored fleet's bows seaward toward the approaching squadron. The commandant, undaunted, used the first rule of war: surprise. He raised fighting sail and beat loudly to quarters. Next, he sent the schooners *Ariel* and *Scorpion* boldly out, firing their guns.

Barclay couldn't believe what he saw. He was too late to catch them on the bar. This was not the way he had wanted it. The American fleet, rated slightly stronger in numbers but weaker to his in firepower, was charging toward him! Had one day made the difference? That extra day for the banquet? What had gone wrong with his intelligence agents? The new British flagship, *Detroit*, was still not ready, it was sitting at Malden without guns. No, the veteran of Trafalgar decided. He would pick the time and place when the conditions favored him. To Perry's great relief, the ruse worked; Barclay came about and headed back.

That evening, the fifth of August, the Erie fleet set out on its shakedown cruise. Returning three days later without having sighted the British, the squadron was brought up to manned strength with the arrival of Master Commandant Elliot with a hundred officers and men from Black Rock.

On August 12, Perry took his forces to a commodious anchorage, nearer the enemy, called Put-in Bay. Gibraltar, one of a cluster of islands off Port Clinton, Ohio, was chosen as a look-out. Perry then stood off Sandusky Bay and fired signal guns to arrange a meeting with General William Henry Harrison of Tippacanoe fame. The general had over 8000 American soldiers at

Camp Seneca in readiness for a thrust north.

Harrison came aboard *Lawrence* during a rainstorm with his aides and twenty-six Indian chiefs of local tribes. A joint army-navy campaign was discussed and Harrison filled Perry's losses to cholera with thirty-six men, mostly Kentucky riflemen. Perry sailed across and challenged Barclay, but to no avail. During this stalemate the Americans had cut off lake traffic to Fort Malden, putting Barclay's men on half allowance. Meanwhile, his Indian allies were turning upon him. Tecumseh, the great Shawnee warrior, went in a canoe to Fort Malden and entreated the British to go out and do battle with the Americans. Perry's presence was injuring the credibility of the British with their Indian allies.

Escaped American prisoners brought word to Put-in Bay that Barclay's flagship was finally ready. Perry briefed his eight captains, assigning each one a specific enemy ship to engage, and emphasized the tactics of close-in bombardment so as not to lose the advantage of his short carronades. Before adjourning the meeting, Perry exhibited his flag again. "When you see this run up to the main royal top, it will be your signal to fire. I will leave you tonight with the words of Nelson." Perry looked each one of his captains in the eye. "If you can lay your enemy close aside, you cannot be out of your place . . ."

"Lieutenant DeWitt."
"*Lieutenant?*" Carson gasped.

"I wouldn't have brought you over from *Porcupine* for nothing. At the meeting earlier this evening, Captain Elliot asked for a replacement for one of his officers, who is down with lake fever. I have no one to spare him. I don't know what went on between you and Commodore Bainbridge when he took *Java*, but it makes no difference now. You've started from the bottom and proven yourself. Just where would our ships be now but for your Dutch camels? Or would you rather not have a commission again?" Perry's cocker spaniel, lying below a chart-covered table, opened his eyes at the change of his master's tone. "DeWitt, I've inquired about you and been reassured your resignation had nothing to do with incompetence. Don't worry. I won't hold it against you if you refuse . . ."

A broad grin spread across Carson's tanned, squarish face. "Sir, I'd like to scream 'wahoo' but the hour is too late . . ."

"Then it's settled. Look, even the ship's mascot wags his tail!"

At sunrise the next morning, September 10, a long, drawn-out cry of "Sail, ho" drifted down from the maintops and was echoed from the lookout on Gibraltar.

"What does he look like?" Perry was among the first on deck.

"Clump of square-rigged . . . and some fore 'n aft, sir." The response turned heads seaward, eyes straining at the small white forms that floated above the horizon, distorted by the heavy summer air. The specks grew and diminished in the shimmering sun, then seemed to lunge closer, throbbing larger and larger under a bright, cloudless sky, imperceptibly sliding to windward.

"You'll have to engage to leeward, sir," cautioned Lieutenant Forrest.

"I don't care," responded Perry, looking older than his twenty-eight years with a new growth of beard. "To windward or leeward, they shall fight today." Calling the quartermaster to bring the battleflag, he mustered the crew aft and encouraged them to the task at hand. "Brave lads," he finished, "shall we run it up?"

"Aye, sir!" The cries rose in unison and cheers repeated along the single file of nine ships, led by the schooner *Scorpion* with her little battery of one long 12 and a 32 carronade.

Cooks passed among the crews, handing a bit of food to each man. It was already noon and stomachs were rumbling. Powder boys scattered sand on the decks and hammocks were stowed in the nettings as the gunners stood grim and determined. Even the commandant's nineteen-year-old brother stood by, armed and ready.

As the squadrons moved slowly toward one another, the strains of "Rule Brittania" were struck up by *Detroit*'s band and carried across the lake. The anthem culminated in a loud cheer as a 24-pounder belched flame toward *Lawrence*, almost a mile and a half away. The shot splashed short.

Barclay's plan was to use his 25-to-15 long

gun advantage to soften up the Americans at a distance. As they drew closer, it became evident that Perry's plan to engage singly would have to be changed. *Scorpion* and *Ariel* picked up the enemy's lead ship, the schooner *Chippewa*, but Barclay's flagship and *Queen Charlotte*, with a total of 19 broadside guns to *Lawrence's* 10, combined their fire against Perry. Then the schooners *Hunter* and *Lady Prevost* veered in for the kill, ignoring the *Niagara*, which stood back when it should have caught up with *Queen Charlotte*, of similar rating. Captain Elliot remained astern of the slow *Caledonia*.

After almost two hours of long-range pummeling from combined broadsides, Perry's brig had been reduced to a wreck, with only one gun operative and more than half her crew killed and wounded. Perry's officers and men were cut down right and left of him. Such was the slaughter that Perry had called down to the surgeons to operate a deck gun. Blood seeped through the deck and into the wounded's cockpit below.

The carnage became hysteria as Lieutenant Yarnall, his face bloodied from a scalp wound, brushed past a shredded hammock with the feathery down of cat-tail mattress stuffing covering him, sotted in his blood. The wounded and frantic sailors were shocked into curdling laughter at "the devil-owl among us." A Seneca brave, who'd danced on deck in full ritual costume before the first shots splintered the brig, lay horrified on the lowest deck he could find. The ship's complement of negroes had second thoughts about receiving the gift of freedom at such risk. Of the original complement of 103, over 80 had been hit, 22 mortally.

Elliot, who had been ordered to close in earlier, had not done so. Instead, he had called for *Caledonia* to go to *Lawrence*'s aid and he stood off. It was clear to some that the captain had obeyed his orders *too* well by staying in formation while his designated adversary had not. It was only when *Lawrence* fell back, a floating hulk such as *Guerriere* had been, that Elliot went into action. He sent a boat over to the *Lawrence* for extra shot to replenish his own. Carson DeWitt and the other officers stood by, helplessly urging Elliot into the thick, but with no success. The *Niagara* stood off, using only its two long guns. It had hardly received a hit, and none of her crew had been wounded.

Aboard *Lawrence*, Lieutenants Forrest and Brooks of the marines were down. The latter suffered a hip shattered by a cannon ball. So intense was his agony that he begged Perry to shoot him, but he died within an hour. Perry's young brother was also wounded and went below as round shot flew through the wounded's cockpit. Midshipman Lamb's mangled arm was no sooner bandaged than a 12-pounder crashed through the hull and killed him instantly. Six shot entered the surgeon's room during the action.

Aloft, the Kentucky riflemen had wrought havoc on the enemy but it was not enough. Captain Barclay had lost his remaining arm, but the British, tasting victory, bore down.

Seeing Elliot's *Niagara* passing by, Perry laid aside his blue nankeen jacky's coat and put on his epaulettes of rank. He left wounded, faithful Yarnall to hold out or surrender and ordered the gig unlashed and lowered. With his battle pennant, four oarsmen and his younger brother, he made for the brig. Enemy cannon and musketry peppered around his boat, splintering oars and pitting the gunnels, but his luck held. At one point the rowers stopped, demanding that he sit down and be less of a target.

After fifteen minutes Perry climbed the gangway of *Niagara*—to the mortification of Captain Elliot, who had thought him dead.

"How goes the day?" asked Elliot.

"Bad enough," replied the smoke-blackened Perry. He sent his older subordinate off in a small boat to bring up the stragglers. He immediately ran up his square pennant and hoisted the close-action signal. Setting more sail, he made for the British line, a half mile distant.

With a burst of speed, *Niagara* caught Barclay's flotilla by surprise. Expecting victory, the British instead received broadsides right and left from double-shotted 32 carronades. So complete was the British confusion that *Detroit* and *Queen Charlotte* ran into each other, allowing Perry to rake both of them. The entire American squadron had finally come up and engaged. When the black smoke had lifted, only eight minutes after Perry's dash, Barclay's flagship struck her colors in surrender. Her action was immediately followed by three ships, while *Little Belt* and *Chippewa* veered off in an attempted escape to leeward. *Scorpion* and *Trippe* made after them and brought them back at night.

The battle over, Perry laid an old letter on his navy cap and wrote on the back to General Harrison, telling him of the capture of two ships, two brigs, one schooner and one sloop.

Witnesses described a "religious awe" that settled over the *Lawrence* as the reinstated flagship received the ritual surrender from Barclay's lieutenants. Perry requested that the British retain their swords and inquired of the enemy's wounded. As the *Lawrence* limped away from Western Sister Island, the master commandant lay down on the deck among the slain, arms crossed and holding his sword. There he fell asleep "as sweetly as a wearied child."

As twilight descended over Put-in Bay anchorage, services for the dead were held and each of the slain, wrapped in a hammock and weighted with a 32-pound shot, was slipped into the clear lake. All, that is, except the dead officers.

Carson DeWitt, his bare chest dressed for splinter wounds, watched glumly from *Niagara*. What would the blacksmith Corcoran have to say about officers getting a proper shore burial while the crew was thrown overboard? Then he recalled the battle with *Guerriere*, after which the slain Englishmen were cast overboard with neither ceremony nor shrouds. Here, the victors and vanquished had shared the fruits of war: a common watery grave for sixty-three crewmen.

The following day, accompanied by *Detroit*'s solemn musicians, a funeral was held and the five slain officers laid to rest in a clearing by the bay. Guns were fired and the funeral gigs were rowed in careful cadence. The wilderness lake was hushed, adding to the solemn grandeur.

The nation rejoiced from Maine to Florida and west to the Mississippi. Never before had an American fleet defeated a British one. The ripples of Erie spread round the world. Even Field Marshall Wellington refused an offer to command the British Forces in Canada because of American control of the lakes. Perry's victory was as complete as that of the British over the French at the Nile; it erased the stigma of General Hull's surrender of Detroit the year before and set the stage for Harrison's invasion of Canada and the retaking of Michigan.

Regarding the defeat, a London newspaper commented that "the flotilla in question . . . was not the Royal Navy, but a local force—a kind of mercantile militia."

September 26

Arouse and save your wives and daughters!
Arouse and smite the faithless foe!
Scalps are bought at stated prices,
Malden pays the price in gold.

A thousand Kentuckians sang around camp-
fires of the massacre at River Raisin. They sang
of revenge upon the British General Proctor,
who allowed his Shawnee allies to butcher almost a hundred Kentuckians for their scalps.
The Indians had then returned to Fort Malden,
where they were paid "market price" for the
bloody locks.

The Kentuckians were part of the large force
that was camped on Middle Sister Island, hav-

ing left their horses under guard on the Ohio shore. Proctor's scouts had exaggerated the number of "Raisin Rememberers," which did not help the general to sleep that night.

Tecumseh, the great Shawnee warrior chief, was already furious that he had not been told of Barclay's defeat, and he became even angrier after being made to wait for days on a fruitless look-out on Bois Blanc Isle. He spoke out at Amherstburg, chiding Proctor before a gathering of chiefs.

"We have heard the great guns but we know nothing of what has happened to Barclay, our one-armed father. We are astonished to see you packing your belongings. You, who told us to remain here and work our lands, you said you would never leave British ground. We must compare your conduct to that of a fat dog who puts his tail between his legs and runs when frightened.

"The Americans have not yet defeated us by land. We therefore wish to remain here and fight them. Give us the arms that our great father, the King, sent for his red children . . . We pledge our lives to the Great Spirit. If it be his will, we shall leave our bones upon our lands."

Such was the tomahawk waving that General Proctor agreed to fall back only to the Moravian towns along Thames River, where he would make a stand.

Five thousand men, some in frontier leather and others in the militia uniform of various states, crowded on sixteen armed vessels and a hundred small army boats on a balmy Monday morning. By nine, the armada was halfway to the enemy shore.

The forces landed at Hartley's Point, on a duned sandy beach, in three columns: regulars on the left, Colonel Ball's legions and the Indian allies in the center, and the Kentuckians and Perry's sailors on the right. They charged over the dunes with cries of revenge and brandished bayonets, tomahawks and cutlasses, but the enemy was nowhere to be found.

Marching toward Amherstburg late that afternoon, the columns saw clouds of black smoke rising ahead of them and encountered a troop of elegant ladies who begged for protection and leniency. They were assured that the Americans would not plunder or burn their houses. The ladies, looking askance at the hundreds of savagely attired Wyandot and Seneca, returned timidly to their homes.

At Amherstburg, it was found that Proctor's rear guard had left scarcely an hour before, after setting the storehouses afire. General Harrison elected to camp in the town since he had not enough horses to pursue the mounted enemy detachments.

Colonel Ball and Captain Perry found horses to equip a troop of twenty and they raced north on the St. Clair Road to save what bridges they could from the British torches. Pulling up at the first bridge, they routed a small enemy platoon of bridge burners with one volley of muskets and extinguished the smoldering tinder.

The second bridge, at Essex, had been partially burnt, but was still crossable. Colonel Ball thought it best not to venture further, as the terrain was wooded and presented a danger of ambush. Carson DeWitt volunteered to scout a few miles further to assess the navigability of the Thames River. He exchanged his uniform for a linsey-woolsey jacket and a coonskin cap.

"DeWitt," Captain Perry said, shaking Carson's hand, "perhaps we can get a gunboat or two upriver to soften up Proctor. Good luck! Who knows. Maybe you'll even find your brother."

"Thank you, sir." Carson examined the flintlock of his pistol, stuck it back in his belt and put his boot heels to his mount's flanks, then galloped over the charred bridge, holding his sleeve up against the blinding smoke.

From a pine-groved bluff overlooking the bridge, a lone Shawnee watched the American troop turn back, then scampered his pony diagonally downhill to the road. From there, he rode a safe distance back as he followed "the blond rider who changed his coat."

Magnus DeWitt counted out the equivalent of twenty-four American dollars in British specie, stacking the coins on a barrelhead between his cocked pistol and a pair of matted straw-colored scalps.

The half-naked Shawnee eyed the three stacks. "Onondaki no count redcoat money. Want twenty-four American gold pieces!" He ran his fingertips over the gleaming steel edge of his belted tomahawk.

"This is better than American money, and it comes to the same value." Magnus's hand moved slowly up the barrel's side, toward his pistol.

"Onondaki bring two scalps. Want twelve dollar each."

"Go to Tecumseh—ask him if the major lies."

The Indian grunted, then scooped up the coins and put them into a leather pouch.

"Mmmm, these look like good ones." Magnus examined the scalps and dropped them into a sack beside him. "I hope they weren't too young."

"Old enough to shoot gun." The Shawnee leaned over the barrel and looked into Magnus's strongbox. "How much gold you pay for big news?"

"That depends." Magnus slapped a coin down, keeping a plump finger on it.

"American general rides with thunder canoe soldiers."

Magnus's eyes narrowed and his tongue wet the corners of his thick lips as he reached deep into the strongbox.

Word was received that British provisions were being moved on Lake St. Clair to the Thames, so Perry dispatched the major portion of his squadron in pursuit under Captain Elliot.

The hero of Erie followed aboard *Ariel*, but the enemy had already escaped to the Thames with artillery and stores.

General Harrison pressed forward rapidly along Lake St. Clair's surrounding roads, which were intact, Proctor not expecting pursuit by land. Harrison was informed by British deserters that their general, with 700 regulars and 1200 Indians, was camped at Dolsen's farm, near the mouth of the Thames.

The Kentuckians marched boldly forward. Three of Perry's shallow-draught sloops followed up the river until the rapids and Indian sharpshooters on the high wooded banks began to tell. The commandant posted a guard and debarked once more as a foot soldier.

General Proctor and Tecumseh took up stations at Chatham while Harrison's columns camped near Bowles's farm. Much of the vicinity had been put to the torch but the Americans salvaged a thousand British muskets and some cannon along the route.

After a gory skirmish in which many Indians were killed as they harrassed Kentuckian riflemen at a bridge, Chief Walk-in-the-Water quit Proctor and offered his sixty Wyandot braves to Harrison. He was told to get out of the way, so he went back to Detroit. Harrison's scouts found the enemy dug in on solid, high ground between the Thames River and an impassable marsh.

Lieutenant DeWitt, after reporting his reconnaissance, had joined the mounted Kentuckians in a stealthy approach through thick woods at the main British line. The bugle blared a charge and the Kentuckians increased their gait, whipping low branches aside, then dispersing at the first British volley. But instead of retreating, they charged again, before the eight hundred Brown Bess muskets were ready. With cries of "River Raisin," the coonskin cavalry vaulted into the British line, scattering the redcoats in all directions. In five minutes, the regulars had been taken, many throwing down their muskets rather than facing their own savage allies in retreat.

The battalion with which Carson rode had the worst of it. They were pitted against Tecumseh, who kept firing until the last second and wounded many Americans, including Colonel Johnson. The Americans dismounted to do combat among the bushes and undergrowth. For some eight minutes, tomahawks and bayonets flashed in the thickets that lined the river and blood spattered on the fragrant honeysuckle. Another regiment was sent against Tecumseh's flank, sending the Indians into chaos as their leader fell, a pistol ball through his head.

Carson, alone in a ravined tributary, had gotten the better of a tattooed Shawnee chief in a fierce contest of scalping knife and pistol bayonet. Upon withdrawing his weapon from the dead Indian under him, he was faced with the flaring muzzle of a British blunderbuss. The figure that held the weapon wavered in the leaf-speckled forest light. There was a grin on the brown, stripe-streaked face as a finger tightened on the brass trigger.

During that instant, that fragment of a second that is eternity, Carson found time to think of Sarah and his son, almost as if he'd rather do that than consider the reality that faced him. Suddenly, a bright flash obscured everything else from his sight and he lost consciousness, shriveling into a black vortex in which there was no memory, no feeling, nothing. . . .

Warm sun filtered through the treetops. Carson blinked awake and realized he was seeing the world through only one eye. He reached for his head and felt a bandage. That was good—bandage over his sightless eye. Turning his head to the side, he saw other forms with white dressings.

"You were damn lucky, Lieutenant." It was the educated voice of a surgeon, the sickly sweet aroma of morphine attending it. "Powder burns, mostly. You'll be fit as new soon."

"What happened?" Carson raised his head and made sure he still had two arms and two legs.

"You were found beside two dead Indians. One was a Shawnee chief. You'd gotten him with your bayonet. The other had his head split open. None of our Indians have claimed doing it."

The next day news spread of Tecumseh's death. A body, entirely naked, had been found in the swamps, strips of skin pared from its thighs. It was rumored that Kentuckians had made razor strops of the strips. Some claimed that the chief's braves had disguised the body before the souvenir hunters had come upon it, dressing it in plain deerskin coat and pantaloons so that it could later be carried away for ritual burial without harrassment. Nearby was found an American pistol bearing the mark "H. Albright," one that Tecumseh had been seen to wear in his belt.

Among the prisoners were several Indians who were kept separate from the British. One was of fair skin and hair and had an aquiline nose—quite unlike the others, though he had scars and tattoos about his face and body, and his attitude and trappings were no less savage.

Carson's eyes met his but neither man changed his demeanor. The lieutenant sensed that any sign of recognition would endanger the fair savage by branding him as a traitor to his tribe.

"We found the half-breed in your area, Lieutenant. Lucky for you we did; his tomahawk was bloody and you were next. Breeds are the worst kind." The marine corporal spat on the ground in front of the sitting braves, whose hands were tied behind their backs and ankles lashed together.

"What do you plan to do with these savages, Corporal?" DeWitt passed among them. The fair one bent over, and as he did so Carson saw the skin just under the waistband on his back. He saw it: the snapping turtle tattoo!

"We Kentucky people got a little thing we're

gonna do tonight about rememberin' th' Raisin. These here Shawnees are some o' them that did it."

Carson said nothing. There were some things that officers didn't want to know about.

Later that night, after taps, three braves escaped while a group of Kentuckians was drinking captured rum and admiring new razor strops around a campfire. Some cut rope-ends were found, along with the marine corporal whose head ached from a blow.

In October, after the British had retreated from Mackinack and General Harrison was pursuing the remainder of the British forces north of Lake Ontario, Carson returned to the *Niagara* and found a letter waiting for him.

> *My dear brother:*
> *When you read this, I shall have left the Erie for new trapping lands west of Huron. My Indian wife and I agree there is little for us and our three children in the white man's valleys.*
>
> *I am content that we met and were of service to one another. I have written to our parents and hope they will understand, as I trust you will. My choice has been made, and perhaps more good will come of it than of schooling and wealth. It takes families to bridge the enormous chasm between races of man.*

Our address will be sent when we know it.

All the best,
Caleb (White Bear)

Carson went home to the Hudson valley, where he spent a restful furlough pampering himself with Sarah's southern-style homecooking, playing with his son, and pulling easy duty in the New York navy yard. Thanks to Perry, his commission had been re-instated with no penalties of grade and seniority. Perry's letter to the secretary of the navy got immediate action, along with his own promotion to commodore.

The mansion at Hastings-on-Hudson had never been as bright and festive as during the snowy holidays. Even Clarissa Hunter DeWitt had succumbed to the magic of her daughter-in-law's smile. The happiest of all was Schuyler DeWitt. His illness conquered after physicians had failed, the lean son of royalist Alastair DeWitt was once more proud of his lot, and he beamed at the very sight of his new daughter-in-law and grandson.

1814

September 2

WASHINGTON HAD BEEN burned. The infamous Admiral Cockburn had personally set Dolly Madison's magenta drapes afire. Only Commodore Joshua Barney's sailors had put up a battle against the British on the road to the capitol. After blowing up their gunboats, which had been cornered in the mud at Pig Point on the Patuxent, Barney and his 500 sailors dragged their cannon over twelve miles of swamp to Bladensburg, where they dug in while the militia fled—giving the battle the ignominious title of "The Bladensburg Races."

As the city that had spawned a navy that was the scourge of His Majesty's commerce, Baltimore was next.

Commodore John Rodgers, the senior American naval officer, had been born in Havre de Grace, Maryland. His home was one of those plundered by Cockburn's forces. Both Porter and Perry came to his side to defend Baltimore. They'd served under him aboard the Baltimore-built frigate *Constellation* during the quasi-war with France in 1798.

Perry's renown had eclipsed that of his venerable and ranked senior officers because of his Erie exploits. No other officer had ever humbled a British fleet, much less led an amphibious assault on a fort and ridden against Tecumseh. Porter was legendary for his prowess in the Pacific. After missing Bainbridge at Cape Verde and Noronha, he had gone around the horn and captured twelve ships in the Pacific before succumbing to superior forces in Valparaiso. Both Perry and Porter had inspired the nation's poets and balladeers with their exploits.

General Sam Smith was among those defending Baltimore. A respected veteran of the American Revolution, he'd fought at Long Island, covering General Washington's withdrawal to Valley Forge, and seen action at Brandywine and Monmouth. He hadn't lost, but he hadn't won either. Now, over sixty, he saw to it that the citizens, including free colored men, built complex fortifications on Laudenslager's Hill, mounted with ample cannon under the command of Commodore Rodgers. He activated redoubts around Fort McHenry and strengthened the battery at Lazaretto Point, across the harbor entrance, using both navy and army resources.

To cap the effort, doughty Sam "borrowed" two dozen private fishing boats and sank them in a jagged line across the channel as a barrier. These would be refloated later, at government expense. He then sent a barge downriver to relay signals from the city heights to Fort McHenry.

The defenders of Baltimore in turn called for their lieutenants, one letter going to the New York navy yard. Sarah DeWitt was ecstatic over returning to her city and her mother—and bringing a grandson and a shipwright along.

September 12

THE OFFICER strode across the beach toward
a detail of Commodore Barney's sailors, who
were cleaning their massive guns. Behind
the earthwork parapets under the shadow of
Fort McHenry, fifteen French 32-pounders were
cradled in timber mounts.

"Guess who, my friend!"

Carson spun around. "God damn!" He em-
braced the Frenchman, then punched him sol-
idly on his shoulder. "What are you doing at an
army fort?"

"Napoleon. He sent me to shoot his cannon."
He rolled his eyes at the racks of shot. "How is
my godson and your beautiful Sarah?"

"Just fine. They're staying with her mother at Fell's Point."

"Ah, good. That's where I sent Lucy to get rooms for us. This fort is no place for a lady. You should see her now, with long hair and lots of dresses. She looks like a girl!"

"What are your plans, Claude?" Carson led his friend around back of the fort and over a dry moat through a dank brick tunnel.

"Lucy and I have enough prize money to start a business. Maybe we'll go to New Orleans, where I have an uncle. Or maybe we'll stay in Baltimore. You still like to build boats?"

They climbed an incline to the ramparts of the star-shaped fort and walked past the cannon and mortars. "After this is over," Carson said, "there's going to be a lot of trade, especially with the East Indies. And this is the place to build fast boats. I've seen plans for ships based on pilot schooners that will revolutionize the whole system, make merchants into millionaires."

"Maybe we'll start building ships together!"

Behind the 16-foot-thick earthen walls faced with red brick and granite, over a thousand men were quartered in a space that normally held two hundred. Three long two-storied barracks, a smaller officers' building and a round-topped stone structure lined the inside perimeter of the five-pointed star. The stone building, a powder magazine, was designed to deflect overhead shot. Twenty-one guns were mounted, only half of which pointed downriver through stone-rimmed loopholes. The fort was protected on its entire perimeter against attack from any direction.

Six hundred infantry were camped outside the walls, stationed in tents and makeshift huts. The ground was muddy from the previous night's heavy rains. This circle of defense was charged with repulsing amphibious attacks. Barney's men manned the "water battery," composed of 36 guns that were ringed around the fort in clumps of four. The 15 French guns in the battery faced the water.

To either side of the water battery, armed scows, barges and gunboats plied the channel in front of and behind the sunken barrier boats. Hanging limp over the seaward bastion on this summer Monday was the gigantic 36-by-30-foot fifteen-starred American flag that had been ordered by Commodore Barney a month earlier, before he was wounded at Bladensburg.

The fort bustled and hummed. It was complete with bakers, cooks, blacksmiths and slave cleaning women. In General Armistead's headquarters, a newspaper lay open on his desk. A pencil mark circled a small advertisement:

GUNPOWDER!
50 Kegs DuPont & Co. Powder can be sold low, if applied for in a few days.
Brisco & Partridge, Charles St.

On Sunday night, Admiral Sir Alexander Cochrane's armada was seen approaching North

Point, some twelve miles downriver from Baltimore. Two hours after midnight, under a full moon, his fleet's boats were lowered and rowed two miles to the beach under cover of shallow-draft gun brigs. By seven, Admiral Cockrane and General Ross were ashore and the force of 5000 regulars, 2000 marines and 2000 seamen moved north. Each soldier was equipped with 80 rounds for his musket and three days' food rations. Cochrane's flag had been transferred to the shallow draft frigate *Severn*, which he commanded as it went ahead to sound the fortified harbor.

The British advanced up the eastern shore of the Patapsco River, occupying private homes on the route to Baltimore. General Ross and his staff set up temporary headquarters at the Shaw mansion for an afternoon's respite. One of the general's lieutenants met young Eleanor Shaw on a staircase and attempted to embrace her. She leapt out of a window and the aide was put under guard to be sent back to the armada and await a court-martial.

In search of jewelry and prized possessions, royal bayonets prodded any possible hiding place—including a grey sack under a wisteria trellis which loosed a stream of bald-faced hornets upon the hapless plunderers.

Mrs. Trotten set cabbage plants over her buried silverware, while a detachment of marines found a false cellar at the Sterrett house and helped themselves to a cache of rare wines, candles and bedding. They left a note for the absent owner, an American colonel who was digging in on Laudenslager Hill.

> Captains Brown, Wilcox & McNamara of the 53d Regiment, R.M., have received everything they could desire at this house, not withstanding it was at the hands of the butler and cook, and in the absence of the colonel.

This was written on the back of a letter upon which Mrs. Sterrett had composed her father's gravestone epithet.

General Sam Smith dispatched General Stricker to harrass the British invaders at North Point with three thousand militia.

Ross and Cockrane rode confidently at the head of their columns. In the woods ahead, two seventeen-year-old riflemen of Captain Asquith's Grey Yaegers waited, their long barrels nestled on oak branches overhead. General Ross's white stallion, red jacket and diagonal black belt were galloping into their gun sights.

The general, shot twice, was carried into the shade of an old oak where he called his wife's name and expired. The rifleboys, Danny Wells and Henry McComas, were swiftly and mortally shot before they could reload. Ross's death significantly weakened the British mettle, but not before Stricker was forced back to the entrenchments on Laudenslager's Hill.

As four ships-of-the-line waited in deep water,

an assault flotilla of frigates, schooners, bomb ketches and a rocket brig anchored off Soller's Point, two miles below Fort McHenry.

The five British bomb-ketches were cleared for action. These sturdy craft, under 90 feet long, had two masts set aft of the waist, the mizzen being lateen rigged. Each carried two mammoth mortars on swivels forward of the mainmast. The mortars took projectiles of a diameter of 13 inches and a weight of over 200 pounds—five times the weight of the largest conventional shot, as used by Fort McHenry's French cannon. The giant mortars' range at best elevation was two and one half miles with a 20-pound powder charge. So dangerous was the handling of the weapons that separate "powder boats" were used to load and fuse the projectiles.

Shortly before dawn on the thirteenth, the signal was hoisted from *Severn's* maintop. The lead bomb-ketch was driven two feet down, almost to its gunnels, by the mortar's recoil. Admiral Cochrane smacked his lips under his spyglass as the first bomb, a speck catching the rising sun, reached its trajectory apogee and screamed down on the five-pointed fort.

"Come on, *chérie*, we give you more powder." Claude Chassagne set his match to the pan of his 42-pounder as the crew turned away and ducked. The last quoin had been kicked out from below the breech and the gun was at maximum elevation.

Colonel Armistead looked down eagerly from his perch on the ramparts as Chassagne fired. He focused on the British rocket brig *Erebus*, two miles distant, which was spitting out 32-pound projectiles, singly and in frightening clusters that streaked fiery trails toward the fort. The colonel's face turned grim as a shot splashed far short of *Erebus*.

"I bet the British know we can't reach them. That's why they let us get the guns from Napoleon." Chassagne sat down dejectedly as a barrage of shot screamed overhead and exploded near the fort wall. A commotion ensued in the infantry perimeter behind his gun. "*Mon Dieu!*" He crossed his heart when he saw it. A woman who'd brought food to her soldier had been cut in half by shrapnel.

Yet another shell had hit the southwest bastion, dismounting a 24 and killing or wounding seven men. Having battered the fort for eight hours, Admiral Cochrane observed what he thought was confusion on the parapets and put up signals for three bomb-ketches and *Erebus* to close in for the kill. There was also the message from Colonel Brooke, who had replaced Ross on land:

> Need support fire at Laudenslager. Yankees are too well entrenched for infantry assault.

The hill was a mile and a half north of the fort. Even with a 20-pound powder charge the ketches would have to close in within a mile of the fort's guns. Cochrane sent them in.

"Hold your fire," Carson DeWitt shouted as he noticed the bombardment vessels turn their bows. The fort was silent. Only the enemy's missiles were to be heard, exploding above the tattered flag, splashing short and screaming beyond.

"Maybe they think we've given up, eh?" Chassagne patted his gun on the breech as the crews crouched low behind the parapets. Word was passed to the long 24s atop the fort to stack extra shot at the ready. Only the neighing of horses tethered behind the fort broke the silence.

Then came a shuddering crash from the interior. A 200-pound shot had landed on the powder magazine, shattering stone from its roof and crumbling a wall. It was a miracle. No explosion—a dud!

Closer and closer, the vessels bore in under sail and oar, firing as they moved in past Curtis Bay, past Colgate Creek. Armistead dared not signal the battery at Lazaretto Point. He hoped they would wait for his guns to open up. When he saw the ketches in line with Ferry Point, he knew they were only a mile away—within range of his medium batteries as well as the cumbersome 32s. He gave the signal and forty guns went off as one long rumble, belching smoke and fire as if the brick and stone of the fort itself were in flame.

Caught in the deadly cross-fire, the bomb-ketches came about but *Erebus* kept on coming, rockets tearing out of small ports below her gun deck. The brig listed as she was struck by shot, then lost headway and fell off toward the Ferry Bar, her spars riddled. Only a small fleet of frantically rowed launches saved the brig from destruction by towing her downriver.

Admiral Sir Alexander Cochrane was wrong. Fort McHenry was far from surrendering.

FELL'S POINT

W HERE IS SARAH?" Lucy Brewer skittered
behind the desk and looked in the dining
room.

"She was here a little while ago." Young Seth
Lewis was picking out one word at a time in
the *Baltimore Patriot*. "It's Tuesday—she goes
out to her private island sometimes on Tuesday."
He riffled to the forecast column. "Full moon.
That means real low and high tides, best time
to go out to her sandbar."

"So that's why she asked me to mind the baby.
She didn't want anyone to know because of the
bombardment . . ."

"She always puts her yellow dress on because

that's what she wore when Mr. DeWitt went out there with her."

"Shouldn't someone go look for her? There may be British soldiers around." The windows rattled ominously with the sound of cannonfire.

"Nah, the paper says Colonel Brooke is marching north to Laudenslager's. And besides, Sarah doesn't like people to go with her. She'll be back when the tide comes in."

"Lord, what is that awful smell?"

"A funny old man with a red hat and bow legs came in before and wanted to know who lives here. He said he was taking a census."

"You told him?" Lucy held her nose. "Ughh, garlic."

"Just about us, I mean me and mom, in case he was a spy."

"Smart boy." Lucy opened up the door and windows.

"You shoulda smelled it when he was here."

Sarah listened to the distant rumbling and prayed to herself. She held a nautilus shell to her ear and drowned out the sound of bombardment. The crescent-shaped beach was her chapel; she felt that something, someone—a god of nature and the sea—would heed her requests on this little sandy island off the tiny town of Canton, a mile downriver from the Fell's Point yards. Drowsing in the afternoon sun, she imagined Carson to be with her, as on that magic day in early May.

She closed her eyes and almost fell asleep,

lying dreamily, her auburn head propped against a sun-bleached ship's plank. The plank was twisted and ragged at one end; several nails were still protruding, worn-down stumps along an edge. What disaster had befallen the ship, she wondered. Was it storm or war? Sarah ran her fingers over the wood grain and was thankful that her husband was safe, in a fort with sixteen-foot-thick walls. Shading her eyes, she could make out Fort McHenry's huge flag over a blue haze. It fluttered only occasionally, as shells burst near it. It seemed impossible that there were people dying on this bright, warm summer's day. She tried to forget but then felt the very sand tremor beneath her fingers.

Sarah sat up and pulled the hem of her yellow calico dress up over her white knees, stretched out and dug her bare heels into the moist sand, wiggling her dainty toes. It was not like a Lewis to be so pale at the end of summer. Was there still time for a tan, so she'd be more desirable to Carson? Sarah watched a fiddler crab shuffle sidewise, past the black leather pumps she'd taken off while wading out to the beach to be alone with her memory of that day with Carson. Oh, how fine it was to be married. . . .

A shadow suddenly loomed over the sand, moved onto her legs. A man behind her. A tricorne hat—

Sarah whirled around and looked into the bloodshot eyes of a stranger, a man who was old but whose bulky body was far from frail. His mouth was open, showing teeth with yellow edges as his lips pulled back in a harsh smile.

Sensing his intentions, she screamed, but the sound was lost in the empty distance. Before she could get up and run, the stranger flung himself at her and wrapped the crook of his velvet-sleeved arm around her throat. Clumsily fondling her, he dragged her backwards into a stand of high beach grass. She felt his hot, garlic breath behind her ear. Clawing and kicking, she was thrown down and the panting stranger fell bodily upon her, ripping her dress at the neck. She cried out, her screams mingling with those of the seagulls.

Getting one arm free, she scratched wildly at his face, pulling his bifocals and breaking the frame so that they hung from one ear. Enraged, he struck her on the cheek and pinned both her flailing arms to the sand, then gave a raspy laugh.

"I like 'em to fight," he said. He brought his lips close to hers but she turned away in disgust. "One thing fer sure—a DeWitt always knows how t' pick 'em." He forced his mouth on hers.

Sarah kicked ferociously as he ripped her dress open at the collar, popping buttons to the sand. The sun beat down on her legs and she realized her dress was up over her thighs. Hard as she beat at him, it made no difference. She couldn't move for his weight on her and she screamed hysterically as he worked his way down across her body, tearing her drawers down and roughly shoving his hand between her legs.

Suddenly, she felt his hand fall away. His weight shifted and a curdling moan rang out as he rolled off in agony, writhing and clutching his left foot. The contortions of his limbs had brought on the scourge of gout. He ripped his wet boots off as Sarah crawled toward the shore. The land bridge was already submerged; the tide was rising fast. Frantic, she got up and ran but was caught from behind, the assailant striking her a blow that made her woozy.

"This time, you won't get away." The tricorned man stumbled and splashed, dragging her back by her hair and neck. She brought up her knee to his groin and he lashed so strongly with pain that they both fell into the surging tide. Kneeling, he closed his gnarled hands about her throat, pushing her head under water.

Then his eyes bulged as a second attack came on. Sarah felt sand in her grasping hand and she slammed it into his face, blinding him. Breaking from his grip, she bolted away, picking the shallows and bars she knew so well. Turning back, she saw the pitiful figure staggering after her. Not knowing the terrain, he slipped into a deep area and was immersed up to his blue shoulders. He screamed for help, thrashing with the agony of yet another attack as the tidal bore rushed toward him.

Sarah crawled up on the mainland beach of Northwest Harbor, sputtering and coughing out seawater. The tide had run high up on the island and the crescent beach was gone.

A DeWitt, he'd said. The shivering young

mother realized only then. It had to be Carson's uncle, the one he said was not right in the head, the one who—

Sarah decided to wait until dusk before going home. She would slip in the back door and clean up, put on a fresh dress. Her face hurt and she knew it must be bruised, but she would say that she'd slipped on a rock. For the first time, she was glad that Carson was not home, would not see her like this. Her ordeal would be forgotten; Magnus DeWitt had brought shame enough on his family.

On the island, the long waves coming in from the sea lapped over the fiddler crabs' burrow, dragging Sarah's shoes as they receded, sucking them back with the undertow. The next low, rolling surge, coming in to the crump of the distant mortars, carried with it a kelp-strewn maroon tricorne hat and left it among the high-tide flotsam.

THE NEXT DAY

Two DEAD BRITISH deserters hung limp from the main yards of the frigate *Weser* as crewmen and soldiers alike stared in horror from their anchored ships.

"Let that be a lesson to those with similar ideas." Standing on the quarterdeck of his flagship, *Tonnant*, Vice-Admiral Sir Alexander Cochrane surveyed his fleet, which lay out of Yankee cannon range off North Point.

"Father," Captain Sir Thomas Cochrane addressed the admiral, "I do hope we're not going to Philadelphia next."

The white-haired officer shrugged and leaned out on the taffrail where his words were less apt to be overheard. "Too well fortified. If we couldn't take Baltimore, it would be suicide to attempt the larger cities. New York City has twice as many guns as Baltimore, and six times as many militia. Besides, our men are tired. We don't have an experienced general and we're short on supplies."

The rakish young captain popped a sweet into his mouth. "Ross made a mistake, didn't he—aside from getting killed?" Sir Thomas chewed noisily while watching a boatload of wounded being transferred to a hospital brig.

"Ross should have landed on the west bank, but he insisted on attacking through the Laudenslager defenses."

"Much more dramatic. You know the army! But then, he might just as well have been shot on the other side too, with his white horse."

"Fording the river would have been difficult, but once across . . ."

"Father, you'll advise Melville, of course, that the operation was hindered by interservice squabbles, that *we* didn't pick the landing spot."

"Of course."

A subaltern saluted as he approached. "A letter for you, sir. Just arrived on the *Vesta* from London."

"Thank you, Lieutenant." The younger Cochrane snatched it from the courier. "Looks like official orders."

The admiral fumbled for his glasses. "You read it."

After breaking the seal, Thomas mumbled over the first few standard sentences. "Ah . . .

'You are to proceed to Jamaica and rendezvous on November 24 ... Lord Hill with 7000 peninsula veterans and a rifle company ...'"

"No cavalry?"

"None. When are we leaving this dreadful place?"

"Tomorrow, at dawn."

"Good, I can use some rest and sunshine."

The admiral watched mutely as his son was rowed back to his frigate, *Surprize*. Then he went below to compose a letter.

September 15

B ELLS CLANGED CHEERILY.
The British fleet was under full sail, heading south into the broad Chesapeake, and
much of Baltimore had marched, ridden or
sprinted to Hawkin's Point to see them off.

Dressed as a country gentleman, Commodore
Joshua Barney had come despite the musket
ball in his hip. Propped up in the back seat of
a surrey, he beckoned toward Carson DeWitt.
"That's a fine boy you have, Lieutenant. I'll bet
he'll be a navy man when he grows up, eh?"

Sarah looked up at the gentleman and thought
she recognized the man from nearby Elkridge.
He put a finger to his lips, cautioning her not to
reveal his identity.

"That's up to his mother." Carson handed the baby to Sarah, who nodded protectively.

"Hmmm," the commodore reflected. "Well, I guess they won't be back round these parts anymore." He squinted at the diminishing sails. "Wonder where they're goin'." Barney tried to get up but winced from the pain in his side.

"Wounded?" Carson asked, concerned.

"Just one damn Limey ball. Best leave it be, my surgeon said. Damn, if I were a couple of years younger, I'd jump outta here and steal a schooner and chase 'em!"

"I think that's a fine idea, Mr.—" Chassagne paused uncertainly.

"Barney. Call me Joshua."

"Commodore!" Carson sputtered and snapped to attention. "DeWitt here, sir."

"Chassagne, sir."

"At ease, men. I'm off duty. Now about that schooner . . ." Barney noticed the expressions on Sarah's and Lucy's faces. "On second thought, men, I think I'd wait a few days till things simmer down a bit. We ought to give Cochrane and Ross a sportin' head start with their slow boats."

"Thank you, Commodore Barney." Sarah nudged Carson and they bid farewell and turned back toward the city.

Barney woke up his colored driver. "Gideon, ol' boy, let's go back to the farm. It's time I took my medicine."

SECOND IN THE DRAMATIC NEW FREEDOM FIGHTERS SERIES:

Muskets of '76

by Jonathan Scofield

Secret agent Matthew Bell embarks on a journey into danger that takes him to the very heart of the British camp, knowing that he cannot fail—or the American Revolution will be lost.

His mission takes him into many strange places—the boudoir of the British commander's lusty mate, the midst of a raging, rapacious mob of British mercenaries, the cell of a traitorous Yankee general. Helpless, he sees his friend Nathan Hale led to the scaffold, as he awaits his own torture.

Here are the bitter battles of rebel and redcoat, Washington's brutal winter at Valley Forge—and the gallant mission of John Langley Hunter and Deborah Bell to snatch Matthew Bell from the jaws of death and dishonor.

#6 IN THE
FREEDOM FIGHTERS
SERIES

Storm in
the South

by Jonathan Scofield

In the early months of the savage War between the States, with the tides of battle running strongly in favor of the South, Nelson Hunter Vaughan, a young Confederate soldier, wages his own inner struggle.

He loses the two women he loves to his dashing but ruthless cousin, Jared, and is stalked by fear and shame at the siege of Fort Sumter and the Battle of Shiloh. But a locket with the portrait of a mysterious beauty leads him through a twisted and tortuous path to true love, redemption and glory.

BE SURE TO READ
STORM IN THE SOUTH—
COMING IN AUGUST
FROM DELL/BRYANS